FLAVOR
OF THE MONTH

Praise for Georgia Beers

Fear of Falling

"Enough tension and drama for us to wonder if this can work out—and enough heat to keep the pages turning. I will definitely recommend this to others—Georgia Beers continues to go from strength to strength."
—*Evan Blood, Bookseller (Angus & Robertson, Australia)*

"In *Fear of Falling* Georgia Beers doesn't take the obvious, easy way… romantic, feel-good and beautifully told."—*Kitty Kat's Book Review Blog*

"I was completely invested from the very first chapter, loving the premise and the way the story was written with such vulnerability from both characters' points of view. It was truly beautiful, engaging, and just a lovely story to read."—*LesBIreviewed*

The Do-Over

"You can count on Beers to give you a quality well-paced book each and every time."—*The Romantic Reader Blog*

"*The Do-Over* is a shining example of the brilliance of Georgia Beers as a contemporary romance author."—*Rainbow Reflections*

"[T]he two leads are genuine and likable, their chemistry is palpable… The romance builds up slowly and naturally, and the angst level is just right. The supporting characters are equally well developed. Don't miss this one!"—*Melina Bickard, Librarian, Waterloo Library (UK)*

Calendar Girl

"*Calendar Girl* by Georgia Beers is a well-written sweet workplace romance. It has all the elements of a good contemporary romance… It even has an ice queen for a major character."—*Rainbow Reflections*

"A sweet, sweet romcom of a story…*Calendar Girl* is a nice read, which you may find yourself returning to when you want a hot-chocolate-and-warm-comfort-hug in your life."—*Best Lesbian Erotica*

The Shape of You

"I know I always say this about Georgia Beers's books, but there is no one that writes first kisses like her. They are hot, steamy and all too much!"—*Les Rêveur*

The Shape of You "catches you right in the feels and does not let go. It is a must for every person out there who has struggled with self-esteem, questioned their judgment, and settled for a less than perfect but safe lover. If you've ever been convinced you have to trade passion for emotional safety, this book is for you."—*Writing While Distracted*

Blend

"You know a book is good, first, when you don't want to put it down. Second, you know it's damn good when you're reading it and thinking, I'm totally going to read this one again. Great read and absolutely a 5-star romance."—*The Romantic Reader Blog*

"This is a lovely romantic story with relatable characters that have depth and chemistry. A charming easy story that kept me reading until the end. Very enjoyable."—*Kat Adams, Bookseller, QBD (Australia)*

"*Blend* has that classic Georgia Beers feel to it, while giving us another unique setting to enjoy. The pacing is excellent and the chemistry between Piper and Lindsay is palpable."—*The Lesbian Review*

Right Here, Right Now

"The angst was written well, but not overpoweringly so, just enough for you to have the heart-sinking moment of 'will they make it,' and then you realize they have to because they are made for each other." —*Les Reveur*

"[A] successful and entertaining queer romance novel. The main characters are appealing, and the situations they deal with are realistic and well-managed. I would recommend this book to anyone who enjoys a good queer romance novel, and particularly one grounded in real world situations."—*Books at the End of the Alphabet*

"[A]n engaging odd-couple romance. Beers creates a romance of gentle humor that allows no-nonsense Lacey to relax and easygoing Alicia to find a trusting heart."—*RT Book Reviews*

Lambda Literary Award Winner *Fresh Tracks*

"Georgia Beers pens romances with sparks."—*Just About Write*

"[T]he focus switches each chapter to a different character, allowing for a measured pace and deep, sincere exploration of each protagonist's thoughts. Beers gives a welcome expansion to the romance genre with her clear, sympathetic writing."—*Curve magazine*

Lambda Literary Award Finalist *Finding Home*

"Georgia Beers has proven in her popular novels such as *Too Close to Touch* and *Fresh Tracks* that she has a special way of building romance with suspense that puts the reader on the edge of their seat. *Finding Home*, though more character driven than suspense, will equally keep the reader engaged at each page turn with its sweet romance."—*Lambda Literary Review*

Mine

"From the eye-catching cover, appropriately named title, to the last word, Georgia Beers's *Mine* is captivating, thought-provoking, and satisfying. Like a deep red, smooth-tasting, and expensive merlot, *Mine* goes down easy even though Beers explores tough topics."—*Story Circle Book Reviews*

"Beers does a fine job of capturing the essence of grief in an authentic way. *Mine* is touching, life-affirming, and sweet."—*Lesbian News Book Review*

Too Close to Touch

"This is such a well-written book. The pacing is perfect, the romance is great, the character work strong, and damn, but is the sex writing ever fantastic."—*The Lesbian Review*

"In her third novel, Georgia Beers delivers an immensely satisfying story. Beers knows how to generate sexual tension so taut it could be cut with a knife…Beers weaves a tale of yearning, love, lust, and conflict resolution. She has constructed a believable plot, with strong characters in a charming setting."—*Just About Write*

By the Author

Turning the Page

Thy Neighbor's Wife

Too Close to Touch

Fresh Tracks

Mine

Finding Home

Starting from Scratch

96 Hours

Slices of Life

Snow Globe

Olive Oil & White Bread

Zero Visibility

A Little Bit of Spice

Rescued Heart

Run to You

Dare to Stay

What Matters Most

Right Here, Right Now

Blend

The Shape of You

Calendar Girl

The Do-Over

Fear of Falling

One Walk in Winter

Flavor of the Month

Visit us at www.boldstrokesbooks.com

FLAVOR
OF THE MONTH

by
Georgia Beers

2020

FLAVOR OF THE MONTH
© 2020 By Georgia Beers. All Rights Reserved.

ISBN 13: 978-1-63555-616-2

This Trade Paperback Original Is Published By
Bold Strokes Books, Inc.
P.O. Box 249
Valley Falls, NY 12185

First Edition: April 2020

Credits
Editore: Ruth Sternglantz and Stacia Seaman
Production Design: Stacia Seaman
Cover Design by Ann McMan

Acknowledgments

When this book materialized in my head, it was originally about pie. And then as I wrote and got to know the characters, it became about… not second chances so much as forgiveness. I found myself exploring the age-old question, "Can people change?" Or are we doomed to make the same mistakes over and over? Do we deserve to be forgiven for our mistakes or is lost trust gone forever? Do those mistakes define us? Or can we come back from them and prove ourselves worthy again? I know what you're thinking: is this a romance or a discussion on existentialism and philosophy? I promise you it's a romance. I also promise that there's pie. So, really, it's all good, right?

And now on to the things I repeat each and every time I write these acknowledgments, as they are things that really, really bear repeating.

Thank you to Radclyffe, Sandy Lowe, and the entire staff at Bold Strokes Books. This publishing a book thing could be really difficult and stressful, but you all make it run so smoothly and easily, and I consider myself very lucky to be on board.

This was my first outing with Ruth Sternglantz as my editor. The entire process was different, yet comforting, and I thank her for that. I look forward to many, many more discussions on romance. Stacia Seaman (who I refer to in my head as Eagle-Eye Stacia) did her usual stellar copy editing and I'm forever grateful that she helps make me look good.

I couldn't do any of this without my daily support system: my dear, dear friends Melissa (who also served as my title guru and came up with this one), Carsen, Rachel, Nikki, Kris, Fiona, Aurora, my family, and more. These are people who get me, and there is nothing in the world more comforting than that. I've said it many times, but writing is a terribly solitary job. And even though I love my quiet alone time, it's comforting to know that I have people a mere keystroke away if I need them. I love all of you guys!

Finally, and always, I can never say thank you enough to my readers. Your emails, your Instagram photos and collages, your reviews and podcasts and messages, they all keep me going on those days when I'm pretty sure I have zero idea how to write a book. Thank you from the bottom of my very, very grateful heart.

PROLOGUE

Y ou know she's only trying to get in your pants, right? Tell me you're not this naïve."

Snark. That's what Charlie heard in Emma's voice, right through the phone line, clear as if she was standing in front of her. It was a sure sign she was getting angry. A coping mechanism when she heard something she didn't want to. Or something that hurt. A child slapping her hands over her ears and shouting *La, la, la* at the top of her lungs.

"Wow. Thanks for that vote of confidence." Trying to make Emma feel bad about her words wasn't something Charlie was proud of, but she did it. Mostly because it was the only way *she* could keep from feeling bad. A weird, vicious cycle.

"You've spent three semesters telling me all about her reputation, how she's known for snagging a new girl every time she does a visit at your school, and now you're going to run off to New York City with her? Are you fucking kidding me?"

Charlie flopped down onto her dorm room bed, phone pressed to her ear, and leaned back against the concrete block wall that was painted what might once have been a sunny yellow but had faded and aged and looked less like sunshine and more like vomit now. Her sigh was loud, purposefully, trying to downplay Emma's concern and the obvious worry that came with it. Emma was giving her very little credit, and that pissed her off. "I'm not running off with her. It's a *job*. A business opportunity."

"Mm-hmm." How Emma was able to fit oodles of skepticism into that one small sound, Charlie would never know. "You know she gets away with her behavior because she's a woman, right?"

"What?" Were they seriously going there now?

"Come on, Charlie. You know as well as I do that if Darcy Wells was—I don't know—*Daniel* Wells, you'd find him creepy, and you'd run in the other direction."

"I don't think that's true." Yes, it was. Absolutely true. Emma knew her so well—something Charlie used to love, but lately it had shifted somehow. Felt smothering, like she had no privacy, no right to her own thoughts. Ridiculous, she knew, but still. It grated. And in that moment? She hated how right Emma could be. The anger began to simmer in the pit of her stomach, a sour, bubbling liquid.

"It's totally true." Always right.

Take a breath. Count to five. She didn't want to fight with Emma, but it seemed like that's all they did lately. Exhausting and depressing. Trying a different tack, she softened her voice and said, "I just wish you could be happy for me. This is an amazing opportunity, you know? It's a big deal, Em."

Emma's sigh was weighted. Defeat? Like most of the wind had been taken out of her sails. "I know," she said, and her voice was quiet. "And I *am* happy for you. And I'm so proud of you. It's just…" Another sigh, an almost unnoticeable crack in her voice. "I miss you."

Again, they were doing this. Going to different colleges had been harder on them than they'd expected, though neither wanted to admit it. The hanging on at this point was merely a formality, a way to avoid admitting defeat. They'd done okay freshman year, but things only got harder after that. Classes and new friends and homework and off-campus projects took up more and more time. Texts became spaced out, more sporadic. Phone calls and FaceTimes were few and far between because who had time for either? Visits, aside from going home during the holidays, were nonexistent, as they were seven and a half hours from each other, and only Charlie had a car, and not a terribly reliable one.

Yeah, the distance had taken a toll. A big one. Farther and farther they'd drifted, and now they were barely hanging on.

Dwelling was not an option. Ignoring was easier, though Charlie was aware how unproductive that was. She'd given herself time to be sad about the whole thing, but she knew that Emma was a shining star at her culinary school, that she was going places. It was grueling, the hours, the pace, and the last thing Emma needed was a needy, clingy girlfriend whining for more time. That's what Charlie told herself. Plus, this opportunity had cropped up for *her*. Darcy Wells, well-known entrepreneur, wanted Charlie to come work for her in Manhattan. *Manhattan!* A chance to not ever have to go back to Shaker Falls. An opportunity to finally leave small-town life behind and do something. *Be* something.

"I miss you, too," she said, and it was the truth. Friends since they were kids, inseparable all through high school. They'd discovered their sexuality together. "But this is a big deal for me. I can't pass it up." Could she hear Emma's brain working? The wheels turning as she absorbed the words, tried to figure a response? Emma was a person who thought before she spoke, always. She took her time, weighed pros and cons, ran scenarios in her head.

"I know it is. I get it. I do. You know me—I just worry."

"You do."

"Be careful around her, okay? You're so trusting, and she makes me nervous."

"I will. I promise." It wasn't an easy admission for Emma, and Charlie knew it. She could picture Emma googling everything she could find about Darcy Wells—she probably already had—and there was a lot out there. Darcy was successful and wealthy and famous in certain circles and ridiculously attractive...and she wanted Charlie. For work. Of course. For work. It wasn't anything beyond that. Charlie was sure of that. Almost. Kind of. Okay, maybe not really.

"Just...don't become her flavor of the month, okay?" Emma tried to play it off as a joke, but Charlie knew her well enough, heard the fear in her voice, and she tried to shake it away. This was the right thing. They'd already drifted. They just had to drift a little bit more, and they'd each be able to move on with life. It would be better for both of them.

It wasn't that Charlie didn't love Emma. She did. Absolutely. She always had. Emma and her mom had moved to Shaker Falls when she and Charlie were eight years old. They'd been instant best friends. They'd had each other's backs. First kiss, first sex, first love, all Emma.

There was no doubt Charlie loved her.

But she wanted more. More than what they had. She wanted a future beyond their small little lives.

Emma was going places, would end up in some fancy high-end

restaurant cooking up creatively delicious meals. Charlie had no idea where, but she knew Emma would make a name for herself. And Charlie was going to do the same thing. It had simply become clearer and clearer over the past year that they were most likely going to do it in different cities. And not as a couple.

Charlie wanted more, and that's what Darcy Wells was offering. On a silver platter. How stupid would she be not to jump on a chance like this?

"Hello? Earth to Charlie." Emma's voice yanked Charlie back to the present. "Did I lose you?"

"No, I'm here. Sorry." Charlie cleared her throat at Emma's choice of words, felt the weight of them, the pain, the sadness. "No flavor of the month. Got it. Promise."

It was time to move on, to move forward, to slowly loosen her grip on her old life and reach out for the shiny new one that was so close, she could taste it.

It was the right thing to do. For both of them.

Wasn't it?

CHAPTER ONE

Five years later

The peace. The solitude. The extra time to think. Charlie had forgotten how much she loved to drive.

When you lived in Manhattan, a car was pretty much unnecessary. Cabs, Ubers, the subway, car services, walking…there were any number of ways to get around that didn't involve having your own car. Her old beater had over a hundred thousand miles on it, and paying to park it cost almost as much as rent—well, rent in a normal apartment in a normal city, not rent in NYC—but today, she was thrilled she hadn't gotten rid of it. She wasn't sure what it was, but something had made her hold on to her old Toyota Corolla even though she didn't need it, and as she sat in the driver's seat heading north, she was suddenly unendingly grateful for it. The first hour or two? Tension. But then things relaxed. Traffic eased up. Tall buildings gave way to houses and trees, then houses spaced farther apart and even more trees, then the occasional field of cattle, lush green grass, and fresh air. That relaxation lasted for the next two hours as she drove along, windows down because the air-conditioning hadn't worked in two years.

Relaxed and laid-back…until she realized how close she was to her destination.

Nervousness and dread mixed into a sour and icky cocktail and took up residence in the pit of her very empty stomach, a steady thrum of trepidation until she caught sight of that familiar brown wood sign that read *Welcome to Shaker Falls!* Complete with an exclamation point, as if she should be overwhelmingly excited to be there. She wasn't.

The sign was old, still nicked in places, and the gold paint accenting the writing had faded in the sun. As she drove past it, the nervous anticipation kicked up a notch or twenty, and the thrum morphed into a pounding, the dread sloshing around in her stomach like chop on a lake on a super windy day. She turned down the stereo, making Cardi B quiet for a change, and she actually considered pulling over so she could throw up on the side of the road.

Two years.

She hadn't been home in more than two years.

A small, harmless detail of her existence when she still lived in New York City, when she was busy with her life there, doing things she enjoyed, living in a way she'd only dreamed of. It wasn't *that* far away from Shaker Falls—just five hours by car. And it wasn't like she was some ungrateful absentee child who'd vanished. Not at all. She was a good girl. She talked to her parents once a week, invited them to visit anytime. And they had. Twice. And they'd looked overwhelmed and mostly freaked out the entire time. Charlie didn't know why she was surprised by that—they'd each been born and raised in Shaker Falls, Vermont. Small Town, USA. She'd so wanted them to love the city the way she did, but that just hadn't happened.

"The big city's not really for us, honey," her father had tried to explain, and he really did seem to feel bad about it. But truer words had never been spoken. It made Charlie sad when she realized she was relieved to see them head home. Relieved for them. Relieved for herself.

And she hadn't been home in more than two years.

Now? Now, that seemed like kind of a horrifying factoid. Two years? How did she let that happen? Who does that? What well-loved kid leaves and doesn't come home to visit for years? She'd missed Thanksgivings. Christmases. Her mother had certainly been heartbroken to have one of her kids absent over the holidays. As she drove, Charlie felt like Shaker Falls itself was looking at her with accusation, scolding her for staying away so long. Welcoming her back, yes, but with a healthy dose of side-eye and a hug that was just a *little* too tight.

Life, man. She still couldn't believe the turn things had taken. Then, *Nope. Not going there right now.* Focusing on the road and her surroundings was better.

Shaker Falls was the epitome of a small town. It had two traffic lights and one center street that held most of the businesses in a single stretch. A coffee shop, a couple restaurants, two banks, The Muffin Top bakery—which was new, she noticed—and various others. She always described it by telling people it very much resembled a town in a Hallmark Channel Christmas movie, and then she'd laugh and shrug and say things like *Such a cliché!* But it was true.

Not much had changed, but a *few* things had, she took note of as she slowed way down, knowing how strict the local cops were about the thirty-miles-per-hour speed limit. The last thing she needed was to be pulled over before she even showed her face anywhere—news traveled way too fast in a small town like Shaker Falls. The gas station had been remodeled and *finally* took credit cards? About damn time. The playground equipment at her old elementary school was completely new and modernized, all dark wood and blue plastic, the space underneath a deep black, indicating rubberized ground so clumsy kids didn't crack their skulls open when they fell off the monkey bars. Her memory tossed her an image of Stevie Todd, who broke his arm when they were seven years old and thought hanging from their knees at the very top was a fantastic idea. The dry cleaner was the same, as was the J-Cup Coffee Shop, where Charlie had written many a term paper, hoping to be able to concentrate away from the chaos of her house while drinking the world's worst coffee. The old diner on the corner was gone, replaced by a new restaurant, the whole building redone to look sleek and updated and slightly out of place next to the older storefronts. Painted a sophisticated dark green with a burgundy awning hanging over the wooden double doors, it was inviting, and Charlie found herself inexplicably wanting to have dinner there. Big brass handles shone in the early summer sun. EG's, it was called.

And that was it. All of it. She was through town and heading to the 'burbs, which was what anything outside of downtown Shaker Falls was called. Which meant pretty much everybody lived in the 'burbs, including her parents.

Heart pounding, she turned onto Elm Street, and there it was. Their house hadn't changed at all, and for a moment, she felt like she'd driven through some sort of a time warp, back to early summer nine years ago, back to when she first left for college. How was it possible not a single thing was different? The simple white siding, the black shutters, the open front porch, the pots of red geraniums and white petunias her mom worked so hard on every year without fail, her pride and joy. Always geraniums and petunias. Always red and white.

"The house where time stood still," Charlie muttered as she pulled into the driveway, her hand hovering over the key but not turning off the ignition. Emotion suddenly felt too close to the surface as she sat there in her car, everything she owned in there with her, filling the trunk and the back seat. Her brain made her stop and absorb that, take it in: she was twenty-seven years old, and everything she owned fit in her Toyota Corolla. Not even crowded in—she could still see out the back window just fine, and the passenger seat was clear, save for her purse and a McDonald's bag that still held the lunch she'd thought she wanted, but couldn't manage to eat. Her breath caught in her throat, and that emotion welled up, made her swallow painfully.

I am so not ready for this.

That one hit her hard. Right in the gut like a fist, so suddenly and so acutely, she felt tears spring into her eyes and made a small sound as she gasped for breath. She hadn't predicted any of these circumstances, hadn't expected to be discarded like an old tissue, and in the blink of an eye. She hadn't expected to be fleeing back home, back to tiny Shaker Falls to live with her parents, and a wave of panic, dread, and shame washed over her. So big, so powerful, she fully expected it to drown her right there in the driver's seat as she slapped ineffectively at the window with an open palm, unable to save herself.

What the hell happened to my life?

It wasn't the first time she'd asked herself that question, and she was pretty sure it wouldn't be the last.

Maybe I should just put the car in reverse, back out of the driveway, and go. That was the next thought that grabbed her. By the throat, tightly, squeezing. *Maybe I should just drive away. To someplace else. Anywhere but here.* Her hand was on the gearshift, her foot pressing the brake, when a gleeful shout cut through the summer air and froze her in place.

"Charlotte!"

And then it was too late.

❖

"I am so, so happy you're home." Charlie's mom couldn't keep her hands off her. "My eldest." Or her lips. Loud smacking sounds filled the kitchen as she leaned over again and kissed Charlie's cheek four times in a row.

"All right, Mom. All right." Charlie wanted to be annoyed with her like she'd always been as a kid. Like how you hit that age when the last thing in the world you want is visible physical affection from your parents, lest your friends see it and torment you endlessly later. But she couldn't. Much as she didn't want to be there, embarrassed as she was to be in her situation, affection from her mother seemed to be just what she needed, and she was soaking it in, even if she didn't want to admit it to herself.

"My babies will all be home for dinner tonight." Charlie's mom pulled out the chair next to Charlie's and took a seat. "Do you know how long it's been since that's happened?"

Charlie did know. She knew exactly: two years and two months. The last time they all ate together was when they'd gathered for a sort of makeshift family dinner during Charlie's last visit home. It was just the family—Charlie's parents, her younger brother and her younger sister. But her mother looked so wonderfully happy right now, Charlie didn't want to spoil it by taking the wind out of her sails. Instead, she reached across the table and squeezed her hand. "It's good to see you."

Her mother had always been a very beautiful woman. There was no denying it, especially when she let loose with a full-on smile. When they said somebody lit up a room? That was a legit fact when it came to Vicky Stetko. Charlie had seen it, even as a kid. Her mom could've been a model, easily. Even now, at forty-eight years old, she turned heads. Blond hair in a shade of gold that people paid good money for, unique hazel eyes that she'd passed down to Charlie—luckily, because Charlie didn't get the hair or the long, shapely legs. When her mom smiled, it accented a set of dimples that made her seem much younger than she was. Charlie didn't get those either. Her hair was almost always pulled back in a ponytail or a twist of some sort to keep it out of her way as she cooked, cleaned, crafted, gardened, or did one of the endless activities that made up the day of a homemaker, and today was no different, the ponytail swinging as she hopped back off the chair at the sound of the oven timer.

"Mom. Did you seriously make cookies?" Charlie asked, pretty sure she was unsuccessful in hiding her delight. The warm, spicy scent had hit when she walked in, but she was twenty-seven years old and not supposed to get excited over things like cookies, so she hadn't mentioned it.

Her mother shot her a look over her shoulder that said *Is that a real question?* as she slid out a sheet of Charlie's very favorite molasses cookies. She'd had them from the best bakeries in New York City but could honestly say that nobody's compared to her mom's.

"You're, like, a walking cliché of a stay-at-home mom, you know that, right?" Charlie grinned at her.

Her mother shrugged, smiled as she turned away toward the counter, and Charlie thought she saw her expression dim just slightly. She pulled out a spatula and said, "I'm about to break the first rule of cookie baking, which is to let the cookies rest on the sheet for a minute before transferring them to a cooling rack, but my oldest girl is home, and molasses cookies are her favorite, so…" Another shrug, and she let the sentence hang as she slid the spatula under two cookies, moved them to a small plate, and set the plate in front of Charlie. Then she poured her a glass of milk and sat back down to watch her eat.

Warm cookies and a glass of milk. That's how Charlie's mom welcomed her home.

Was there anything better?

Charlie felt a pressure in her chest, a squeeze of her heart, and just like that, she was ten years old again, home from a long, upsetting day of school. The inviting smells of her mom's kitchen, the warmth and the feelings of safety they evoked, her mother sitting with her elbows propped on the table, chin in her hands, waiting Charlie out. It's how she always did it. She never had to force Charlie to talk. She'd just wait, knowing that sooner or later, Charlie would. Her mom had more patience than anybody she'd ever met.

The cookie was warm, the center soft, the blend of spices perfection. As she chewed, those memories of home and childhood wrapped around her, hugged her close, made her feel protected enough to let her guard slip just a little. Annoyance hit when she felt her eyes well up, even though she'd kind of expected they would. Her mom had that effect, too.

"Are you doing okay, honey?" The words were soft, the tone tender, and that was all it took. It was always all it took.

Tears spilled.

Without a word, her mother slid her chair around, the legs scraping the floor, until she sat next to Charlie and could wrap her arms around her as Charlie tried—and failed—not to cry. "Shh. It's okay, my girl. It's all okay. Let it out."

And Charlie did.

Crying quietly in her mother's arms, it occurred to her that it was the first time in months she felt safe, felt loved.

Sometime later—a few minutes or a few hours, Charlie really wasn't sure—she felt the tiniest bit better. Wiped her tear-streaked face with the back of her hand, blew out a breath of relief. Of course, next came the embarrassment, finding a home in her head, settling in, just as it usually did, as this was the order of things. She hadn't given her mother many details, just the basics, and she wasn't ready to give them now either.

"That girl wasn't good enough for you," her mother said, an edge to her voice as she handed Charlie a tissue that she seemed to have pulled out of thin air.

"Mom," Charlie warned, not ready to go there yet, but secretly loving the Mama Bear tone.

"Well, she wasn't." Fingertips brushed some of Charlie's hair away from her face, tucked it behind her ear like she did when Charlie was little, a gesture that seemed to comfort them both. "I'm your mother. Mothers are allowed to say that." Charlie gave her a watery smile, and her mother gestured with her chin at the small plate. "Eat your cookie."

Charlie did as she was ordered, finishing both cookies and the entire glass of milk while her mom sat with her. Charlie didn't mention that it was more than she'd eaten in several days.

When she finished, Charlie blew out a breath as if she'd just worked really hard on a huge meal and told her mother, "Okay. I'm going to get my stuff out of the car and bring it upstairs."

"Actually, I have a surprise for you." There was a sparkle in her mom's eyes as she said it.

Charlie furrowed her brow, puzzled. "You do?"

"Follow me."

Growing up, Charlie had shared a room with her sister Sherry, who was five years younger. Their brother Shane fell between them at two years younger than Charlie, and they'd had their own rooms in the three-bedroom house until Sherry came along. Shane had moved out two years ago, so Charlie naturally assumed she'd stay in his room, as Sherry still lived with their parents, and their old room was now hers.

But instead of taking Charlie upstairs, her mother opened the basement door and headed down the stairs. Charlie followed, curious, and when they got to the bottom, she gasped in wide-eyed wonder.

Everything was different. There were large windows and a set of sliding glass doors on one wall of the walk-out basement, allowing access out into the large backyard. Bright and open, the space had started as a playroom. All their Fisher-Price toys, Shane's train set, Sherry's dollhouse, her Easy-Bake Oven, it all lived down there. As they grew, their father, a contractor, changed things around, and it became a rec room of sorts. Berber carpeting, a big sectional couch, TV and DVDs, PlayStation, Xbox, the board games Charlie loved, they were all still there, but not front and center like usual. Now, that stuff was shifted to one side of the room and looked like a makeshift living room. Up against the far wall was a double bed, made up in a deep eggplant colored comforter with ivory and lavender throw pillows, and a large dresser with five drawers. One of those assembly-required racks for hanging extra coats or clothes you don't wear anymore stood in a corner, empty hangers waiting patiently to be draped with Charlie's things. Her father had added a second full bathroom down here years ago when he realized three teenagers sharing one bathroom could very possibly start World War Three.

Charlie stood there in awe, looking at what was essentially an adorable and roomy studio apartment, minus a kitchen.

She turned to her mother, tears in her eyes *yet again*, which annoyed her, *yet again*, and asked, "You guys did this for me?"

Her mother nodded, waved a hand dismissively as if it was no big deal to haul a bed and dresser through the backyard, as well as shifting everything that already occupied the space into a whole new layout. "Well, you're home now, and we wanted you to be comfortable and to have your own space."

"This…this is amazing, Mom. Thank you so much." As Charlie hugged her, she decided not to correct her on the *you're home now* part. Charlie had no intention of staying, but she also had no idea how long she'd need to be there.

Anger, frustration, joy, hesitation, love, worry. They hit her all at once. A veritable stew of feelings, and Charlie had had her fill of that particular meal, thank you very much. She swallowed down that now-familiar ball of emotion that had become a regular fixture in her throat as she stood and took in her new digs, her new life, and she sighed quietly, could only think of one thing. One question that plagued her.

Now what?

CHAPTER TWO

Vicky Stetko's roast chicken was legendary in her house. *Legendary.* Charlie had watched her make it hundreds of times, and it wasn't like she did anything odd or secretive—that Charlie knew of—to make it so. It was just, to quote Shane, *freaking food of the gods.* Charlie's waning appetite wasn't something she could easily hide, though, and she was already trying to figure out how she was going to trick her mother into thinking she ate more than she did once they sat down to dinner.

Two chickens had gone into the oven right after they'd finished with the cookies, and the scent of them, of the roasting seasonings and spices, wafted down to the basement as Charlie pulled clothes from her suitcases and put them away, set her toiletries up in the bathroom. Her mother's offer to help had been sweet, but Charlie promised her she was fine and knew her mom had other things to do.

Half of that was true.

She dropped down onto the bed—its firmness telling her it was probably brand new—and tried not to think about how she'd gotten there, but her head summarized for her anyway. Long story short: her girlfriend left her for somebody else and pretty much threw her out. Life had been good, for the most part. They'd been happy, for the most part. Charlie was. For the most part. Well, she thought she was. God, did she even know anymore? Everything she'd thought she was sure of, she suddenly wasn't. Having the rug pulled out from under you was a horrible cliché, but that's exactly how she felt. *Exactly.* She'd been standing there on the rug of her life, perfectly content, unsuspecting, and whoosh! It was yanked from under her feet, hard, sending her crashing to the floor, blinking up in a shocked and painful heap of confusion, all *What the hell just happened?*

Darcy had happened. That's what.

Darcy Wells ran one of the most successful marketing firms in the country, and she spoke at Charlie's college four times during her junior and senior years, back when Charlie was working toward her degree in business and advertising. To this day, she had no idea how she managed to snag Darcy's attention, but she had, in a big way. Despite the stories going around about her, Darcy Wells swept Charlie right off her feet. Charlie had always thought that was just a silly figure of speech, something only talked about in romance novels and rom-coms, but she was so wrong.

This was the part where she sarcastically laughed at all the clichés about balance…the rug, the sweeping. Apparently, she couldn't stand on her own. With a sigh, she threw a sweatshirt onto the laundry pile on the floor.

It helped to understand that Darcy Wells was a woman who got exactly what she wanted, exactly when she wanted it. Always. A simple fact, but an important one, and if Charlie had been privy to it sooner, she might've saved herself a lot of pain. But she'd been with Darcy for over four years, and she still didn't know how she did it, how she just had whatever she desired fall right into her lap. Maybe she was a witch? Had magic powers of some kind? Knew sorcery? Sometimes, Charlie definitely wondered.

The internship had come first. Darcy had sweet-talked Charlie into interning at her office in Manhattan. Which, if she was going to be honest, didn't really take much. It was Manhattan, for God's sake. Four months after that, she'd talked Charlie into her bed…not that Charlie needed much convincing there either, because there was nothing about Darcy Wells that *wasn't* magnetic. Next, she talked Charlie into moving in with her, into her Manhattan penthouse. That was a mere three weeks after they'd slept together the first time, which made Charlie cringe now. *Three weeks? That was it? Seriously?* Charlie could admit, though, that she fell hard for Darcy, settled very comfortably and easily into that new life, and before she knew it, four years had flown by.

Pinpointing when the new girl showed up was still something

Charlie hadn't quite been able to do. She should have anticipated her, should have been on the lookout, but Charlie had already outlasted all Darcy's past girls, so she naïvely assumed she was The One for Darcy.

God, was *that* a stupid thing to think.

Commotion upstairs tugged Charlie's train of thought back to the present, thank God. Stomping of feet, exclamations of greeting, the sounds of dishes and cutlery. Ready to be done with the unpacking and sad reminiscing, she abandoned her things and headed upstairs into the kitchen.

"Sharlie!" Her brother Shane always called her that, insisting that she'd ruined the perfect alliteration their parents had created with Charlotte, Shane, and Sherry by insisting she be called Charlie. He started it when he was around ten, and it stuck. She was his Sharlie now, and she always would be, and she was good with that. He opened his arms and swooped her into a bear hug. He smelled of the outdoors and motor oil and guy.

Shane was a big dude. Tall, broad, muscular. Charlie grabbed his full sandy beard with both hands, tugged on it. "What's this, Paul Bunyan?"

"Part of the new uniforms," he said with a gleam in his eye.

"You'd think it actually was," their mom said. "I think every firefighter has grown a beard over the past couple of months."

"Beards are in." Charlie noticed Shane staring at her. "What?"

He shrugged. "It's just been so long since I've seen you, it's hard to believe you're really here. You look good."

Charlie's heart squeezed. "Thanks, Shane." He was lying, of course. She did not look good and she knew it. She'd lost a bunch of weight, which would normally thrill her, but she'd gone past sensually slim and into sickly thin a couple weeks ago. Dark circles under her eyes had become part of her daily wardrobe because she couldn't seem to get a full night's sleep. She hadn't exercised in ages because her emotional state had drained her energy, so much of her muscle tone had gone soft. No, she did not look good, but she loved her brother for saying she did.

"Where's that girl of mine?" Brad Stetko's voice boomed through the house the same way it boomed everywhere. He was not a quiet man, that was just fact. "Is she here?" The side door slammed closed and in the next minute he walked in, his blue eyes twinkling with happiness when they found her, and then filling with unshed tears.

"Aw, don't cry, Daddy." Charlie went to him, let him wrap her in his strong arms and hug her tightly until she had to ask for breath. Her dad was a big guy, too, just like Shane, and of her parents, he was the emotional one, crying at the drop of a hat, which melted Charlie's heart every time. He cried the first time she started in a high school volleyball game. He cried when she graduated from high school and then again when she finished college. And she was told he was practically inconsolable for more than a week when she'd moved to New York. Brad Stetko was six foot three, two hundred and forty pounds, a contractor by trade who looked like he could kick the ass of anybody who glanced at him sideways. He also wore his heart on his sleeve, loved his family fiercely, and wasn't embarrassed when Christmas movies made him tear up.

Finally letting her go, he laid his big calloused palm against her cheek and looked her in the eye. "It's good to have you home, Bug." A moment passed, and then he blinked, pulled his gaze from Charlie's, and said, "Where's my woman?"

Her mom rolled her eyes as he went to her and kissed her. High school sweethearts, her parents had gotten married and started a family very young and were still sickeningly in love with each other. Charlie found herself both filled with love for them and also insanely jealous that she was pushing thirty and hadn't found that kind of connection for herself yet. Here she was, back at square one.

Within twenty minutes, the four of them were sitting down to dinner, laughing and stuffing their faces as if Charlie had always been right there in her designated chair, as if she'd never left and it hadn't been two years since she'd been back. Finding a small bit of appetite, she put the last tiny new potato into her mouth when the side door opened, closed, and a voice called out, "There'd better be chicken left."

People found it hard to believe Sherry and Charlie were sisters. It had always been like that. First of all, they looked nothing alike. Sherry was tall. Charlie was of average height. Sherry had dark hair and their dad's blue eyes. Charlie was more of a dirty blond—who had come up with that description anyway? she'd always hated it—with their mom's hazel eyes. Sherry was long and lean and small-breasted, where Charlie was curvier and…not small-breasted. Secondly, they acted nothing alike, completely different personalities. While Charlie was outgoing, an extrovert, talkative and curious about others, Sherry related better to animals than people, had little patience for crowds, was happier on her own or with her very small group of friends than at any kind of party or large gathering. All that being said, she and Sherry had been very, very tight. Or they used to be.

Sherry came into the dining room and saw her sister. "Oh, hey. You made it." A hug from behind kept Charlie from getting up, a quick squeeze of one arm around her shoulders that was much less of a warm greeting than Charlie was expecting. Sherry went around the table, sat in her usual chair, and reached for the chicken.

"I did. How are you? Mom said you've got a new job as a vet tech?"

Sherry nodded as she forked some chicken onto her plate. "It's going pretty well so far. Hey, Dad, can you look at my car? It's making a weird noise."

Apparently, that was all Charlie was going to get from her little sister, as Sherry turned back to their father and discussed the timbre and pitch and rhythm of whatever sound her car was making, apparently, a metallic knocking of some sort. Charlie wasn't all that surprised— she hadn't been expecting party horns and confetti—but more than a passing glance would've been nice. A sip of her water helped to stifle a disappointed sigh.

Welcome home, she thought.

❖

One a.m. Eyes wide open.

Unsurprising, as it was par for the course of Charlie's life at that point: hardly eating, barely sleeping because her brain just would not shut off, constantly working to try and figure out exactly how she'd ended up in the situation she was in, having gone from luxury Manhattan penthouse to her parents' basement in a matter of weeks. Add to that stress the cool reception from her sister *and* the fact that she needed to find a job, at least for a little while until she figured out her next step—and what the hell could that next step possibly be?—and sleep was beyond elusive. While she'd always been in her own head a lot, this had gone way past normal for her. *Out* of her head would be nice, on occasion.

The new bed was firmer than she was used to, but the bedding had all been washed to a softness that felt lovely, and it smelled like fabric softener and home, so she cuddled down into the pillows as she lay in the dark, scrolling on her phone…which was not the best way to harness sleep, if all the studies were correct.

Scroll, scroll, scroll.

Thank God she'd never changed her phone plan from her parents' to Darcy's, which was something Darcy had suggested more than once. One of the only things Charlie hadn't instantly jumped on board with. Why not was something she still wasn't sure of. It had been so easy to follow Darcy, to do whatever she wanted, to agree with everything she said. For a while, it was all Charlie wanted to do: please her. Make her happy. For a while, she had.

Memories swirled in the darkness, came into focus, then faded like smoke. Not for the first time, she tried to remember exactly when she'd first felt that niggling in her gut. That tiny seed of dread that kept telling her she was failing, that she, in fact, *wasn't* making Darcy happy any longer, that Darcy was tiring of her, that she was looking over and around and beyond Charlie for something different, something new, something better. Fear was tricky, though. Tucking the niggling away, ignoring it, pretending it wasn't a thing seemed like the only thing to do.

Dumb.

Second-guessing herself was one of her finest talents, so before she could do that, she typed out a text, a simple *I miss you*, and sent it to Darcy.

Nothing.

Charlie felt herself beginning to spiral downward as she let her memories take over—another common occurrence in the wee hours, lately—when her phone pinged. Her heart leapt. Darcy? Maybe she missed her after all. Maybe she was making sure Charlie had made it safely. Maybe she wanted to tell Charlie she'd made a huge mistake, that she wanted to talk about working things out. Charlie looked at the screen.

Not Darcy.

Why wasn't Charlie used to that feeling by now? The letdown.

The disappointment. Common enough at that point that she should be, and really, she'd known the text wasn't going to be Darcy. Felt it in her heart.

She read the text.

Heard you were back in town. Yes? Let's get together!

If Charlie had to name somebody to fill the role of new BFF in her life, Amber McCann would be her pick. Close friends in high school, they had stayed in touch despite going off to different colleges. Not instantly liking Amber wasn't an option in life, couldn't be done. She was sweet, bubbly, and kind, and her presence filled the room with happiness and fun. They had drifted a lot when Charlie moved. No, that wasn't true. *Charlie* had drifted when she moved, and it was right then, in that moment in the dark, that she realized just how much she'd missed Amber.

Yes! I'd love to see you. When? She hit Send. Waited. Amber always was a night owl, so getting a text from her anytime after midnight wasn't at all surprising.

OMG, I can't believe you're still up. Hi! Tomorrow? I have an appointment at 5...is 3:30 too early?

Something to look forward to. It was just what Charlie needed. *I'm in. Where?*

Amber's reply came within seconds. *Chug?*

Charlie felt the smile bloom on her face as she read. Chug was older than both of them, and if you looked up the words *dive bar* in the dictionary, an illustration of the dingy, dark interior of Chug was probably right there. It was also a staple in Shaker Falls. *Perfect. See you there at 3:30. Can't wait.*

Amber sent back a smiling emoji followed by two beer steins clanging together.

Kind of amazing how having something to do the next day shifted Charlie's mood. While sleep still felt elusive, she was able to set the phone aside and pick up a book. The same book she'd been reading for the past three and a half weeks, but still. A book.

Man, lack of concentration blows. Hard.

She managed to get through almost an entire chapter before the words blurred, her eyelids grew heavy, and she drifted off into a light sleep.

CHAPTER THREE

Chug's dive bar status still lived on. That was Charlie's first thought as she walked in. Stale beer and the faint stench of cigarettes were the ruling scents—weird, because there hadn't been smoking in public places for a long time now. Going to Chug had always been a ritual of sorts, a rite of passage for local kids who finally turned twenty-one—not that there hadn't always been dozens of kids with fake IDs, because she was sure there were, Shane being one of them. She scanned the bar and wondered why, almost laughed out loud at what a dump it was. *Why did we want so badly to be able to get a beer here? Kids.* She shook her head, but the smile was there on her face anyway—she could feel it.

She stood for a moment and let her eyes adjust. Like any dive bar worth its salt, Chug was very dark, and coming in from the sunny day outside left Charlie momentarily blind. She blinked several times, waited, then heard a voice from the end of the bar working hard on a Southern accent.

"Why, if it isn't Miss Charlotte Stetko. As I live and breathe!"

More blinking. More adjustment. And there she was. Charlie felt her smile grow, spread across her face as she finally focused on her friend. Amber got off her barstool as Charlie approached, held her arms open for her, and as they hugged tightly, she was instantly transported back to high school. Amber was short, a little plump, and Charlie had to bend slightly. She still smelled the same, like the citrusy body spray she always wore, and she looked the same, her brown hair still straight and reaching just past her shoulders, blue eyes bright and inviting. Hugging her was like coming home, and Charlie's eyes welled up unexpectedly.

Amber held her at arms' length and Charlie noticed the wetness in her eyes, too. "Look at us," Amber said with a watery smile. "Two blubbering messes." She paused, just looked at Charlie, then playfully slapped at her. "I missed you, you bitch."

"I missed you, too."

Charlie took the stool next to hers, and they were two of only four customers, which wasn't really surprising given it was still midafternoon. The same grizzled bartender, wiry beard gone silver now, came over and stood, waited for Charlie's order. She pointed to Amber's draft beer. "I'll have what she's having."

They touched their glasses together and each took a big swallow. The beer was surprisingly cold and hit the spot.

"What did you do today?" Amber asked, as if they had seen each other just that morning and were now catching up.

Gratitude. For the normality of the question. Charlie grinned at her. "Well, let's see. I spent the day dodging questions from my mother and absorbing the fact that I am twenty-seven and living in my parents' basement. All I need is some acne, an Xbox, and a bag of Doritos, and I'll be high school me again. That was pretty much the extent of my day. How about you?"

Blink. Another blink. Then Amber burst out laughing. That was the other thing about Amber McCann: she had the best laugh on the planet. It was loud and surprising and contagious, and within seconds of hearing it, you were laughing, too.

"My life is so boring compared to yours," she said. "I sold a house, showed three more, and signed a contract with a new client."

"I did one load of laundry. You were way more productive than me." Charlie sipped her beer, and then they both turned as the door opened and a short blast of light filled the bar. A new customer came in and took a seat. Turning back to Amber, Charlie said, "So, real estate is your thing, huh?" With her bubbly personality and trustworthy demeanor, Amber was a born saleswoman. She could sell ice to an Eskimo.

"Number one salesperson in the region, two years in a row."

"Wow! That's awesome." Charlie gestured to the bartender. "Next round's on me."

They spent the next hour catching up, talking about their families, other people they knew. Charlie was so far out of the loop, she found it almost embarrassing, but Amber simply caught her up and gave her very little grief about abandoning everything Shaker Falls without so much as a backward glance. Which was pretty much what she'd done.

"So what happened?" Amber finally asked, as Charlie knew she eventually would. "New York didn't work out for you?"

What had happened? That was the big question, wasn't it? The one she didn't really want to answer, but also the one that she needed to, owed it to her friends. Even though Charlie wasn't sure how to verbalize it all, for Amber, she tried. "I was an idiot."

A tilt of the head, a look that said Amber didn't believe her for a second.

"I got caught up."

A slight nod this time. Happier with that wording, it seemed.

"I fell in love with somebody, and I was ready to do anything for her. Anything. And in the course of doing that, I completely lost my way. Lost myself." Charlie took a sip of her beer. "I didn't know it at the time, but…" Big inhale. Slow exhale. "Yeah." She shook her head as she gazed into her glass.

If Amber was disappointed with such a weak attempt at an explanation, she let it go. "Well, I can tell you that I'm super happy you're back. And because I love you and have missed you more than you probably realize, I'll wait until we see each other a few more times before I shred your ass over how quickly you dumped all your friends for your shiny new life in the big city."

Ouch. Charlie's head snapped around to her, but she was sipping her beer, looking away. Resignation. Okay. That was a fair shot.

And Charlie was thankful for the waiting period because she wasn't ready to be hit with both barrels. Fair or not. Not yet. They were deserved, she knew that. In a role reversal, she'd feel the same as Amber. But she wanted to at least be up on her knees when those shots hit, not still lying on the ground in the fetal position. No, they could talk about that another time. So Charlie did what any intelligent person avoiding the truth tended to do: she changed the subject.

"Lots of new storefronts on Main, I noticed."

Amber nodded without missing a beat. "Right? Doesn't the gas station look great?"

"It does. First thing I noticed."

"The pumps take credit cards. We're no longer living in the seventies." Amber held up her fists, shook them in victory.

"The J-Cup looks the same." The local coffee shop was the place the kids of Shaker Falls hung out until they were old enough to come to Chug. "Does the coffee still suck?"

A snort. "Please. Of course it does. Bob will never put a dime into that place to make it look pretty. As long as Shaker Falls stays too small for a Starbucks, he doesn't have to." Bob was an old man who grumbled and griped, as if the last thing in the world he wanted to do was run a coffee shop. Yet he'd done exactly that ever since Charlie could remember.

"And the diner's gone," Charlie said, then caught something glint in Amber's eyes.

"Oh yeah, that's been gone for about six months now. The owners retired and sold. Remember the Jefferses?"

A nod. "The restaurant there now looks kind of fancy."

Lips pursed, Amber looked like she was thinking. "Not so much fancy as…a little upscale. Nicer than a diner, anyway." She grinned and looked at her beer. "I've eaten there several times, and the food is fantastic."

"Yeah? I'll have to check it out."

"You should. Emma owns it."

Smack! Was there a glass door nearby? Had Charlie just walked face-first into it? Because that's what it felt like. All forward progress stopped. All focus brought to said door. In that moment, she realized she'd been avoiding one particular subject without consciously admitting she was avoiding it, and she'd avoided it with everybody. Her parents. Her siblings. Amber.

That subject was Emma Grier.

"*Oh*," Charlie drew out and all but slapped her forehead as the restaurant name EG's suddenly made sense. Emma Grier. Charlie's first love. The first person whose heart she ever broke. Badly.

Amber seemed to watch all the emotions that played over Charlie's face intently, at one point even tipping her head to the side in what looked a hell of a lot like amusement.

"She owns it, huh?" Charlie pulled herself together, did her best to act casual and nonchalant, which was probably destroyed when she took an enormous slug of her beer. Amber was doing that half-grin thing, the kind where you didn't want to laugh outright at a person, but also, you kind of did.

"Yup. She owns the restaurant—well, the whole building—and has an apartment above it. And she's the head chef. She was working in Burlington for a while for some really well-known chef."

Charlie had heard that at one point and had just assumed Emma was still there. "And she came back to Shaker Falls?" She said it like that was the stupidest decision ever and immediately regretted it when she saw the flash of anger fly across Amber's face. "I mean, rather than continuing to work for a well-known chef. Cause that seems like it would be good. For her career. And stuff." Charlie's attempt at redemption seemed to work. A little.

"Her mom needed her."

"Oh." Charlie nodded, that familiar and intense wave of sympathy splashing up in her stomach. Emma's mom. Always really nice. Always a little messed up.

"Anyway, you should check it out." Apparently, it was Amber's turn to change the subject, and Charlie tried to hide her relief. "So, how long are you staying? What will you do while you're here?"

There was no solid answer to either of those questions, and how interesting that Amber was the first person to assume she wasn't going to hang around in Shaker Falls for long. Charlie fudged an answer as best she could, suddenly wondering if she was disappointing Amber somehow. Maybe it was just her, but she felt…weird. Not good enough. They talked about a few more mundane, superficial things before Amber gave her cell phone a glance and claimed she needed to run.

This time when they hugged, that odd sense of falling short was gone, and Amber seemed nothing but happy to see Charlie again. She could admit to being totally relieved, and she squeezed Amber tightly, promised they'd get together again soon.

She actually meant it, too.

Charlie watched her friend leave, then sat quietly and finished her beer.

EG's wasn't far from Chug. Nothing was, really, not in tiny Shaker Falls. Walking distance, easily. It was a nice day. Sunny. Not quite the dinner rush yet. Just checking things out, satisfying her curiosity, that's all she'd be doing. Right?

She scoffed, unsure why she was even bothering with the justifications. She knew where she was headed. She knew why.

There really was no question.

❖

Ninja-like. That's how Charlie walked in. Slowly. Quietly. As if she was making some sort of attempt to sneak in unnoticed. Which she kind of was, and the first thing she became aware of was the amazing smell. Garlic. Butter. Basil. Her mouth filled immediately as she realized how hungry she actually was. Well. That was new.

EG's was small. Intimate was a good word for it. On the left a U-shaped bar. Sophisticated. Made of something nice, something resembling cherry or mahogany—shout-out to her father for teaching her to identify different wood—and burnished to a gorgeous shine. An old-fashioned brass rail ran the length of it, and the barstools had backs and looked comfortable enough to spend some time sitting on. To the right were about fifteen tables, a blend of round and square that kept the small space interesting. White tablecloths covered them, small votives and bud vases in the center of each.

It was barely five. Still a bit early for dinner, unless you were part of the early bird crowd like the two elderly couples seated at tables toward the wall. The bar boasted seven guests that Charlie could see: a group of four guys in suits and ties, obviously grabbing an after-work cocktail, laughing about their jobs, their wives, their kids, or all of the above. Two women who might have been doing the same thing. One lone gentleman nursing what looked like a Scotch, neat.

Another step farther in, a look around at the décor, trying to take it all in and also not care, both at the same time. It was weird, and she tried not to think about what she was doing as she scanned some of the art on the walls, some paintings, some photographs, but all evoking the same feel, the same mood: relaxation, comfort, home. Charlie found herself wanting to take a seat, settle herself at one of the small round tables, and have comfort food delivered to her. That's how the atmosphere made her feel.

It was nice.

"Did you want a table?" a gentle voice asked, and Charlie turned to face a young woman. Maybe eighteen. She smiled, and Charlie realized as she took in her black dress that she was probably the hostess.

"Oh." An unintentional clearing of her throat, as if she'd been caught doing something she shouldn't have been, which was almost true. "No. No, I'm good. I was just…um…" The sentence dangled.

"Charlie? Is that you?" The voice was not gentle. It was rough. Booming. Vaguely familiar, and it cranked up from the past like a phoenix rising out of the ashes.

Charlie leaned around the hostess to see the source, and her eyes went wide. Tucked around the corner of the bar, the petite woman had gone unnoticed in Charlie's initial scan. Charlie knew her, yes, but she'd also aged about thirty years since she'd seen her last.

Emma's mother.

Damn it.

Charlie had hoped to skulk in and then skulk back out with no one the wiser. Celia Grier had just shot that plan all to hell.

"It *is* you!" she said, loudly enough that every bar patron turned Charlie's way. "Come here. Let me look at you." She gestured Charlie to her with a too large rolling of her too thin arm. Celia had never been about subtlety.

Charlie had no choice. She couldn't just turn and run—though she seriously thought about it—so she gave the hostess an apologetic smile and then headed toward the bar. She was still two or three steps away from Celia when the woman reached out, grabbed her, and yanked her into a hug. She smelled like cigarettes and gin, exactly like she always had. Some things never changed.

"I can't believe it's you." The usual raspy voice, though extra enthusiastic. Overserved. That's what Emma always called it when Celia had too much to drink. Loud. Overaffectionate. Embarrassingly proud of her daughter. All signs she'd been overserved. Charlie knew them well because Emma knew them well.

Celia didn't seem super drunk right then, just at that level of contentment where you're almost boneless, almost too happy and relaxed, arms sort of flailing, but she looked much worse than Charlie remembered. Alarmingly thin. A gray pallor to her skin that was new to Charlie. A pronounced gray part visible in her reddish-brown hair. Dark smudges under her blue eyes looked like she put them there on purpose in preparation for playing center field. Charlie recalled Amber saying that Emma had come back to Shaker Falls because her mom needed her, and now Charlie thought she understood why. "What are you doing in Shaker Falls?" Celia asked, hauling Charlie out of her memory bank. "We didn't think you'd ever come back."

Charlie noted her use of the word *we*, wondered who she meant, though she was pretty sure she knew. A shrug. Vague was better. "My situation changed."

Celia nodded as if she completely understood that. "Does Em know you're here? Lemme get her." She slid off her stool and disappeared through a swinging double door before Charlie could utter a word.

Crap.

The panic was instant. Charlie's heart began to pound. Sweat beaded on her upper lip, palms dampened. She hadn't seen Emma in more than five years. She hadn't talked to her in more than three, and that's because the last time Emma called, she didn't answer. No, that was a lie. The last *seven* times Emma called, she didn't answer.

Twenty-three-year-olds were stupid. And selfish. Those were facts.

Looking around frantically, trying to decide if it would be considered rude if she simply fled, ran out of EG's and never returned, she was stopped by that voice.

"Well, would you look at that? It *is* you. Huh."

A hard, hard swallow, a slow turn of her head, and Charlie faced her. Emma Grier. Her first love. The person who used to know her better than anybody in the world. Who probably still did.

"I was sure my mother was mistaken, just saw someone who looked a little bit like you, but..." Her dark eyes raked over Charlie, quickly and not kindly. "Nope. It's really you."

"It's really me." Charlie's voice was a croak. Croaks were *so* impressive. God, she wanted the floor to open up and swallow her whole. With yet another clearing of her throat, she held her arms out to the sides, presenting herself. Let them drop. "Hey, Emma."

How unfair was life when five years went by and Emma looked like *that*? Stunning. Head-turning. She always had been. She could stop Charlie in her tracks just by looking like herself. In that moment, she realized Emma still could. Trailing off midsentence was something Charlie had perfected. Happened every time Emma walked into the room. And right then? Charlie realized she still possessed that power. It was one of the many mysterious things about Emma Grier: She never looked rumpled. She never looked tired. Or maybe that had just been Charlie seeing her through the rose-colored lens of young love. Apparently, that lens was still in perfect working order because, much as Charlie hated to admit it, Emma still took her breath away. In her white chef's coat and hat, there was a sexy air of authority floating in the dining room. Her dark curly hair was pulled back and was much longer than Charlie remembered. And her skin. Charlie didn't even want to go there because that irresistible urge to touch her was shockingly still a thing. It literally made Charlie's fingers tingle. Even after so much time, Charlie had to consciously keep her hands at her sides, ball them into fists.

"Well, give her a hug, why don't you?" Celia must've nudged Emma because she sort of took a stutter step toward Charlie, an odd look on her face. Reluctance. There was no way for Charlie not to see it, and man, did it sting. She hated that.

"It's okay," Charlie said, holding her palms toward Emma, halting her in place, relieving her of doing something she evidently didn't want to. "No worries. This place is really nice." It was a valiant effort at a subject change, the awkwardness reaching unbearable levels. It worked, though. Emma's face lit up. Charlie's relief at that pissed her off.

"Thanks. It took a lot of work, but here we are."

"Best restaurant in town," Celia offered, and Charlie had forgotten for a moment that she was still sitting right behind Emma.

Emma's eyes cast downward. "Well, that's not hard in a town this small."

"I've heard good things," Charlie said, stretching the truth a little bit. But when Emma brought her gaze back up and that light was back, it was worth it.

"Yeah?"

"Oh yeah. Hey, can I look at a menu?"

With a nod, Emma grabbed one from the hostess stand and handed it over. It was nice. Heavy. Like a faux-leather portfolio. Only two pages—appetizers, soups, salads on the left, entrées and desserts on the right. A wide variety of dishes, which ranged from simple comfort food to more exquisite cuisine, the small menu had quite a span: lobster mac and cheese and shepherd's pie to chicken cordon bleu and surf and turf.

Charlie's mouth watered at almost everything. On the list of appetizers, her gaze stopped on the roasted asparagus topped with a fried egg, and just like that, she was eighteen again. In Emma's mom's tiny kitchen after midnight, Emma showing her the wonder of roasted asparagus. When Charlie told her she didn't like asparagus, Emma swore to her that almost anything was made better with a fried egg on top. Charlie remembered her piling stalks of asparagus fresh from the oven onto a plate, sprinkling a little salt, a little pepper, and topping it with the fried egg. One simple cut and all that gorgeous yellow yolk dripped down and through and around the asparagus. Charlie finished it, every last bite, and wanted to lick the plate clean, it was that good.

She looked up at Emma now and could see that Emma knew exactly which dish Charlie was thinking about. She could tell by her ghost of a smile. "The asparagus," she said unnecessarily and pointed.

Emma nodded once, her eyes skittering away from Charlie's in… embarrassment? She wasn't sure. "It's popular."

"Still one of the best things I've ever eaten in my life."

Emma looked right at her then, finally. A moment. A definite moment. Of sorts. Kind of. Well, for Charlie at least. Emma's eyes were still the deepest, most intense dark brown she'd ever seen, and for a second or two, she let herself remember how they used to hold her, how she only had to look into them to feel any shift in her world tilt back to level again.

"Emma, can you help me back here? I'm having an issue with the rib eye."

With that simple request from somebody who peeked his head out of the kitchen, the hint of any spell was broken. Emma's expression morphed into one of apology—not quite a smile, not quite a grimace, but some weird combination of the two. "It was nice to see you, Charlie." Polite. Not terribly genuine. Charlie still knew her well enough to know when she was saying what she was supposed to, not what she actually felt. Especially since she said nothing that remotely resembled *come back soon* or *I hope you come in for dinner sometime*. Funny how memory worked. It was rather clear Emma wouldn't be heartbroken if she never stepped foot in her restaurant again.

Could Charlie blame her?

Yeah, the answer to that was no, she absolutely could not.

CHAPTER FOUR

Charlie *fucking* Stetko.

Of all the people in the world, the last person Emma ever thought she'd see stroll into her restaurant? Like, ever? Charlie fucking Stetko. Didn't Charlie say she would never come back to Shaker Falls? Emma snorted quietly at the irony. She'd said the same thing once upon a time, yet here she was.

Chopping onions. A great, mindless chore. Years of culinary school and then working in the tense and demanding environment of a high-end restaurant Emma could chop onions and barely pay attention. Chopping had become second nature to her, and she did it when she needed to think. Even if she didn't need anything chopped.

Charlie fucking Stetko.

Different. That's how Charlie looked to her. Still heart-stoppingly beautiful—Emma had resigned herself long ago to the fact that she'd always think so—but different. Smaller. Deflated. Maybe a little broken. And while some part of Emma smirked at that—why wouldn't she?—a bigger part hated it. She had loved Charlie once, loved her deeply and with everything she had, and despite the pain Charlie had caused her, she didn't want to see her unhappy. She still cared about her and that was okay.

Two and a half years of therapy. That's what it had taken for her to be able to say that.

Emma grabbed another onion, expertly peeled it, and set to chopping. It was her eyes. There was something in Charlie's eyes. Those gorgeous hazel eyes that Emma had always felt so safe in. So loved. Now they held something…sad. That was it. That was the word.

Charlie was sad. Emma wasn't sure if other people would notice, but she knew those eyes better than she knew her own, even after all this time, and they carried something heavy in them. The realization felt heavy to Emma as well.

No. No, no, no.

Her knife stopped for a moment. Hovered above the onion. No, she couldn't think about this. She didn't *want* to think about this. It was long ago. Years. Charlie had crushed her, had run off to New York and had done exactly what Emma had warned her about. She got sucked in by that Manhattanite shrew, just as Emma had predicted she would. Granted, she had not expected it to last for years. Rather, she'd predicted a fling. A few months. Maybe a year, and then it would be over, Charlie would have it out of her system, and they'd figure things out.

But that hadn't happened. Charlie hadn't come back to her. They hadn't even stayed friends, though Emma did realize that was probably a good thing, for a while. She had spent years working through it all. Her friends didn't seem to understand the depths of her feelings for Charlie. There'd been a lot of *You deserve better*, and *You can have any girl you want*, and *Just let her go*, but none of that had helped because Charlie had been *it* for her. The One. Capital *T*, capital *O*. She'd been so sure of it.

Ridiculous and naïve.

That's what Emma had been. Her therapist would disagree, tell her to stop beating herself up for loving somebody deeply, but Emma just felt stupid, because it had become pretty obvious Charlie hadn't felt the same way about her. It was the only explanation.

"Hey, Em?" Sabrina Tate's voice cut into Emma's thoughts and Emma looked up. Her bartender was tall, very sexy, and right then, her dark eyes held worry and a hint of confusion. "You okay?"

A curt nod. Chopped onions into a hot pan, the sizzle of them in the oil creating one bar of the music of her kitchen.

"I think your mom's ready to go."

Translation: Your mom has had more than enough to drink. Emma knew that, and she gave another nod. "I'll get her an Uber." She took out her phone, did so, and reported the make, model, and driver to Sabrina to pass along—the same make, model, and driver, Tom, that usually came, since a town as small as Shaker Falls didn't exactly have a bevy of Uber drivers. Then she picked up her towel and grabbed the hot handle of the pan, tossing the onions expertly. She could feel Sabrina still standing there. Waiting for something more. Expectant. Always so expectant. But Emma didn't look up from the pan until she knew she was gone.

Sabrina.

Yeah, she was an issue all of her own.

That rabbit hole was a dangerous one. Emma was far too familiar with it. Before she could get sucked in, Jules, one of her waitresses, burst into the kitchen with an order, the way Jules burst in anywhere she went. The girl had more energy and presence than anybody else Emma knew. It made her very likable as a waitress, if not a little bit annoying when you were feeling pensive.

"One filet, one pork tenderloin," Jules reported, knowing she didn't need to announce the orders because they showed up on the screen mounted near Emma's head. She just liked to and always did when she entered the kitchen to get salads for her customers.

"Got it." Emma got to work on the dinners, happy to push Charlie *and* Sabrina out of her mind, at least for a while.

❖

Exhaustion. You got used to it. Who knew?

The first couple of weeks EG's was open, Emma would end up so utterly wiped out, she wondered if she'd ever be able to wake up in the morning. It surprised her, the bone-melting fatigue that had set in. After all, she'd apprenticed under a high-profile chef, worked grueling hours for him for nearly two years, yet had never felt so completely clobbered at the end of her shift. Not the way she did when she headed up to her apartment after a busy night at her restaurant.

Gabe Battaglia, one of her instructors in culinary school and a man who'd become an advisor and friend, finally explained it to her in a way that she understood.

"You're running the whole show." He'd said it simply, gruffly as he said most things, and with such nonchalance that it surprised Emma.

"Yeah. So?" This wasn't news.

"You're running the *whole show*." He stressed the last two words the second time. "Believe me, that carries a lot more weight, whether you realize it or not. You have so much more on your plate—forgive the pun—than cooking and creating. You've got the staff and the inventory and the planning and the money…For fuck's sake, the money alone is enough to drive a person mad."

She got it then. Crystal clear. Like a bulb went off and illuminated what she hadn't been able to see. There was so much more to deal with as the owner/proprietor. Not that she didn't know this going in— she was a smart woman and she hadn't gone into restaurant ownership blind. The opposite, actually: she'd studied and researched and read and read and read probably way more than she'd needed to before she decided to purchase the place. She'd gone into this business with her eyes wide-open. She'd just never bargained for the level of exhaustion she faced.

Now, it was closing in on midnight, and she was on her couch in her apartment, upstairs, above the restaurant. Laptop open on her thighs, glass of Bordeaux within reach, glasses perched on her nose while she went over the books. Sabrina had tried to garner an invitation to join her—she'd tried hard, really, and Emma had to give her kudos— but she had stood firm, told her she had a bunch of work to get done. Not a lie at all, as evidenced by the spreadsheet gracing her screen. But also not the entire truth.

Because the entire truth was: Charlie.

Charlie was on her mind and had been since Emma had walked out of the kitchen and found her standing in her restaurant.

So many emotions had run through Emma's mind then and had continued to speed a circular path in her brain for the entire evening. Emotions at NASCAR. That's what it felt like. Round and round and round. She'd been able to push them into a corner, at least for a little while, so she could focus on her cooking, on her customers, but she'd been very aware that they were there, waiting, revving their engines, and that they'd come blasting out as soon as the last plate left her kitchen.

And they had.

Confusion was first, which surprised her, because why not anger? She'd expected anger. She'd expected that the most. But it was confusion, as if seeing Charlie standing in her restaurant made zero sense in the grand scheme of life, as if Charlie was a figure that had been slapped onto the wrong painting, out of place and confusing to all onlookers.

Charlie had seemed confused, too. That was…well, it wasn't surprising, if Emma was being honest. Like Charlie, she had also vowed not to return to Shaker Falls, yet here she was, with her own business, obviously announcing some semblance of permanence. No wonder Charlie'd had that divot over her nose, the one that always formed when she was thinking hard or couldn't figure something out. Emma had wanted to reach out and smooth it with her thumb the way she used to when they were studying in high school.

Why is she here? Why is Charlie back in Shaker Falls?

Just visiting, probably. That made the most sense. And that would definitely be best for Emma. The last thing she needed was to run into the woman who'd shattered her heart into a million pieces on a regular basis. No, thank you.

Her phone pinged, which was a good thing, as it yanked her out of her head and back into reality. Present day. The now. And the now included her mom texting her to say good night.

Sleep tight, Emma-love, the text read. She'd spelled everything correctly, which was always a good sign. It meant she'd either gone easier tonight than on most of her nights off, or if she hadn't, she'd recovered a bit. Whichever it was, Emma felt that old familiar relief, and her tense muscles relaxed just a bit.

You good? Emma typed back.

Yep! That was followed by a barrage of various emojis. Her mother was enamored of them and way overused them. Which was super cute and made Emma grin most of the time.

Good night, Mom. I love you.

Emma set the phone aside and pulled off her glasses, rubbed the bridge of her nose. She was tired and emotionally drained, and what she needed was her bed. Maybe tonight, she'd actually sleep.

She'd seen Charlie.

She hadn't fallen apart.

Okay, good. That's done, and hopefully, she'll head back to the city and I won't have to see her again anytime soon.

CHAPTER FIVE

S leep still hated Charlie.
     She was still having tons of trouble getting a decent night's
sleep at her parents' house. But it wasn't because of her overworked
brain, well, not always. It wasn't because she was uncomfortable. The
basement, basically her own apartment, was perfect and above and
beyond anything she'd expected. No, she couldn't complain about that.
She had everything she needed down there; it was kind of awesome. But
still, sleep played a brilliant game of hide-and-seek…and was winning.
     It was the quiet.
     In the five years she'd lived in New York—first in a miniscule
apartment with six roommates, then in Darcy's penthouse near Central
Park—she'd surprisingly grown used to the sounds of it. They didn't
call it The City That Never Sleeps for no reason. It truly did not. Traffic,
car horns, sirens, shouting. All hours, day and night, it went on, and
after a while, it became a sort of soundtrack that she had come to
expect, though it took her a good six months before it felt normal. So,
lying there in her parents' basement in Shaker Falls, Vermont, gazing
out the sliding glass doors at the silent and peaceful woods beyond the
yard, everything just felt *so quiet*. Eerily so.
     Charlie missed the city. She missed her quote-unquote *friends*
there, noting that she'd started putting quotation marks around the word
in her head because she had only heard from one of them since she
left. She missed the king-size bed she was used to and the warm body
that had been in it with her. She missed the charity work she was just
starting to get into. She missed the business world that she was just
starting to get into.

And Darcy. God help her, she missed Darcy.

That last one was the hardest. She missed Darcy and hated admitting it. To herself or to anybody else. Despite what Darcy'd put her through, despite the way she'd done things, despite the fact that Darcy had left her with very little money and no place to go, Charlie missed her anyway. She hated her and she loved her and she missed her and that made her angry. She'd texted her when she'd first gotten into bed. Just like before. *I miss you.* She'd gotten no response. Just like before.

It was probably safe to assume that was still one reason she couldn't sleep, in addition to the quiet.

Another was pretty obvious: Emma.

Of all the ways she'd envisioned seeing Emma again, walking into a restaurant in tiny Shaker Falls and seeing her in her chef's coat, all authoritative and distant, wasn't really one of them. Though it didn't really make sense that it wasn't.

Charlie sighed and shook the image of Emma's gorgeous face and smooth skin and lack of enthusiasm over seeing her aside and turned to gaze out the sliding glass door.

Black to deep blue to indigo to light pink. The colors morphed and shifted as she lay there watching. Eventually, movement above her in the kitchen caught her attention, as did the heavenly aroma of coffee, and she decided she might as well get up and get some caffeine into her system asap. Work. A job. She needed to find some kind of temporary employment while she figured out her next move and how to get back to the city. The agenda for the day. While her parents wouldn't hear of taking any money from her for rent, Charlie was no freeloader. If they wouldn't take rent, she'd find other ways to pay them back. Buy groceries, fill their cars with gas, take them to dinner, whatever she could do to show her gratitude. But in order to do any of those things, she needed money, which meant finding a job.

Not something she was looking forward to.

In the kitchen, she found Sherry. Charlie had expected her dad. "Morning," she said, her voice husky. She cleared her throat.

"Hey," Sherry said, not looking at her. Her purple scrubs were cute, Charlie noticed, as she filled a big blue travel mug with coffee.

"Look at you, all doctor-y." Charlie felt herself well up with pride. Sherry had wanted to work with animals since she was about five years old. A bird had flown into their bay window and lay stunned on the lawn, its wing possibly broken. Their dad wanted to put it out of its misery, but Sherry begged him to let her take care of it. And damn if she didn't nurse that bird back to health until it was able to fly away on its own. Her patience was astounding, and when Charlie looked back on that whole thing, it was so obvious Sherry was meant to be doing exactly what she was doing. "How's life as a vet tech?" Charlie asked, pulling a mug from the cupboard.

"It's good." Sherry poured soy creamer into her coffee, shouldered a bag, and left out the side door with nothing else to add. She wasn't really a morning person, never had been, so Charlie decided to chalk up her icy demeanor to that, even though she suspected there might be more to it.

Resigned and a little disappointed, Charlie doctored her own coffee with too much sugar and just enough cream to make it slightly less than black. As always, that first sip was magic, the caffeine racing through her system, poking and prodding it awake.

Little by little, the house came alive. Her mother came down only a few minutes after Sherry left, gave her a kiss good morning, and pulled eggs and bacon from the fridge. Every morning since Charlie could remember, her mother had cooked bacon and eggs for her father's breakfast, and she was pretty sure her mom could do it with her eyes closed by now. Eggs over easy, bacon extra crispy, white toast now multigrain toast—a change he'd agreed to in order to keep the bacon, Charlie recalled—coffee, and orange juice. Every day. Charlie's father was a creature of routine, there was no doubt about that, and she smiled to herself.

Contentedness and comfort were like a warm throw draped over her shoulders as she sat sipping her coffee, the morning rituals of the Stetko household taking place around her. There was something hypnotic in it, and though she tried to elaborate on the feeling in her mind, the simple conclusion was that it was all very…peaceful. Comfortable. Familiar. Her mother's unhurried movements, her father appearing in his work pants and flannel shirt, placing kisses on Charlie's head and her mother's lips. For the first time in years, she admitted to herself that she might have missed this. Maybe. Just a little.

Her dad ate his breakfast while scrolling on his phone.

"No newspaper, Dad?"

"What am I, a dinosaur?" he asked, his eyes never leaving the screen in his hand.

Charlie grinned as her mother set a plate in front of her. Scrambled eggs, two slices of bacon, no toast. Charlie looked up at her, opened her mouth to speak.

"Eat," her mother said, a hand held up to keep Charlie quiet. "You're way too skinny."

"Agreed," her dad said, still not looking away from his phone, which was dwarfed by his enormous hand. She wondered when her rather old-fashioned father had come into the twenty-first century. It was weird. But in a weirdly good way.

Charlie surprised herself by eating every last bite of breakfast, her dad leaving in the midst of her chowing down like she hadn't seen food for days, as her mom sat at the table with her tea—she hated coffee—and watched.

"Why are you grinning at me?" Charlie asked.

Elbow propped on the table, chin in her hand. "Mothers love to see their children eat. It's a thing."

Charlie chuckled. "Oh, I see."

A soothing aura. That's what her mom had. She'd noticed it, thought about it a lot when she was younger, no way to really explain it. When people were around her mom, they were relaxed. She had that effect somehow. So even though there were elements of shame and frustration at being home indefinitely, sitting with her mother calmed those feelings, as if she took the weight of whatever was sitting on Charlie's shoulders off. At least for a few moments.

"You got plans today?" her mom asked, then sipped her tea, the little red tag hanging down the side of the mug identifying it as English Breakfast.

"Gotta make some money."

"Oh!" An upheld finger, a disappearance from the kitchen. Charlie could hear her rummaging around in a drawer in the dining room, and when she returned, she slid a business card in front of her.

The Muffin Top. Small Town Bakery. Sandy McCarthy, owner/operator.

Charlie looked back at her mom, raising her eyebrows in question.

"Sandy's a friend of mine. She's so sweet. Been divorced for a bit and finally decided to bite the bullet and do something she always wanted to do. A few months ago, she bought that old bakery you worked in when you were in high school, remember? She's looking for help. I mentioned you were coming home and what a terrific baker you are, and she said to send you over."

"Oh." Charlie wasn't sure what she felt in that moment. A bit of excitement to have a possible job opportunity? A smidge of nerves worrying that she wouldn't know what she was doing? A little embarrassment that her mother had been talking about her to people she didn't know? Charlie wondered how detailed her mom had gotten about why her big city daughter was suddenly returning to the nest.

"She needs help with pies," her mother said with a twinkle in her eye, unaware of the swirling in her daughter's head. "She tested out a few and they sold like crazy, but they're not her strong suit. You're just what she needs."

Baking was something Charlie was good at. Very good. She didn't really know why she'd gravitated toward it, but she had. She loved to bake just about anything. Cookies, cakes, muffins, breads. Pie, however, was something she'd always had a knack for.

But there was a slight problem.

"Mom, I haven't made a pie in years. Literally." Darcy would never have something homemade if she could buy the best instead. And let's face it, living in Manhattan meant you could pretty much buy the best of anything you wanted if you had the means.

To her mother's credit, she tried to hide the flash of surprised disappointment as it zipped across her face, but Charlie knew her well enough to catch it, and it bummed her out.

"Well," her mom said, recovering quickly, "I doubt that's something you'd just…forget. It'll come back to you. Maybe go see Grandma for a refresher."

Not a bad idea at all. Charlie needed to see her grandma anyway. She'd already been home almost a week, and if she didn't go see her soon and she found out, her mother would get an earful.

"I think I'll do that." Charlie stood back up, cleared her dishes and put them in the dishwasher, then grabbed the card off the table. "Thanks, Mom." She kissed her mother's cheek and headed downstairs to shower.

And just like that, she felt almost energetic, something she hadn't felt in a really long time. Being dumped, kicked out of your home, and forced to move back in with your parents was a pretty good way to feel weak, powerless, and flattened. Energy was something she'd become rather unfamiliar with. But not today. Today, after waking up with little direction for the hours stretched out in front of her, she had a plan. She would go see Sandy McCarthy at The Muffin Top about a job, and then she would visit her grandmother and hope she'd be up for making some piecrust.

Maybe today, things would start looking up.

Today, Charlie had a purpose.

CHAPTER SIX

E normous potential.
   That was the first thing Charlie thought about The Muffin Top. Enormous potential. It was a good-sized space for a bakery: not huge, but not tiny and cramped. Plenty of room to grow, if that's what Sandy McCarthy wanted. The glass case was large enough to hold a decent variety of baked goods, but not so big that it was in danger of looking empty if they didn't keep it crammed full, something very important from a marketing standpoint. The front of the bakery, when you first walked in, was decorated in pink and white, with fun oil paintings of cupcakes and muffins along the walls in all different bright colors. There were five small round tables with three chairs each, though Sandy told Charlie during her interview that people didn't really hang around, so Sandy wondered if the tables were a waste. Coffee had seemed a no-brainer solution—she'd suggested Sandy sell it, so people would want to sit and sip it with their baked goods—and Sandy had looked at her like she'd just given her the cure for cancer.

Then she hugged Charlie and hired her on the spot.

My God, bakeries open early...

Charlie was not a lazy person by nature, and while she enjoyed sleep—true, more in theory lately than in practice—she wasn't one of those people who thought getting to work by nine was torture. However, she *did* think that getting to work by four thirty came pretty close. Wow.

She'd showered quickly, hoping that the water beating on her would help wake her up, then threw on old jeans, a white V-neck T-shirt that she didn't care about, and pulled her hair into a ponytail. It was the best she could do at oh-dark-thirty.

If Charlie thought sleeping at her parents' was hard because of the quiet, seeing the main stretch of Shaker Falls before sunrise was almost eerie. There was literally nobody to be seen as she drove. Not a soul. No other cars, no people, no activity whatsoever. It made her think of various horror movies from her childhood where a meteor passed over the town or some horrific virus decimated the population and she was the only one left. Thinking up survival techniques helped keep her awake until she pulled into the back parking lot of The Muffin Top and had to refocus.

Sandy only had one other employee, her niece Bethany, who was home from college for the summer. Charlie hadn't met her yet, but when a small Honda Civic pulled into the spot next to hers and a bleary-eyed teenage girl in jeans and a worn Patriots T-shirt got out, she assumed she was about to.

"Hi," Charlie said as she shut her car door, the sound seeming to jerk the girl to attention. "Are you Bethany?"

She squinted at Charlie as she nodded.

"I'm Charlie. New employee." She stuck out her hand. Bethany looked at it for a good five seconds before shaking. Yeah, the girl was tired. Charlie thought back to her time in college and how alarmingly little sleep she'd gotten the entire four years. Her first week home for summer vacation, she had never wanted to leave her bed.

"Hey," Bethany said, then headed toward the back door of the bakery without another word. Charlie followed.

Sandy was the opposite of Bethany in the morning, and after having interviewed with her, Charlie had suspected as much. Sandy was bright, bubbly, and friendly, and also seemed just a little bit frazzled at all times. *Slightly flaky* was how Charlie's mother described her, but with affection. Instantly likable was how Charlie did. She was in her forties, tall and lanky, and had pin-straight chestnut brown hair. When she smiled her very wide smile, her dimples lit up her whole face and made you want to smile right back at her.

"Good morning, staff," Sandy said as Bethany and Charlie entered, then giggled at her own joke. She wore black leggings and a white T-shirt, a pink Muffin Top apron tied over it. Her hair was in a ponytail, and she wore zero makeup, as far as Charlie could tell. She seemed ridiculously wide awake.

Bethany grunted a greeting—at least that's what Charlie thought it was—and she smiled in reply. Despite the lunacy of the hour and knowing this was just a temporary thing, it surprised her to realize that she was happy to be there.

The Muffin Top smelled amazing. Charlie wasn't sure why that fact surprised her a little bit—it was a bakery, after all—but it did. Maybe because it was so early? She stood still and simply inhaled the scents of flour and dough and chocolate and cinnamon, all making her feel warm and hungry.

Charlie had just registered that the scent of cinnamon was most prevalent and was making her mouth water, when Bethany said, "They're ready. Excellent."

Puzzled, Charlie furrowed her brow as she turned to see Sandy, oven mitt on one hand, pulling something out of the oven. The scent of cinnamon became more intense, and Charlie became hungrier as Sandy set down a tray of huge cinnamon rolls.

"Oh my God," Charlie said softly before she could catch it, and Sandy chuckled.

"I like to get my day started with a little blast of sugar and the warmth of cinnamon. I did it once, and it somehow became tradition."

Bethany already had a small plate and a spatula in her hands. She dug out a roll, and it steamed as she set it on her plate, then handed the spatula to Sandy, who dished one out for Charlie.

"You do this every morning?" Charlie asked. Was there drool on her chin? Did she look like some Pavlovian dog? Because good God, the smell was divine. Her grandma had taught her that humans ate with their eyes first, and just looking at the soft doughiness of the roll, the perfectly golden top, the brown swirls of cinnamon running through it told her how amazing it was going to taste. She glanced around for a fork when she saw Bethany pick her roll up and take an enormous bite, despite the fact that it must have been hot. Bethany's eyes stayed closed as she chewed, and Charlie swore she could actually see her waking up fully.

Screw it. Charlie followed suit. And it *was* hot. Burn-the-roof-of-your-mouth hot. But also freaking delicious. Sounds came from her throat. Embarrassing sounds. Humming. Moans of delight. The dough was pillowy soft and light, the amount of cinnamon perfect—not overwhelming and not too subtle.

"Oh my God," Charlie muttered, fingers in front of her full mouth.

Sandy beamed as she lifted her own roll. "You like?"

"Oh my God," she said again, then took another bite.

"Welcome to The Muffin Top. There's icing in the fridge if you want it." Sandy grinned, and the pride she had in her bakery was unmistakable. For a moment, envy surged through Charlie. Sandy had what she wanted. She was making it a success. She'd taken something she loved—baking—and turned it into her livelihood. Pretty cool. Pretty goddamn cool. Sandy handed Charlie a pink apron with the Muffin Top logo—a smiling, dancing muffin with stick arms and stick legs and a pink paper cup acting as its dress—screen printed across the front. "All right. Let's get this day started."

The first couple of hours, Charlie got to know the place, learned her way around the kitchen and the shop itself. Bethany, fully awake now and actually in possession of a very approachable personality, pointed out the whiteboard on the wall where Sandy would write a to-do list for the day and showed her the ropes: which baked goods were made first, where all the spices and other ingredients were kept, what to do if something was running low. They pulled anything left over from yesterday out of the giant refrigerator and boxed it up, reduced the price, and put it out on the day-old table in the shop area. What didn't sell today would be picked up by a local food bank. Then Bethany gave Charlie a quick lesson on the cash register, which she grasped pretty fast.

By six thirty, when Sandy unlocked the front door and switched the sign from *Closed* to *Open*, a few early birds came in, and by seven thirty, the shop was quite busy. Cinnamon rolls, croissants, and muffins were the popular morning items, Charlie noted. Sandy had made most of them as Bethany showed her around, so the freshness couldn't be beat. Then she watched Bethany whip up a batch of blueberry scones— *so much butter, oh my God*. While Charlie wasn't new to baking at all, watching how quickly the two women worked and how well they knew each recipe was pretty intimidating.

At the same time, her business schooling had started to tickle the back of her neck as she paid attention to possible profit-building opportunities. Where Sandy could make more money. Where she might be losing it. Coffee was definitely something that needed to happen. Charlie kept her phone in the back pocket of her jeans and, anytime an idea came to her, jotted it down in her notes. Old habits.

By nine, things had tapered off a bit. She and Sandy were standing behind the glass display case when Sandy turned to her. "Okay, we're in a lull. How're you feeling?"

"Well"—Charlie pointed at the front of the shop—"I just now noticed that the sun is up and there's daylight out the windows."

Sandy laughed. "Yeah, that happens when we have a rush." She studied her for a moment. "Does my new employee feel like making me a pie?"

Charlie's face lit up—she could feel it. "Hell, yes. What kind?"

"Let's start with something simple. Cherry?"

"On it." Adrenaline shot through her as she headed back to the kitchen, Sandy following.

"You can work right here." Sandy indicated a large countertopped workspace off to the side, more spacious than any kitchen Charlie had ever baked in, that was for sure. Even Darcy's gourmet one. "Bethany showed you where everything is, but ask if you can't find something. I'm not going to watch over your shoulder." Charlie felt her own relief at that, because she kind of expected Sandy *would* watch over her shoulder, and the idea of somebody observing her every move made her nerves jangle. "If we get a sudden rush, I might need your help, and I could call you away. Just know that."

Charlie nodded, not worried at all. She'd interned in one of the busiest marketing firms in New York City. Being pulled away from her cherry pie to ring up some sugar cookies wasn't going to rattle her.

She'd taken photos of several of her grandmother's recipes during her visit, just to refresh her memory, and she called the one for cherry pie up on her phone.

She got started.

❖

"You sure you're okay?" Alec Haberman, her sous chef, had asked the question three times now, and Emma wanted to be annoyed by that, but she just couldn't. The nicest of nice guys, Alec was simply voicing concern, and Emma knew it.

Can't blame him, she thought as she caught a glimpse of her own reflection in the large stainless steel pot he carried past. Dark circles highlighted—lowlighted?—her eyes, her coloring was dull, and it was glaringly obvious to anybody who gave her a passing glance that she'd gotten little sleep. So many things in her head that wouldn't leave her alone, wouldn't let her relax.

"Yeah, I'm fine. Just didn't sleep well."

Alec gave a nod and went to work on the base for the chicken potpie that would be tonight's special.

A yawn pried Emma's mouth open wide and she grunted a sound of annoyance. This was why she couldn't open for lunch. She'd need to get started even earlier, and she just couldn't imagine doing that. Not now. Not yet. But she'd get there. She wanted to get there.

Emma wiped her hands on a towel, tossed it to the counter, and went to the walk-in freezer, where she stepped inside and closed the door, leaving it ajar a few inches.

A ritual of sorts.

When life got to her, when things beyond her control were weighing her down—today it was Sabrina...*again*, her mother...*always*, and Charlie...*unexpected*—she went into the freezer and closed her eyes. She let the fog swirl around her as she took in three deep breaths. Slowly. Deliberately. In. Hold. Out. Two more times. Then she opened her eyes, shook her arms out as if she was a boxer about to step into the ring and do battle. She rolled her head around, taking satisfaction in the grinding and popping of her spine as she worked out all the kinks. One more deep breath and she was ready.

End of ritual.

She stepped out of the freezer, caught Alec's eye as he shook his head.

"It always freaks me out when you do that," he said with a chuckle.

"I know." Emma grinned at him as Jules walked in the back door.

"Hi, gang," she said cheerfully. Everything she did she did cheerfully. Everything she said, she said cheerfully. Emma joked once that when you looked up the word *perky* in the dictionary, there was a picture of Jules next to it. Jules sniffed the air. "Oh, that smells wonderful. What are we making?"

And so, the day began. This was how it always went. Honestly, it wasn't a bad gig, and she knew it. She was lucky. She was the boss. At barely twenty-eight, she owned her own business. It was quite an accomplishment, and she often had to remind herself of that. She let the feeling of success wash over her as she and her tiny staff got to work.

Sometime later, Emma pulled the first batch of her chicken potpies out of the oven. Five of them. The smell was heavenly, rich and meaty. The crust was baked to a golden brown. She set the tray on the counter to let them cool.

"Okay," she said. Alec looked up from the clam chowder he was making. Jules was working on salad ingredients. "Lunch is served. Let's see how we did." When the pies had cooled, the three of them sampled one, digging forks in, looking critically to each other.

"Mm. That's delicious," Jules said as she chewed.

"The base needs a bit more salt," Emma commented, then looked at Alec, who was nodding. "The chicken is nice and tender, though."

"Peas were a good call," Alec said.

"Agreed."

"And your crust is on point."

"It came out good." Emma turned to Jules. "Wrap two of them up and run them over to Sandy's place. See what she's got for us."

"You got it, boss."

Inventing and experimenting. Tweaking and adjusting. This was the part of cooking Emma loved the most. Making changes. Adding. Subtracting. Until it tasted perfect, whatever it was. Getting her out of her own head was simply an added bonus. She could set aside things that had been weighing on her. She'd been known to make the same dish a dozen or more times until she felt it was the best it could be. It was all about focus.

As Jules put the potpies in a bag and headed out the door, Emma got to work on the next batch. Comfort food at its finest. Her specialty.

"These are going to be a hit," she said, not really to Alec, just in general. But he nodded with enthusiasm.

"Definitely."

❖

Nerves tickled up and down Charlie's spine like fingernails, as it had been a long time since she'd made pie on a regular basis, and she found herself wanting to impress Sandy. She took a big, fortifying breath and got to work.

Five years old. That's when she first started to help with the baking. Helping in the kitchen was something that caught her young attention early on, but only with regard to baking. She didn't really enjoy cooking actual meals, but cookies? Cake? Pie? Sign her up.

It took her a while to figure out why that was. Why did she love to make dessert, but hate to cook anything else? Why did she loathe her mother asking her to get dinner started but would happily make a batch of oatmeal raisin cookies at ten o'clock at night? It wasn't until her freshman year in college and her first visit home over Thanksgiving that she figured it out. She hadn't expected to be homesick at college—and she didn't tell her parents how badly she was because they'd warned her it would happen and she was eighteen and, like all teenagers, didn't want them to be right—so she was quietly thrilled to be back in the house she grew up in, preparing for the holiday. She had no desire, really, to help with things like the stuffing or the sweet potato casserole or even the turkey. But she was all about making the pumpkin and apple pies. She watched her mother toss various ingredients into her stuffing, not measuring anything, just tasting and adding, tasting and adding. It wasn't until she pulled out her mother's beat-up binder full of recipes to get what she needed for the pies that it struck her: rules. She was a huge follower of rules. She liked them. Preferred them. A good girl. She waited for the Walk sign when she crossed the street, even if no cars were coming. She had never in her life cut in line, nor had she ever littered. She was a rule-following girl who grew up to be a rule-following woman, and baking was all about rules.

That being said, she'd made enough piecrust in her life by the time she was in The Muffin Top that she didn't need a recipe to follow. Sugar, butter, flour. A little salt. Maybe a dash of milk, depending on what kind of pie she was making. Maybe replace the butter with shortening—her grandmother still used lard, which could be hard to come by, but made the crust friggin' delicious. Maybe a combination of butter *and* shortening. Piecrust was one of those things in baking that seemed deceptively simple but could be the most difficult thing in the world. Even now, her mom bought premade piecrust because she felt like she could never get it right when making it from scratch. Charlie's grandmother was horrified by that and took great pride in the fact that her granddaughter wouldn't hear of such a thing. Lies. Charlie had to confess, at least privately, that she would buy a premade crust at the store in a heartbeat if she didn't have time to make one from scratch. But she would never, ever tell her grandmother…or let her taste that pie because *she would know*.

Charlie's favorite part of making piecrust was when all the ingredients were incorporated, and she had to fold it over and over with her hands. It wasn't quite the same as kneading bread—she had to be a bit gentler so as not to melt all the butter or shortening with her body heat—but there was something about the feel of the dough in her hands, the rhythm of the work. It cleared her head, much as she imagined running or yoga might for others. The feel of the dough, soft and smooth and pliable, the motion of folding it and pressing it, pushing her body weight against it, then repeating. It was almost hypnotic.

She'd never baked in a bakery before, and having all the ingredients—more than she needed—right at her fingertips was a luxury Charlie could absolutely get used to. Same with the tools. Plus, Sandy had all the newest equipment, which was awesome. She had a pastry blender, so Charlie didn't have to use two forks like her grandma taught her. Endless mixing bowls and spatulas, all pink. There were stacks of cookie sheets and pie plates and muffin tins. Four huge ovens. A blast chiller. It really was a dream kitchen. The workspace was huge, and there was plenty of room for her to spread out and not get in anybody's way. She separated the pie dough into four evenly sized balls, wrapped them in plastic, and put them in the enormous fridge to chill while she turned her attention to the cherry filling.

Two hours later, she was using a pastry cutter to make strips of dough for the latticework on the tops of the pies. Sandy told her that she didn't have to go that far the first time, but if there was one thing Charlie had learned in marketing, it was that presentation is key— again with the *We eat with our eyes first* that her grandma had taught her—and when you thought about a cherry pie, you saw a pie with a latticework top crust. She wanted Sandy's customers to be so drawn to the prettiness of the pie that they couldn't resist at least a slice.

A tiny bell tinkled, indicating a customer had come in the front door. Charlie barely noticed it earlier that morning when they were bustling, but when things were slower, the little bell had a light and cheerful sound. It reminded her of Tinker Bell from *Peter Pan*.

"Hey, you," she heard Sandy say. There was a large window in the kitchen so staff could see people in the front and people in the front could see what the staff was baking, but Charlie's workstation was off to the side. She had no clear view of the front, but she could hear what went on pretty well.

"Ready for lunch?" It was a woman's voice, one Charlie didn't recognize, and she tilted her head to the side, listening, curious.

"You have no idea. What's today's special?" Sandy asked, and then Charlie could hear the rustling of what sounded like a paper bag.

"Chicken potpie," the woman said, the pride in her voice evident. "It's fabulous. Wait till you taste it. Emma outdid herself, I think."

Emma?

"Oh my God, that smells *amazing*." Bethany.

"Here are the shortbreads," Sandy said. "And listen, I've got a new employee making cherry pie back there. Tell Emma I'll send one over, and you guys can see what you think."

"Pie, huh?"

Sneaking a peek made Charlie feel a little bit like a creeper, but she did it anyway. The woman was young. Very young. Maybe college age like Bethany. Stocky, curly red hair pulled into a ponytail, and bouncing slightly on the balls of her feet, as if she couldn't contain her own energy. "Yeah, definitely send it over. I'll tell Emma it's coming. And let her know what you think of the potpie." Her voice faded a bit as she turned and headed out the front door, the little bell tinkling again. Charlie swallowed down whatever weirdness it was that had formed a lump in her throat and got back to work. She was sliding the two pies into the oven as Sandy came into the kitchen area—Charlie could feel her behind her.

"Wow, those are beautiful," Sandy said, her voice quiet as if she worried she'd disturb Charlie's movements.

"Thanks."

"When they're done, we're gonna box one up, and you can run it across the street for me."

Charlie swallowed. "Across the street?" Sandy wanted *her* to take the pie over?

"Well, kitty-corner across the street. Ever been to EG's?"

"Not to eat, no." Charlie hoped her face didn't betray all the weird things she was feeling. Also, *why* was she feeling all those weird things?

"Oh, you have to," Sandy said, buckling her knees slightly, obviously illustrating her weakness for Emma's cooking. "Emma

Grier is a genius in the kitchen. A certified *genius*. Occasionally, she sends over lunch for us, whatever she's putting on special that night. I send cookies or lemon bars or something for her to serve with after-dinner coffee. It's a nice trade-off. She's been asking about things like cheesecake and pie because she doesn't have a full dessert menu yet, but I haven't been able to accommodate her." She smiled at Charlie. "Until you." She grabbed two forks from a drawer and handed one to her. "Today is chicken potpie, and I can only imagine how good it'll be. Come and eat. You've been working nonstop since you got here."

Charlie didn't have to imagine how good Emma's chicken potpie would be because she'd made it for her more than once when they were younger. Emma's mom wasn't terribly reliable, and she was a horrifyingly bad cook, so meals fell to Emma. Charlie was pretty sure Emma's love of cooking came out of necessity.

She joined Sandy and Bethany at the cookie workspace where Sandy dished the two potpies onto three plates. It was still steaming, and the delectable aromas of chicken and vegetables were so different than the usual sweet scent of the bakery that it felt almost tangible. Like if Charlie reached into the air, she could literally touch the smell.

The three of them dug in, and at first, there was absolute silence. Then three different levels of moaning began. It was comical, and they looked at each other, then burst into laughter. Yeah, Emma's chicken potpie was *that good*. Charlie was unsurprised that it was delicious but was very pleasantly surprised by the sophistication of the dish. When they were young, Emma had made standard chicken potpie. Chicken, potatoes, carrots. This potpie, however, was not only a step above, it was several flights above. Chicken, potatoes, carrots, yes. But corn and peas and a blend of savory spices that lifted it up from simple comfort food to something more…elegant. Mature.

Color her impressed.

About an hour later, the entire bakery smelled like cherry pie, warm and sweet and inviting. Charlie took them out of the oven, and after they'd cooled a bit, Sandy cut into one, dished herself a small slice, and tasted. Strangely, she was almost as nervous over that moment as she'd been the first time she'd pitched a marketing idea to Darcy, an uncomfortable desire for approval hanging over her like a gray cloud. She watched as Sandy chewed slowly, savored, tilted her head to the side as if thinking. Then she took a second bite and her gaze met Charlie's.

"Your crust is outstanding," she said, and relief washed through Charlie, almost making her knees buckle. "Light. Flaky. Delicious, but not so strong it overwhelms the pie. The filling might be a tad sweet, but that could just be me." Bethany came back from the display area and Sandy held out a forkful of pie. "Taste this."

Bethany did as ordered, and her eyes closed as she moaned. "Oh my God, that's good."

"Right?" They stood looking at each other, chewing. Amusing. Charlie smiled as she watched. With a nod, Sandy told her to box up the second pie and take it over to EG's. "After that, you're free to go." Her face grew serious. "You worked hard today, and I appreciate that. I think this is going to work out really well."

Lots of mixed emotions happened right then for Charlie. Happiness, pride, relief over getting the stamp of approval from Sandy, a little guilt that she didn't intend to stay. Added to that, worry and nervousness over what she had to do next.

So much for never stepping foot in EG's again.

CHAPTER SEVEN

It was getting close to push time.

That's what Emma called that time about an hour before dinner customers started to appear. There were already folks at the bar for happy hour. She liked that people were starting to pop in after work for a drink. It had been slow getting started, but it seemed like word of mouth had gone around town, and each day, the crowd stayed steady or increased. The profit margin on alcohol was pretty good, so she'd take it. Soon, her early bird customers would start to trickle in for dinner.

The chicken potpie was ready to go. The standard meals were ready to go. The steaks and the chicken dishes and the seafood. Alec had prepped everything that needed prepping, and Jules had the salad area all stocked. They were ready.

"Hey, Emma?" It was Sabrina, looking sharp in her uniform, which Emma tried to ignore. Black pants, a white oxford, a black tie. She'd complained about the tie more than once, said it got in her way when she was making drinks, and Emma could admit that it was a valid objection. But damn if it didn't look good. Also, she probably shouldn't have slept with Sabrina. Boss and subordinate, and all that. But one look at her and that flew out the window. Sabrina was hot. "There's a woman here from Sandy's place with pie?"

"Oh, right." Emma hoped this was the beginning of something beneficial for both her and Sandy. EG's had a nearly nonexistent dessert menu, and she hoped to remedy that before the end of the summer, but she hadn't had the time to sit down and figure out exactly what she wanted to do. Sandy's cookies were wonderful, especially the shortbreads—buttery and delicious—and EG's served them with every order of after-dinner coffee. But she really needed to offer some actual dessert. Mousse. Cheesecake. *Pie*. She wiped her hands on a towel, draped it over her shoulder, and pushed through the double doors of the kitchen out into the restaurant.

And stopped.

But only for a split second because she did not want Charlie Stetko to know how affected she was by her presence. She had to steel herself. Put on her armor persona, as her mother called it when Emma had to be firm with somebody. Square her shoulders. Puff up her chest. Hold her head high.

Charlie was nervous. The darting eyes, the shifting from one foot to the other, the twisting of the ring on her finger all made it obvious. Emma took a bit of satisfaction in it. No, she wasn't proud of that, but so what? Despite the quirks, though, Charlie looked... Emma sighed internally. *Damn it.* She looked good. A little too skinny, but still so pretty. Her dark blond hair was a little shorter than Emma remembered, and her ponytail couldn't hide the gentle wave of it. Those soft hazel eyes had always been home for Emma, and it was hard to believe they could still spark that feeling in her, but that's exactly what they did. *Goddamn it.*

"You're Sandy's new employee, huh?" She purposely forced herself to sound disinterested. Bored, even. Should she yawn? "Jules said there was a new baker. Who'd have thought it would turn out to be you?"

"It's me." There was false cheer injected into Charlie's tone. Emma could tell. And it surprised her that she still knew her that well. Yeah, she was nervous and uncertain, and again, Emma could admit to taking a tiny bit of pleasure in knowing that.

"She's got you making pie." It was an unnecessary statement, but Emma was having trouble finding words. At all. *Steel*, she reminded herself. *Steel. Armor. Be firm.* She opened the box. Nestled inside was an almost picture-perfect cherry pie, complete with the crisscrossed latticework on top. It smelled delicious and was still slightly warm; Emma could feel it through the box. She salivated.

"It's the first one I've made in a while, so they'll only get prettier." Charlie's smile faltered. Oh yeah, she was definitely nervous. Emma could see her throat move when she swallowed.

She reached below the bar and into the utensil holder for a fork.

Which—she didn't let herself stop and reconsider—she stabbed right into the very center of the pie. Charlie's eyes went wide, then a cloud passed over them, and she poked the inside of her cheek with her tongue. To her credit, she said nothing, just watched as Emma put the forkful of pie into her mouth.

Jesus Christ, that's delicious. It was the first thought that came to mind, but Emma didn't let the words escape. Instead, she kept her lips closed and chewed, making a show of being thoughtful about the taste. "It's not bad," she finally said, feigning reluctance. "The crust is a little soggy on the bottom and the cherries are a little bit too sweet. And your latticework needs…work. But you know that already." Little circles of pink blossomed on Charlie's cheeks, and Emma instantly felt guilty, but not enough to stop. "Have you heard of Mama Jo's? It's at the other end of town, near Clifton. Her pies are great. You should check them out."

"I'll be sure to do that." No inflection. No tone. It was pretty obvious Charlie wanted to flee, and she did exactly that, turning on her heel and shoving her way out the door, leaving Emma standing there with the ruined pie.

"Wow, that was harsh." Sabrina's voice came from behind Emma, who'd forgotten she was there. "Even for you."

Yeah, okay. It *was* kind of harsh, though, in her defense, Sabrina didn't know who Charlie actually was. But Emma wasn't about to let it sit on her, to wallow in feeling guilty for being harsh. Charlie had been more than harsh years ago when she'd left Emma in her dust to go build a shiny new life in the big city. That had gone exactly as Emma had predicted. Charlie had gone to work for Darcy Whatsherface and, a few months later, moved in with her. Apparently, it had been super easy for her to forget about any history she'd had with Emma. She'd heeded the siren's call of the Big Apple and the successful older woman without so much as a backward glance. At least, that's what it had felt like to Emma. Now? She only had one question.

What the hell was Charlie doing back in Shaker Falls making pie?

❖

Charlie's college roommate, Lily Bricker, was about the only person she knew in her age group that would rather talk on the phone than text. Charlie never understood why—just got to a point where she realized it was simply Lily's thing, and if Charlie ever wanted to catch up with her, she was going to have to have an actual conversation. On the phone.

Charlie was not a huge fan of live conversation, but for Lily, she always made an exception. Almost always, anyway. Because there were times, she had to be honest, that she'd see Lily's name pop up on her screen, and she just wasn't up for setting aside an hour of her day or evening to talk. She could do other things while having a text conversation. Because God forbid her multitasking self didn't get fourteen things done at once.

That night, though, she was flopped on her bed, her stomach full of her mother's meatloaf, and seriously considering going to sleep before nine. A horrifying possibility, she could admit, but Lily saved her.

"Hey, bitch, what's up?" Standard greeting in Lily's world. She only called you a bitch if she loved you. "You hanging in there in Small Town Land?"

"I miss the city. Not gonna lie."

"I bet." Lily worked at a large, prestigious advertising firm in Boston. "I've got some feelers out with people I know to see who might be looking to hire. Your résumé up to date?" Typical Lily, getting the business-y work stuff out of the way first. As soon as Darcy had dumped Charlie, Lily had offered to help her find another job. Or *a* job, as Charlie had stopped working more than a few hours a week for Darcy's firm, in favor of volunteer work and things the wives and girlfriends of successful people did instead of going to an actual job forty hours a week. It was why she had little money when things ended. She wasn't making much. When Lily had offered, Charlie was still reeling over what had happened, the change in her situation, the need to go into hiding and lick her wounds, so she'd kind of just smiled and nodded and let Lily do her thing. Apparently, Lily had.

"I think so, but I'll take a look tomorrow. I'm too tired tonight."

"Tired? It's eight twenty-seven. What's wrong with you? Are you sick? Did you turn eighty since you've been away?"

Charlie snuggled down into the pillows and filled her in on everything that had happened since her return home. Including her new job and her run-ins—that's how she was looking at them—with Emma.

"Emma's in town?" Lily knew all about their history, the good and the bad. "I thought she went off to culinary school and was like you, never wanted to go back to Small Town, USA."

Charlie's memory tossed her an image of Celia Grier—Emma's mom—sitting at the bar that first day Charlie walked in, slightly overserved, kind of loud and floppy. She also remembered Amber's cryptic explanation for why Emma was in town. "Emma's mother has always had some issues. From what I can tell, Emma decided not to leave her here on her own. I guess. I'm not sure."

"You didn't ask her?"

Charlie snorted. "Yeah, I'm not exactly her favorite person." She told Lily about work, about the pie, about Emma eating right from the middle.

Lily's laugh blasted through the phone like a gunshot. "Oh my God, that's such a dick move. And also kind of awesome, if you think about it."

"Shut up." Charlie had been trying *not* to think about it. "It was definitely a dick move."

"Does she know why you're back?"

"Not from me."

Nose scrunched, lips pursed. That was Lily's thinking face and Charlie pictured it. "Yeah, that's a subject that might take some... finesse."

A yawn cranked Charlie's mouth open. "I am way too beat to finesse anything. I forgot how tiring it is to be on your feet for nine hours a day."

"God bless the desk job, amirite?"

A grunt was Charlie's response.

"You gonna talk to her?"

"Like, give her details?" While Charlie's tone said, *That's the stupidest thing I've ever heard*, her head—she realized in that moment—had been leaning a little bit in that very direction: actually trying to have a conversation with Emma.

"Is that dumb?"

"I don't know." She really didn't. Her energy reserves were so low at that point that thinking about anything beyond watching something mindless on Netflix and drifting off to sleep was just not possible.

She managed to keep herself awake and even engage with Lily for a while longer. Lily caught her up on her job, her new boyfriend, and her tentative plans for taking a long weekend to visit Shaker Falls because she missed her bestie. Charlie had to admit, that was nice. Out of sight, out of mind seemed to be the running theme back in New York, and she'd actually started to think about her marketing career as her previous life. That's what it felt like, so long ago and so far away. But Lily was a tie to that old life. Proof that Charlie hadn't dreamed up the past five years, that they actually did happen.

By the time they finally hung up, it was closing in on nine thirty, and Charlie felt the slightest bit better turning off the lights and clicking on an old episode of *Gossip Girl* on Netflix. She propped her laptop next to her on the bed and settled in.

The alarm was going to go off in six and a half hours, and then she was going to do it all over again.

CHAPTER EIGHT

Charlie was a week into her new job, but she still had mornings of complete disorientation when her alarm went off. Like, she didn't know where she was, what time it was, why there was an alarm, and who was it waking up in what was technically still the middle of the night? She groaned every time when she realized it was all for her.

Showering at night would have been a smart use of her time, so she wouldn't have to in the morning and could sleep for an extra few minutes, but standing under the water that early went a long way toward helping her wake up and *almost* function. So she took a quick one, got dressed, and headed quietly up to the kitchen.

Sherry's presence startled her, and she stumbled on the last step.

"God, you scared me," Charlie said quietly as she pressed a hand to her chest and recovered. Sherry was pouring coffee into a travel mug, and Charlie felt certain she had seen exactly this picture before. "I'm having déjà vu," she said with a grin. When Sherry didn't respond, Charlie asked, "Why are you up so early?"

"I'm assisting in a surgery first thing and want to prepare."

"Really? That's so cool." Charlie grabbed herself a mug from the cabinet.

Sherry screwed the top on her mug and shouldered her bag. "See ya."

"Bye." Charlie gave a half-hearted wave as dejection sat on her shoulders. Okay, it was obvious they needed to talk, she and her sister. Something was on Sherry's mind and she'd never been one to just give it up. You had to move in slowly, crowbar in hand, and pry it out of her little by little. And sometimes, it was freaking exhausting. She'd been that way her entire life, and there'd been a time when Charlie was pretty good at getting her to talk. She wondered now if she still had the skill. Then she wondered at the fact that they were both adults, and why in the world should she have to work so hard to get her sister to say what she was thinking? She sighed loudly in the empty kitchen. That was just it—Sherry was her sister, and Charlie didn't like the weird cold shoulder she'd been getting from her. If she wanted to find out the reason, she was going to have to ask.

With a shake of her head, Charlie filled her own cup with coffee, doctored it up. It was too hot to take a slug, but she did it anyway because four fifteen a.m. was insanely early and she was practically sleepwalking. She needed that blast of caffeine, the sooner, the better.

The smell of Sandy's cinnamon rolls? A lovely thing to be greeted by in the morning, Charlie decided as she walked into The Muffin Top, and it perked her right up. Not fully—hello, four thirty a.m.—but it helped her feel a little bit less like a zombie, especially after shoving one of the rolls directly into her face.

The morning rush was similar to the day before. Many of the same faces. Three people asking Sandy when she was going to start serving coffee. One sophisticated older gentleman with a goatee and a gorgeous head of silver hair chatting Sandy up for longer than necessary. Charlie and Bethany exchanged a knowing look over that. Later, when the usual lull came, Sandy pulled Charlie aside.

"I know you talked about the whole coffee thing. Do you think you could do some research on it? Give me pros and cons or…something?" She made a face that said she was uneducated in this arena. *Luckily for her*, Charlie thought, *I am not.*

"I'd love to," Charlie said, enthusiasm hitting her suddenly and all at once. This was right in her wheelhouse. Unexpected excitement bubbled up. "It's what I do."

"Great. No hurry. Just when you get around to it."

"You got it."

"Ready to make some pie?"

"Absolutely. Suggestions?" Charlie was surprised to find herself actually looking forward to it.

"It looks sunny and gorgeous out today. Let's try a lemon meringue, and then you can surprise me the next time. Deal?"

"Deal."

Lemon meringue pie was pretty straightforward and simple, basically a lot of eggs and a lot of lemon. Which was not to say it was easy to make, because it could actually be a little finicky, Charlie knew. You could make the filling too watery, which would make the crust soggy. Your meringue could be too thin or not stiff enough. There were lots of variables in what was actually a pretty basic pie as far as ingredients went. She was thrilled to find fresh lemons in the fridge, as they made the taste of the pie so much brighter than bottled lemon juice did—she'd made it both ways. She separated the eggs while they were still cold from the fridge, then let them sit for a bit to get to room temperature while she worked on the crust.

"Hey, can you make three today?" Sandy asked from the cookie workstation, where she was mixing dough and Bethany was frosting half-moon cookies as big around as a small plate.

With a nod, Charlie added more ingredients to her bowl of piecrust dough and got to work.

It was when she was making her meringue that she felt Bethany behind her, watching as she used Sandy's fancy bakery-issue stand mixer to beat the egg whites and cream of tartar until soft peaks started to form. Then she added the sugar and the salt and let it beat some more.

"Oh, it's getting all shiny," Bethany breathed, clearly engrossed.

"That's what I want," Charlie told her. When it was finished, she began spreading the cloud-like white meringue over the still warm lemon filling already in the piecrust.

"You don't have to let it cool?" Bethany asked.

"Nope. You want to spread the meringue while things are still warm, and you want to spread it all the way to the crust, so it seals the lemon filling in and doesn't separate." Charlie did so while Bethany watched, then made some decorative peaks with the back of her spatula. "There."

"How do you know how to do all of this?" Bethany seemed almost in awe. "I mean, I've worked here for a while, but I need to follow recipes and be super careful. You're like one of those bakers on TV who never have to look up anything."

"Well, I used to be able to make pretty much any pie without following a recipe. I had them memorized because I baked with my grandma all the time, and stuff just kind of sticks in your brain. But I've been in the city for almost five years, so…" She held up the recipe and fanned it around. "I'm a little rusty."

The bakery never smelled anything but tempting and delicious, and that day, she filled the air with the lovely warm scent of lemons. Three pies went into the oven. They'd only take about a half hour, and she watched carefully to make sure the meringue toasted but didn't burn.

The bell over the door tinkled, and a glance at the clock told Charlie it was very possibly a lunch delivery from EG's. And sure enough, the redheaded girl—Jules, right?—came bouncing in like Tigger, bag in hand. Charlie came out from the back and stood near the counter.

"Hi, Sandy," Jules said, her voice super cheerful. *What I wouldn't give to bottle just a fraction of her exuberance*, Charlie thought. Then she gave Charlie a nod and a huge smile. "Hi. I'm Jules." She held her hand out and they shook as Charlie introduced herself. "I come bearing gifts."

"*Ooh*," Sandy said, drawing out the word as Jules pulled containers from the bag. "What do we have today?"

"Wild mushroom risotto."

Three containers this time instead of two. Wasn't that interesting? Sandy opened one and inhaled deeply. "God, that smells amazing."

"Make sure you tell Emma that. She's a little frazzled today."

"Oh yeah? How come? Everything okay?" Sandy dug a spoon into the risotto, tasted it, and her eyes closed as she savored it.

"She said she was out too late last night." Jules glanced at the two customers at the table by the window and leaned over the counter more. She lowered her voice and added, "I think she was out with a girl because Sabrina didn't look very happy when she came in."

"Who's Sabrina?" Charlie asked before she could think twice about it.

"She's a bartender at EG's," Sandy supplied. "Nice girl."

"She really is," Jules said, still keeping her voice down. "But I think she wants more than being Emma's flavor of the month."

"They've had a thing," Sandy whispered to Charlie. "Emma's gay."

It took all Charlie's willpower to keep from bursting out laughing, because if anybody knew Emma was gay, it was certainly her. Instead, she just nodded.

"So much drama," Jules said, then shrugged and smiled. "What can you do?"

"Tell Emma not to worry. The risotto is fabulous." Sandy held up a spoonful before putting it into her mouth.

"Will do. And she said to send more pie." With that, Jules bounced out of the bakery, and Charlie stood there blinking as her words hung in the air like the scent of the brownies in the oven.

Emma said to send more pie.

"You hear that?" Sandy asked, big smile on her face as she pushed playfully at Charlie. "More pie."

"I wasn't sure if she liked it," she said honestly as she recalled Emma chewing, analyzing, criticizing. "She asked me if I'd ever been to…" What was the name again? She searched her brain for the other bakery Emma had mentioned to her. Taunted her with, really. "Mama Jo's? Does that sound right? Said I should check it out."

Sandy made a face. "Ugh. That woman."

Charlie caught Bethany's eye behind Sandy's back and raised her eyebrows in question. "Do I smell some healthy competition?"

Bethany snorted at the same time Sandy laughed bitterly. "If I had to guess, I'd say maybe forty percent of her inventory is made on the premises. *Maybe.*"

"Really? What about her pie?"

"Frozen." Bethany was putting whoopie pies in the display case, and she spoke without looking up.

"Trucked in from Burlington or some such place." Sandy rolled her eyes. Then she put the last bite of her risotto into her mouth and seemed to study Charlie for a moment. "If Emma told you to go to Mama Jo's, she was yanking your chain, you know."

Charlie felt her eyes widen a bit, as she hadn't considered that. "She was?"

"Absolutely. If you knew Emma, you'd know she hates pretty much anything that isn't made from scratch. Or mostly from scratch."

If she knew Emma. An interesting choice of words, that, and a pretty large clue that Sandy didn't know about her past with Emma, that her mom hadn't said anything. She couldn't decide if she was grateful for that or a little bit disappointed.

Everybody got back to work, and before Charlie knew it, it was time to clock out. Sandy had boxed up two of her pies and put the third in the display case. It hadn't lasted past noon, which made Charlie ridiculously happy.

"Take these over to EG's and you're free." Sandy handed her the boxes. "See you tomorrow."

Charlie nodded. She'd agreed to work a few hours every other Saturday. *So much for this being a part-time gig, right?* She sighed quietly as she headed out the front door, pies in hand.

❖

Definitely attractive. In kind of a sultry way. A little mysterious.

It wasn't really surprising that Charlie studied the bartender a lot more closely this visit. Sabrina. She didn't really look like a Sabrina, though she wasn't really sure what somebody who looked like a Sabrina would actually look like, so that was kind of an odd thought to have.

Sabrina was pretty. Charlie had to admit that. Taller than her. Taller than Emma as well. Brown hair that she'd pulled back into a messy bun. Her build was thin, long limbs and fingers, few curves, but she was quite attractive. She didn't seem at all like Emma's type. And as soon as that thought chugged through Charlie's brain, she realized that maybe she had no idea what Emma's type was now. When they were together, she liked lighter hair, an athletic build. Maybe her tastes had changed. *I mean, really, how would I know?*

Sabrina seemed slightly less cheerful when she greeted Charlie this time than she had last time, and there was a glint of melancholy in her dark eyes. "Hi, there," she said. Indicating the boxes with her chin, she asked, "Pie?"

Charlie gave a nod but, for some strange reason, felt less compelled to flee this time, so she just stood there.

"Emma!"

The shout did not come from Sabrina, and they both flinched at the sound of it, went wide-eyed with surprise. Charlie turned to see Celia Grier sitting on the same stool she'd occupied during her first visit.

Emma burst out of the kitchen then, the swinging door flapping behind her. "Mom," she hissed, quietly enough so Charlie almost didn't hear her. "How many times have I told you, you can't be yelling like that in here?"

"I wasn't yelling," Celia said, and it wasn't until she reached for the glass in front of her on the bar and missed it completely that Charlie realized she was much drunker than the last time. Emma noticed her then, and an obvious shot of shame flashed across her face. Charlie's heart squeezed in her chest as old memories of helping Emma take care of her mother came flooding back.

"You were, and you need to go home now, okay?" Emma's voice had gone gentler as she helped Celia off the stool, catching her arm as she almost went down to the floor like a rag doll, counting on legs that didn't work as well as she'd apparently expected.

"I need my purse," Celia said, grabbing for the bag on the hook under the bar. When she glanced up and her eyes met Charlie's, she gave her a weak smile. "There you are, Charlie. I knew you'd be back."

Charlie didn't stop to think. She simply set the pie boxes down on the bar and took the few steps toward them.

Emma raised a hand, like Charlie was a car and she was a traffic cop, and Charlie stopped in her tracks. "No," Emma said. Her voice was quiet as she glanced quickly around the restaurant, presumably to see who was watching. "I don't need your help."

They stung, those words, and Charlie swallowed. It didn't matter that she understood them. It didn't even matter that, deep down, she'd expected them. They still felt like a slice from a razor blade. Her shoulders dropped and she was startled by how deflated she suddenly felt as she stood there and watched Emma guide her mother through the swinging kitchen doors and out of sight. And then she stood for a moment longer.

With a grimace, she turned back to Sabrina, whose expression, rather than appearing at all empathetic, just seemed annoyed. She shook her head as she caught Charlie's eye. "That woman. I don't know how—or why—Emma puts up with it."

There was so much Charlie could've said right then. So many things she knew that Sabrina very obviously did not. And she wanted to. She should have. She wanted to put that bitch right in her place. But her mind tossed her an image of Emma's upheld hand, the tone of her voice as she told Charlie she didn't need her help, how it was filled with so many things, none of them happy, and so she clamped her mouth shut, not wanting to add to Emma's embarrassment.

"I'll make sure Alec gets the pies." Sabrina gestured to the boxes on the bar.

Charlie had no idea who Alec was, but she thanked Sabrina anyway and pushed her way out of the restaurant, which had somehow started to feel like it was closing in on her, making her feel like she needed to escape. Her heart pounded like that of a claustrophobe in an elevator, and once outside in the fresh air, she took in a huge lungful. She felt so many things in that moment: empathy, regret, wishfulness, shame, sadness. They all came and sat on her and she swore she could feel her feet sink into the ground under their weight. A ball of emotion settled itself in her throat.

She just wanted to go home.

❖

What was the Universe trying to do to her?

"Goddamn it," Emma muttered, shaking her head in frustration over what had just happened, as she gathered ingredients for the garlic herb butter that would be served with the filet mignon tonight. Why did Charlie have to be here? Again?

It was Emma's life, taking care of her mother, and it always had been. It just…was. Didn't faze her anymore. Well. That wasn't entirely true. There was always an element of shame, of embarrassment, when she had to call Tom the Uber to take her drunk mother home so she didn't disrupt business. But the truth was, she would rather have her mom nearby where she could keep an eye on her than at some other bar, drinking and getting hit on by strange men. And today was an exception. She didn't always get *that* drunk. Please. When you'd been drinking steadily for more than fifteen years, you built up a pretty high tolerance. It took a lot of alcohol for Celia Grier to actually appear drunk. A lot.

Charlie had wanted to help.

There had been a split second where, in Emma's mind, they were sixteen again, Charlie was staying overnight because Emma didn't want to leave her mom alone, and Charlie helped get Celia to bed. She'd done it every time, stepped in to help, and never complained. Never mocked. Never balked. It was part of Emma's life back then, and Charlie never questioned it.

Today, when Charlie'd taken a step toward her, it was like no time at all had passed.

That pissed her off.

Because she'd spent a boatload of time moving past Charlie Stetko. Pushing her out of her mind and out of her heart and what did she do? Showed back up and took all that time and all that work and crumpled it into a ball, tossed it in the trash.

"Goddamn it." She blew out one more frustrated breath and gave her head a literal shake, hoping to reboot her brain and focus on tonight's dinner.

"Mm. Taste this." Sabrina was suddenly next to her, holding out a fork with a bite of what looked to be lemon meringue pie. Charlie's lemon meringue pie.

Emma knew better than to hesitate and closed her lips over the fork. The flavors exploded in her mouth. The smooth lightness of the meringue. The tart sweetness of the lemon. The delicate yet firm crust. "Good Lord, she can make a pie."

"And I was civilized and cut a small slice, rather than plunge a fork into the middle like some people we know." Sabrina arched an eyebrow and looked pointedly at Emma. She didn't know the history Emma had with Charlie—she hadn't told her—so the cherry pie incident had seemed strange to Sabrina, but Emma had offered no explanation other than she'd been in a bad mood. Any other details would have meant letting Sabrina further in and she didn't want to do that.

With a nod, she directed Sabrina to take the pies to Alec, so he knew to add them to the dessert menu for the evening, and she returned her focus to her work.

The kitchen relaxed her. It always had. Everything else faded away when she was busy chopping or mixing or sautéing. It really came as no surprise to anybody when she'd chosen to go to culinary school. She'd been cooking for herself since she was a kid, and somehow, coming up with a meal made her feel like an artist. Creative. Original. No different than a painter or a sculptor. She hadn't had the easiest of childhoods or the easiest of lives so far, but she'd found her passion early on, and she knew most people couldn't say that. Gratitude filled her heart almost every day.

Her cell vibrated in her back pocket as she gently stirred the Alfredo sauce for tonight's fettuccini special. She glanced at the screen, then answered.

"Hey, Mom. Make it home okay?" The number of times she'd

asked that exact question had to be in the thousands by now. Tens of thousands. Hundreds of thousands, maybe.

"Yeah. I'm so sorry, honey…" Her mother's voice cracked, and she started to cry.

Emma breathed in deeply as she held the phone away from her ear and let her mother sob out her apology. Another thing she'd heard a thousand times. "It's okay. But I really need you to try and pay attention to how much you have. You know?"

"I'm such an embarrassment. All I do is embarrass you…"

Emma kept stirring so the sauce wouldn't burn and closed her eyes. "Mom…" But there was no interrupting when Celia Grier got on a streak of self-pity. She just had to wait her out.

Her mother was a functioning alcoholic. Had been ever since Emma was old enough to know what that was. There had been endless arguments over the years about getting help, but finally *finally*— Emma understood that her mother would get help when she was ready to and not one second before. No matter how much Emma begged, pleaded, threatened. Her threats were empty anyway, and they both knew it. Her mother was all the family Emma had, and she wasn't going to leave her to fend for herself. Ever. No matter what.

Even if it kills me. Or her. Which it might.

The sobs had devolved into wet sniffles, and Emma knew the sound well: recovery from her emotional outburst.

"It's all okay, Mom. I promise."

They hung up, Emma feeling the same way she always did after similar conversations with her mom: wrung out, empathetic, grateful. And this time, more than a little annoyed. Her mother had obviously been more intoxicated than usual. She needed to have a talk with Sabrina about that.

A glance at her watch told her it was after four. The early birds would start showing up, so she returned her focus to her job.

"How're we doing, Alec?" she called out as she headed to the enormous refrigerator. Inside were the two lemon meringue pies, looking as perfect as if they were props for a photo shoot of food porn. And just like that, her mind went wandering right back in the direction of Charlie Stetko once again.

"Goddamn it."

CHAPTER NINE

D o you have the cookbook Grandma gave you?" Charlie asked her
mother as the family sat down to dinner. "I want to look through
it and check online for some different pies." It was a little weird, she
thought, her dawning realization—or recollection, rather—that she
really, *really* enjoyed baking. No mixers had been touched when she'd
lived in New York. Darcy never understood making something from
scratch when you could just pay somebody to bring it to you. Charlie
had focused on business. On advertising. On image and status and
fashion, and baking had gradually faded into a distant memory.

"You're liking it there, huh?" Her mother set a big bowl of salad on
the table and took her seat. It was the four of them for dinner, everyone
except Shane, including Sherry, who was home earlier than usual.

"Yeah, it's good for now."

Sherry's snort was quiet, and Charlie didn't think their parents
heard it. The look she shot Sherry was ignored, and she seemed to
concentrate intently on her dinner.

"I get the impression Sandy's trying to add an arm to the business
by selling pie to restaurants. She's had me take some over to EG's more
than once."

"Emma's place?" Sherry stopped with her fork halfway to her
mouth and turned to Charlie.

Charlie nodded, chewed her broiled haddock slowly.

"I bet that was fun for her." The eye roll and condescending
expression that followed pissed Charlie right off.

"What's that supposed to mean?" Too much venom in her tone,
but she didn't care.

"What do you think it means?" Sherry snapped back.

"What is your problem?" Sick and tired of the cold shoulder and brush-offs she'd gotten from her sister since the minute she'd come home, Charlie's blood had started to boil. Enough. Enough already.

"Girls. Stop it. Can we just enjoy dinner, please?" Her dad was always the peacekeeper, but that didn't mean his booming voice wasn't startling. He used it to his advantage at work to direct his guys and at home to get the attention of his distracted kids. It was only the softness of his eyes that made Charlie back off, but it was far from over. She understood that Sherry had been upset with her for breaking up with Emma—she'd liked her a lot and, Charlie now suspected, still did—but more than four years had gone by and it seemed a little silly that she'd still be hanging on to that. *I'm your sister, for God's sake.*

"Oh, that restaurant is beautiful," their mother chimed in. "Your father and I eat there a lot."

Terrific. While I was away, the entirety of my family has become BFFs with my ex. "A little heads-up would've been nice. I had no idea she owned it until I walked in."

A couple nods. A hum of sympathy. That's about all she got.

All right. Fine. Whatever. "Anyway, I'd like to come up with some creative pies. Play around a little bit. Sandy seems like she'd be okay with that sort of thing."

"What do you think of the place?" her dad asked, finishing off his brussels sprouts, the only food on the table Charlie completely ignored. If she wanted to eat balls of leaves, she would just go gnaw on the front lawn.

The question was her dad's way of asking her to put her business and marketing degree to work, and she knew it. "I think it's a great little place with tons of potential. I've sort of touched on a couple of things, but I don't want to walk in and start telling Sandy what to do, you know?" It was true. In her head, she could see so much that could be done with The Muffin Top. Shaker Falls was a small town, but it was surrounded by other small towns. And those other small towns were full of people who were willing to drive a little ways to get something they felt was worth the trip. At the same time, Charlie didn't want to be that millennial who came in and started telling somebody from the next generation up all the things they were doing wrong with their business.

"Like that punk I hired that one time?" A grunt from her dad.

"Exactly like that," Charlie said with a small laugh. He'd hired a young guy many summers ago, and all he did was spend his days telling her father all the ways he should be doing things differently. Drove him nuts. Charlie was all for using what she'd learned to help better a business, but she was not a know-it-all, nor did she want to come across as one.

"Baby steps," her father said, and he was exactly right.

❖

Because it was a Saturday and Charlie was only working a few hours, Sandy told her she didn't have to show up at half-past pitch-black. So she slept in until six and was walking in the back door of The Muffin Top by seven.

She was reasonably sure she'd never get used to how wonderful it was to walk into the bakery in the morning and be enveloped by the most comforting scents in life: sugar, butter, cinnamon, apples. Charlie had realized a couple days earlier that the first thing she did when entering The Muffin Top was stop in her tracks and inhale deeply. There was nothing like it.

Sandy was out front, waiting on a handful of customers. Charlie called out a good morning, donned an apron, and checked the list on the whiteboard of things that needed to be done. Then she got to work.

"How do you feel about making some turnovers?" Sandy asked a few minutes later, after she'd taken care of the line. "Just cherry and only one batch." She reached for a little box with recipe cards in it, sifted through, and pulled one out. As she handed it over, she glanced down, slightly sheepish. "One of these days, I'm going to get all my recipes onto a computer or something. Live in the twenty-first century." The bell over the door tinkled, and she went to handle the customers.

Charlie scanned the recipe card, but her head had already veered off toward the idea of creating a recipe database for The Muffin Top. Notes. Her thumbs flew as she jotted a reminder to do some research. Then it was turnover time.

Fewer overall customers, but larger orders. That seemed to be Saturdays. People came in to pick up boxes of cookies, cupcakes, and various baked goods they'd preordered for events. So wrapped up in baking her pies during the week, she apparently hadn't paid a lot of attention to the orders Bethany had been taking at the same time.

Turnovers cooled, Charlie carried a tray out to the front to put in the display case. Pride swelled because damn if they didn't look gorgeous, all golden brown with white drizzled icing and hints of cherry peeking out the corners.

"Charlie! Hi."

Over the top of the tray, Charlie saw the smiling face of Amber McCann, her joy contagious, as usual, and she couldn't help but smile back. "Hey there. How are you?"

"I'm great. The sun is shining. The birds are singing. It's a beautiful day." If Amber held out her arms and began to spin while she sang a lively tune, it would've been perfect. She looked fresh and summery in a green and white sundress, a lightweight white cardigan over it. "I didn't know you were working here."

"For a couple weeks now." Charlie glanced at Sandy, gave her a smile. "What brings you in?"

"Oh, I have an order to pick up. We're having the first barbecue of the season at our place tomorrow, so I ordered an assortment of cookies."

"Yeah? Who's we?" Charlie asked, curious. She realized that, aside from Amber's job as a successful real estate agent, she knew very little about her life.

"Me and Levi. My boyfriend."

There was a boyfriend? Charlie searched her brain for any mention of a boyfriend when she and Amber had met at Chug, but nothing came up. She found Amber's order and rang her up. "Well, you're going to get some nice weather, from what I've heard."

"You should come." Wide-eyed and suddenly excited, a grin blossomed slowly on Amber's face as if she'd just come up with a fabulous idea.

"I'm sorry?"

"Oh my God, yes! Come over. It'll be great. It's very casual and relaxed. Not huge. Levi cooks a mean burger, and he'd love to meet you, since I've been talking about you so much lately."

"Me?" Charlie wasn't sure why that would be.

"Yes, you," Amber clarified. "It's not every day my high school bestie returns home from the big, bad city." Amber's face grew serious, though still remained friendly and open. "I haven't seen you in years, Charlie, and I'd like you to meet the man I love."

Warmth radiated from the inside out at Amber's words. A combination of guilt and happiness flooded Charlie. She'd been mentally weighing the pros and cons. Something to get her out of the house, hanging with people besides her mother. Not knowing anybody there and standing in a corner alone. But after Amber's comment, there was nothing to do but nod and say truthfully, "I'd love to meet him, too. Tell me when and where."

❖

Good numbers, folks sitting at the bar until last call. It had been a decent Saturday night. Emma was satisfied with the sales. Stretched out on the couch with her laptop, a glass within reach of a new Meritage that Dani, her wine rep and good friend, had suggested, she went over it all. The specials had been a hit, as had Charlie's lemon meringue pie, both selling out before eight. She had mixed emotions about that, but overall, her restaurant was doing pretty well. It wasn't gangbusters, but in a town as small as Shaker Falls, it was going to take some time for word to reach other nearby towns, and she had a food blogger with a huge following coming in next week, so a good review might draw an uptick in customers. Emma needed to decide what to cook for him.

Flipping through meal ideas in her head was interrupted by the ringing of her FaceTime app, and she hit the answer button without hesitation. The screen filled with the smiling face of Gabriel Battaglia— typically disheveled salt-and-pepper hair, eyes that held the bright sharpness of somebody who'd been a night owl for most of his life, a face with that slightly craggy, weathered look of a man who either spent too much time in the sun or too many years in an overly fast-paced job. For Gabe, it was a little of both. He'd spent nearly thirty years in the restaurant business before retiring to teach the culinary arts—and learn to play golf.

"Well, hello there, young man," Emma said with a smile as his face came into focus on her screen.

"Ah, bless you, my child, for calling me young. Something I haven't been in a very long time." He seemed to study her through the screen for a moment before saying, "I figured you'd be up."

"Life of a chef, right?" Emma said with a big smile. Talking to Gabe always gave her a boost, lifted her, shifted her attitude. "What's new with you? How'd the semester go?"

"It went well. A couple of very promising chefs in the midst of a mostly average class." Gabe's voice was deep, gravelly. "Tell me, how is EG's doing? What were tonight's specials? Were they a hit?"

These were the conversations Emma loved. That she lived for. Talking to somebody who completely got it was like breathing better oxygen. Oh, she had friends she could chat with. Her mom sometimes. But nobody *really* understood the restaurant business unless they'd been a part of the restaurant business, and Gabe was the best.

They spent the next half hour talking various dishes, specifically the Gruyère mac and cheese Emma had been tweaking for weeks now. Gabe had discovered a new brand of spices that he was crazy about and promised to send Emma some samples.

"And how are things on the home front?" Gabe's voice softened, took on a fatherly tone, which Emma didn't mind at all. When you were the closest thing to a father figure somebody ever had, it was totally allowed. "Your mom okay?"

"Meh." She made a face into the webcam and tipped her head one way, then the other. "Some days are better than others."

"I hear that."

"She does okay, though. Gets herself to work and does well there. Only lets things get out of control when she doesn't have to work the next day. So…progress? I guess?"

"And the foot? Have you put it down yet?" Gentle, Emma had to give him that. It was a question she'd expected but could admit to hoping it would get skipped. Gabriel had been telling her for months that it was time to put her foot down with her mother. Insist that she get help. Not just suggest it. Not slip pamphlets into her mailbox or send her links to AA meetings. *Insist.*

Emma sighed. "The foot is still hovering in the air." Shame filled her, telling him this. She knew it was a silly reaction, but it was there. Embarrassed. Weak.

"Stop that," Gabriel said, a sharpness in his voice. "Stop that right now. You do it in your own time. I'm not pushing. I'm just asking."

Eyes welled and Emma clenched her teeth, willing them to clear. "I know. It's just…" Her swallow was loud in the quiet of her apartment.

"She's your mom."

"Yeah." Emma's voice was a whisper.

"It's okay, Em. Really." A beat went by. Gabe waited, gave her time to collect herself. Then he asked, "So, what will you do with your Sunday off? It's June. It's supposed to be sunny. I hope you're going to get outside and soak up some vitamin D."

"As a matter of fact, I am." The grin came as she sat up a bit, relieved to be talking about something else. "Friends are having a barbecue, so I'm going to their house to hang out on their back lawn and drink beer and eat hamburgers. I'm guessing on the hamburgers, but it seems logical for a barbecue."

"Good. I don't like the idea of you spreading yourself too thin and not allowing yourself any time to just...what was that phrase you always use?"

"Be a person?"

"Yes! You should people tomorrow. Just be a person."

"I will. Promise."

They covered a few more inconsequential things and signed off, and Emma felt lighter, like she'd been carrying a sandbag over her shoulder and somebody had just lifted it from her. That was the result of talking with Gabe, always. A glance at the clock told her it was going on two a.m. She closed up her laptop, finished the last of her wine, and headed for the bedroom.

She needed to get some sleep if she intended to be a person tomorrow. Being a person was hard work.

CHAPTER TEN

O ut of sorts. That was the best way for Emma to describe herself on Sundays. A little bit out of sorts. Especially in the mornings. It was the only day of the week the restaurant was closed—if she didn't have friends who cared about her sanity and well-being, she'd be open seven days a week—and every Sunday, she felt a bit adrift, like a dinghy cut loose from its larger ship.

Sleeping in wasn't really possible for her. Never had been. It was hard to work in a field where being a night owl was necessary when you were actually a morning person, but Emma had functioned on roughly five hours of sleep since she was a teenager, so waking up before seven a.m. when she didn't have to was nothing new to her.

A gentle breeze ruffled her hair as Emma stood in front of the open window of her living room and sipped from her second cup of coffee, strong and hot as the first. Dressed in lightweight gray sweats and a white tank top, her thick hair piled on top of her head, Emma allowed herself to feel relaxed. She inhaled the fresh morning air through her nose, held it, slowly let it out, and tried to decide what she might want to do today.

That question was decided for her when her phone pinged. It was a group text from Ryan Kim, golf pro at Shaker Hills Golf Club and one of her closest friends.

Barbecue at Amber's today. Don't forget. Want me to pick you up?

It was funny how she'd just talked to Gabe last night about the barbecue, but this morning, it seemed to be wiped from her brain. For a split second, she thought about making an excuse, but she'd told both

Ryan and Dani—who'd also received the text—that she'd go. They'd give her so much shit if she backed out now.

While Emma preferred to drive herself so that she could escape when she wanted to, having Ryan drive was usually the better choice. He was a stickler about fitness and health, and he rarely drank alcohol. Having him behind the wheel was always a good call.

Sure, she typed. *Time?*

2ish? I'll grab Dani first and be over.

Emma sent a thumbs-up emoji, then set the phone down, deciding on one more cup of coffee. She'd taken two steps and her phone pinged again. This time, it was Dani. As expected.

A thumbs-up? Seriously? Are you seventy?

Her soft laugh carried through her apartment. The thumb had been a running joke ever since she had sent one accidentally, and Dani teased her mercilessly about it, though Emma wasn't quite sure why. Now, she sent them on purpose. Constantly.

Feels like it sometimes, she sent back. *Hey, bring a couple bottles of the Meritage for Amber. I'll pay you.*

Dani agreed.

Normally, Emma would make an appetizer or ask about helping with the main course. After all, she was a chef and her friends knew that. But Amber was one of the sweetest people on the planet, and she was adamant about not wanting Emma to work in any way, shape, or form on her day off. Since showing up empty-handed was not an option for her, wine it would be.

Third—*and final, oh my God*—cup of coffee in hand, she walked across the hardwood floor to her bedroom and began the loathsome task of figuring out what to wear.

❖

"I don't understand how life is so unfair." Danielle Schwartz stood with her hands parked on her hips, looking annoyed as could be, though Emma knew she was pretending. "How is it that you can wear something so simple and look so gorgeous? How?" She waited for Emma to fold herself into the back seat of Ryan's two-door coupe, then pushed the seat back and got in.

"Listen, somebody with your movie star hair is not allowed to complain," Emma said. Dani had a head of thick curly hair that fell past her shoulders in waves of sunset red.

"Agreed," Ryan said, raising one hand. Then he pulled out of the EG's parking lot and pointed the car toward Amber's house.

"Please. My hair enters a room before I do. Take a good look now because summer is here, and that means humidity, and that means it's ponytails and buns and braids and hats until fall."

"I hear that," Emma said. Most people would be surprised how humid it could get in the summer in the Northeast. "I'm so glad I had the AC installed in my place last year."

They chatted a bit, but the ride was quick, and Ryan was parallel parking on Amber's street before they knew it.

"Who's gonna be here?" Emma asked. "The usual gang?"

"I think so," Dani said with a nod. "You know Amber—there will probably be some newbies. She loves to weave new people into her day-to-day gang."

Irony. Dani never saw it and Emma smothered a grin. Dani and Amber were so much alike in their love of people and their outgoing personalities, it was frightening. Not that either of them recognized it. They were good friends and had been for years, but they could also rub each other the wrong way, which Emma always found fascinating.

Wine bottles in hand—Ryan carrying a six-pack of flavored seltzer—they headed up the driveway and followed the music around to the backyard.

"Hey!" Amber said when she saw the trio come through her back gate. "You made it." She hugged both Ryan and Dani, but seemed to save most of her hugging energy for Emma. Wrapping her up and holding her tightly, Amber said in her ear, "I'm so happy to see you. I miss your face, you know."

Emma squeezed her back, her own heart growing at the warm welcome. She and Amber had been friends in high school—many of the people mingling in the yard had, she could see—but they'd grown closer after college. When many of their classmates were off exploring the world and finding bigger, more exciting places to live, she and Amber had both come home to Shaker Falls not long after getting their degrees. She hadn't expected that to be a bonding thing, but it was.

"Here." Dani held out a bottle of the Meritage. "This is for you."

Emma held hers out, too, and Amber laughed. "You guys. You didn't have to do that."

"Open it and have some," Emma told her. "You'll be glad we did."

"On it." Amber waved toward the small crowd that was hanging in the backyard. "Go mingle. There are munchies on the tables under the tent. Feel free to go swimming if you want. Levi's going to throw burgers, hot dogs, and chicken on the grill by three o'clock." She grinned and the world seemed to glow. "I'm so happy you're here!" She squeezed Emma's arm, promised a quick return with wine, and headed in the back door of her house.

Emma turned to scan the yard just as Dani made a small sound and said, "There's John Garcia. My sources say he's opening a liquor store over near Clifton by the end of summer."

"Your sources? Do you work for the CIA now?"

"Hey, maybe I do." Dani made an exaggerated face, arching one eyebrow comically high as she pointed at Emma. "You don't know." She stuck out her tongue, then beelined for John, who wasn't going to know what hit him, poor dude, and Emma shook her head and smiled at the thought. Her friend was a force, that was for sure.

She had always liked Amber's place, and now that Levi lived there as well, it seemed even warmer somehow, even more inviting. The backyard wasn't huge, but it was a decent size—big enough to hold a small patio, an aboveground swimming pool, a grill that rivaled the cooking area in Emma's own restaurant kitchen, and a small tent covering two rectangular tables of food and drink. She estimated roughly fifteen to twenty people hanging out, but she knew from experience that folks would come and go all day, and by the evening when Levi stoked the fire pit, there would only be a handful left.

"Here you go." Amber returned and held out a glass of wine for Emma. She held up hers. "Cheers." They touched glasses and sipped. "Oh, that's *good*."

"Right? Dani introduced me to it last month, and I ordered a case for the restaurant. It pairs really well with a lot of things."

"Levi mentioned the other day that he wants to come in for dinner again soon, so maybe next week?" Amber's eyes suddenly went wide before Emma could answer, and she whispered, "Oh, wow, I didn't think she'd actually come."

The words were spoken so quietly, Emma wondered if she was even meant to hear them. She followed Amber's gaze and felt her own eyes widen a bit in surprise at who had just walked through the gate.

Charlie.

❖

Charlie waited a split second too long to spin around and hightail it back to her car. Amber saw her, made eye contact. Standing next to her was none other than Emma.

"Shit," she muttered.

How had it not occurred to her that Emma might be there? How had she not thought to prepare for the possibility? How had Amber not told her? She stood there, just inside the gate, six-pack of beer in one hand, pie in the other, and couldn't move. Paralyzed. Legs made of lead. Feet rooted right into the grass. Luckily, Amber came her way. She watched as Emma headed in the opposite direction and went in the back door of the house.

"You made it," Amber said, her face open and happy, and Charlie felt the tiniest bit better due to the Amber Effect. "I wasn't sure you'd come."

Charlie hadn't been, either. If she was going to be honest, that's what she'd say. And if she'd known Emma would be in attendance, she probably wouldn't have come at all. But she'd spent breakfast with her parents, who then went off to church followed by a potluck, and they wouldn't be back until the evening. Sherry was off with friends for the day—and probably wouldn't have talked to Charlie if she'd stayed anyway. And then she was alone. In the house, in the quiet. She was hit with a sudden urge to go somewhere, do something, anything but sit around in that empty house. She remembered Amber's text from yesterday with the reminder about the barbecue, the address to her house, and that had been all the push she'd needed.

Now she was here.

And so was Emma.

"Did you bring me a pie?" Genuine or feigned, it didn't matter. Amber's delight helped Charlie breathe a little easier.

"I did." She held up the box. "Chocolate peanut butter. It needs to go in the fridge if you're not going to cut it right away."

"You didn't have to do that." Amber grabbed a woman who was nearby, handed her the pie to take inside. Then she put an arm around Charlie's waist. "Come on. I'll introduce you to some people."

Relief and gratitude circled when Amber led her into the yard and toward a small group of people standing near some coolers, rather than into the house where Emma had gone. *Is this how it's going to be? We just avoid each other until the end of time?* Charlie stifled a sigh as Amber introduced her to Brian, his wife Tara, a guy named Ryan, and Amber's boyfriend, Levi.

Charlie shook everybody's hands, smiled.

"Here, let me take that." Levi took the six-pack and put it in a nearby cooler, then picked one bottle back out and held it up. "Yeah?" he asked her, and she nodded as Brian and Tara noticed another couple coming through the gate and left, presumably to greet them. Once Levi had popped the cap and handed the beer over, he said, "Amber's told me a lot about you."

Uh-oh seemed to be Charlie's initial reaction on a regular basis now. She kept it to herself and instead said, "Oh yeah? Well, don't believe everything you hear. Amber's a *huge* liar."

"Really?" Levi said, a glimmer in his blue eyes. "She speaks very highly of you."

"In that case, *do* believe everything you hear." She took a slug of her beer as Levi and the guy named Ryan chuckled. "She only speaks the truth, always."

"Levi!" Amber called from the back door. "Can you get the grill started?"

"Yes, dear," he called back, earning laughter from around the yard. "Whatever you say, dear."

And then it was just Charlie and Ryan.

"So, how do you know Amber?" Ryan asked. He was handsome and probably in his thirties. His jet-black hair was neatly styled, and his khakis, docksiders, and navy blue polo shirt made him look like he'd stepped out of the pages of a J.Crew catalog. He took a sip from the can of grapefruit seltzer he was holding.

"We actually went to high school together."

"Really? So, you're from here?"

"I am. But I've been in New York City for several years." Charlie wasn't sure why she felt the need to slip that in, but it had come out before she realized she was going to say it.

"Yeah? You're just back visiting?" Charlie was pretty sure Ryan's questions were innocent, just a guy making small talk with a girl. Despite their intrusive nature.

"For a little while, yes." She took a slug from her beer and shifted the subject smoothly. "What about you? From here?"

"Oh no." Ryan shook his head. "I'm from Philly."

"Wow, really? What brings you to Shaker Falls? A job or love?" She lifted one shoulder in a half shrug and smiled. "It's usually one of those two things that makes us leave home, right?"

Ryan nodded his agreement. "Agreed. For me, it was a job. I'm the golf pro over at SFGC."

"Seriously?" She couldn't contain her delight. They spent the next twenty minutes just shooting the breeze about golf. It was a sport she'd always wanted to learn to play but had never taken the time to.

The day went on, sunny and warm and friendly. Charlie visited with so many people. Some she remembered from school. Some were new. And as the sun began its descent, she was surprised to admit she was having a really good time. Much better than she'd expected. She and Emma had mostly avoided each other, but as the crowd thinned and people started to leave, that became harder to do. She was thinking maybe it was time for her to go when Amber came up behind her, linked an arm in Charlie's, and walked her toward the portable fire pit set up toward the back of the yard.

"You'll stick around for a while? This is the best part—when the acquaintances have gone home, and it's just my favorite people left. We'll sit around the fire, make s'mores. It'll be fun." At Charlie's hesitation, Amber said quietly, "Please? I'm so happy you're here and I'd love for you to stay."

She took in the small circle around the fire pit as she and Amber approached. Levi was stoking the flames. Ryan sat with his legs out straight, feet crossed at the ankle, and laughed at something the woman next to him said. She had a mass of red curls and an infectious giggle— Charlie had heard it several times during the afternoon and it had made her smile, just as it did now. A woman named Kyra—the one who'd taken the pie in for Amber—sat on the edge of her fold-up chair, beer in her hand, listening to a story being told by the one last person around the fire: Emma.

Fighting her instinct to turn and flee—that seemed to be her go-to response to seeing Emma in any situation now—Charlie pasted on a smile.

"Here," Amber said and gestured to an empty chair next to Kyra. "I'll be right back." She turned and headed back toward the house.

Charlie took the offered chair and settled in, then looked up and realized exactly where she'd sat.

Directly across the fire from Emma.

CHAPTER ELEVEN

S o Charlie was staying for a while longer, apparently.

How to react? Emma stifled a sigh and took a sip of her wine, held the plastic stemless wineglass in both hands and turned it slowly in her fingers. She hadn't planned to have all that much to drink, but seeing Charlie walk through that gate had kicked her nerves into overdrive and the size of her sips had increased by quite a bit. Or a lot, as the day went on.

The result? Definitely buzzed and on her way to slightly drunk, at least if she kept up this pace. Charlie took a seat next to Kyra. Dusk was settling down on their little gathering, but Emma could still make out Charlie's face across the fire. She looked uncertain. Nervous. Hesitant.

Good. She should.

Emma grimaced as soon as the words flew through her head. They weren't her. They weren't the kind of person she was...or wanted to be. No, Emma Catherine Grier was not a mean-spirited person. She didn't believe in *deserves*. Nobody deserved to have bad things happen to them, no matter what. Everybody was human. Everybody did things they shouldn't have. Everybody made choices they'd go back and change if they could.

Charlie met her eyes and their gazes held.

Did Charlie have regrets?

The question had tortured Emma for way too long. Months. Years. Hell, still. She still wondered.

Pulling her focus away, she glanced down at her empty glass, then found the wine bottle on the small plastic table between her chair and Dani's. Refilled.

The mood was warm. Friendly. A quieter gathering, a wind down. Levi had the fire blazing and it was throwing off almost too much heat on the warm evening. Emma moved her chair back a few inches, and Levi tossed her a lopsided grin that said *oops*.

"Okay, gang." Amber appeared then, carrying a tray filled with small paper plates. On each plate was a slice of chocolate peanut butter pie. "Charlie was nice enough to bring this pie, and I was ungrateful enough to put it in my refrigerator and forget about it. So here. Eat." She walked around and each person took a plate. She set the tray aside. "Well." Amber didn't so much sit as drop into the one open chair left. She blew out a long, loud breath of what sounded like relief, set her pie down, then reached toward the wine bottle near Emma and wiggled her fingers. "Gimme." She filled her plastic cup, then took a sip, sat back, and smiled wide. "That was fun. Did everybody have a good time?"

Nods and murmurs of agreement went around the circle.

"Nobody leaves here without taking something home. I have enough food left to feed a marching band."

Darkness had settled, but the fire allowed Emma to clearly see the slice of pie on her plate. It was gorgeous, almost didn't seem real. Too perfect not to be a plastic version, the kind they use for photo shoots of food.

"Oh my God." It was Dani and she held her fingers in front of her mouth as she spoke. "This pie is *so* good. You said Charlie brought it?" Dani looked toward Charlie. "Where did you get it?"

"She made it." The words were out of Emma's mouth before she even realized she'd been thinking them, as if her tongue had a mind of its own and no regard for what her brain thought. Why wasn't it possible to grab them out of the air and stuff them back in? That should be a thing.

"You did?" Dani's tone of disbelief was a bit over-the-top as far as Emma was concerned, her normally exuberant personality only magnified by alcohol. Across the fire, she could see Charlie's cheeks redden as she cast her eyes down.

"I did," Charlie said.

"Charlie's a master at pies," Emma said, again wondering how the hell words were being spoken without her permission. "She's been making them since we were teenagers."

"Oh," Kyra said, sitting up straighter. She pointed her fork at Charlie, then Amber, then Emma. "So you all went to school together?"

Dani and Ryan exchanged a look. Emma closed her eyes and silently counted down. Three...two...one...

"Wait a minute, is Charlie the one who...?" Dani stopped midquestion, pressed her lips together.

An awkward silence dropped over the group.

Her past with Charlie wasn't a subject she talked much about. Her friendships with both Dani and Ryan had only begun since her return to Shaker Falls a few years ago, and it wasn't like she sat with them over dinner and said, *Hey, let me tell you about the girl who shattered my heart into a million pieces because I love reliving that story.* She'd given them a bare-bones version—that there had been a girl all through high school and much of college, that she'd left Emma to pursue a career in New York City, that it had hurt. Badly. She never got into just *how* broken she had been or why or for how long. Amber knew because she'd been around to see it. Emma's mother knew, as did Charlie's family. But it wasn't a subject she brought up and chatted about.

Until now.

Across the fire, Charlie was looking down at her pie, a bite on her fork that didn't seem like it was going anywhere near her mouth now. "Yeah," Charlie said quietly as she looked back up and at Dani. "I was the one who."

"*Oh*," Dani said, drawing out the word. "So you live in New York?"

"I...well, I did." Charlie nodded slowly as she gazed into the fire.

She did? Not she *does*? Emma's inebriated brain tried to comprehend the words. She concentrated hard as Amber spoke.

"But you're home now." Amber took a bite of pie.

Charlie kept nodding, nibbled the inside of her cheek.

"What made you leave New York?" Dani asked. "It's such a cool city. If I had a job there, I don't think I'd leave." Her eyes went wide and she clamped a hand over her mouth for a moment. With a wrinkled nose, she asked in a small voice, "You didn't lose a job, did you?"

Even after all these years, Emma still knew Charlie well. She could read her face, take one look and know what she was thinking. And right now, Charlie was feeling frustrated and cornered.

Those things occurred to Emma mere seconds before Charlie blurted, "I did. I lost my job, my home, and my girlfriend. Not necessarily in that order. And now I live in my parents' basement."

Silence fell and lasted for a very uncomfortable moment before Charlie took a big breath and said, "Well, that was awkward. And super TMI. Sorry about that." Then she laughed. It wasn't a genuine laugh— Emma knew that. But it was Charlie's attempt to ease the discomfort. "So. How about that pie, you guys?"

Chuckles went around the fire and the mood elevated considerably, the discomfort dissipating. Gradually, but dissipating. Conversation started up again about the pie, the wine, the fire. Emma met Charlie's gaze across the fire, and Charlie subtly lifted a shoulder as she made a face, and Emma couldn't decide if it was a half grin or a grimace. Maybe a little of both.

Either way, this was new information. Charlie had apparently come home with her tail between her legs after being dumped. It was excellent news, right? The karma Emma had been waiting for for more than four years, right? Charlie had gotten exactly what Emma was sure she deserved, right? But as she studied her, she noticed things. Mainly that Charlie was playing it off, acting light and breezy, nonchalant, no big deal. But her eyes held much more. They held pain. They held shame. They were sad. Maybe nobody else could see that, but Emma could.

Not that she wanted to. She didn't. What she wanted was to laugh. To point at Charlie and shout, *Ha! I told you that would happen! Serves you right!* To be glad that she'd been correct in her predictions. To tell Charlie that's what she got for leaving behind what they had and barely looking back.

But those eyes.

Those soft, sad hazel eyes.

Emma wanted to feel satisfied. Vindicated.

So how come she didn't?

❖

Charlie braced both hands on Amber's bathroom sink, dropped her head down, and leaned. Added a little rocking in there for good measure. Forced herself to breathe in through her nose, out through her mouth, slowly. Deliberately. Lifting her head so she faced the mirror, she spoke quietly to her reflection.

"Well. That was fun. What the hell were you thinking?" She stared for a beat longer, then washed her hands, dried them, and pulled open the door.

Emma stood there.

"Oh. Hey."

"Hi." Emma studied her. She had always done that, looked at Charlie with such an intensity it made her want to squirm. Some things never changed, and Charlie shifted from one foot to the other, uncomfortable.

"Just do it," she said, not meeting Emma's eyes. "You might as well."

"Do what?"

"Say I told you so. It's got to be killing you not to."

Emma was quiet, and Charlie braced. After several seconds, Charlie did look at her. Emma's dark eyes were soft. Kind. Everything about her was. Unexpected, to say the least. "I've never wanted you to be unhappy, Charlie."

Charlie merely tipped her head to one side, eyebrows raised, and Emma chuckled.

"Okay, maybe for a hot minute or two, way, way back." Charlie joined her in the light laughter and Emma spoke again. "But I'm sorry. That you went through that. I mean…" Emma's gaze drifted up toward the ceiling, something she'd always done when searching for what she wanted to say. When she brought her eyes back to meet Charlie's, she shrugged. "I'm sorry you're hurting is what I'm trying to say."

"Thanks."

A second or two passed, and Emma sidled around Charlie so she could use the bathroom. The door clicked shut as Charlie headed for the kitchen to collect her things and call her Uber. It was time to go home.

❖

Charlie was getting used to staring at the ceiling or out the window as she lay in her basement bedroom. Her cell told her it was nearing one a.m. She was going to be a zombie at work if she didn't sleep for at least a couple of hours. But her mind wouldn't shut off. She kept going over the barbecue in her head. The people, the conversations. It had been... surprising.

She liked everybody she'd met for the first time. Ryan Kim was going to give her a golf lesson, and she was looking forward to that. Kyra was fun, somebody Charlie would like to know better. Dani was super high-energy, but entertaining. Levi seemed like a really nice guy, and she loved the way he looked at Amber as if she hung the moon and the sun and was responsible for everything else wonderful in the world. She remembered when she'd looked at Darcy that way.

Had Darcy ever looked at her like that?

Charlie scoffed. "Yeah, right," she muttered into the night. Showing that kind of love for another person? Darcy would see that as weak, akin to exposing her jugular to an enemy, too vulnerable. If there was one thing Darcy Wells was not, it was weak.

She didn't want to spend time thinking about Darcy—a glance at her phone made it very clear that Darcy wasn't spending any time thinking about her—but her mind seemed determined to keep her stuck in that place as it replayed some of the last things they'd said to each other.

"You used to have...I don't know...spark." Darcy threw up her hands as she said it. "You were open and exciting and like a sponge, just ready to absorb anything and everything. That's what drew me to you in the first place."

Charlie stood there with tears in her eyes, not believing what she was hearing. "Seriously? That's your excuse for sleeping with somebody else? I wasn't exciting enough for you?"

"That's not what I meant." Darcy sighed as if they'd had this very conversation a hundred times, rather than this being the first and only discussion.

"No? Because that's sure what it sounded like. How about you explain it to me then?"

And Darcy shut down. Right then and there, Charlie watched it happen, watched any and all emotion leave her face. The walls went up. Doors slammed shut. There would be no explanations, no more conversation. It was over. Charlie knew it in an instant.

"This isn't working for me anymore. You should be out by the end of the week. I'll go stay at Tatiana's."

Charlie gaped at the casualness of it all. The casual dismissal of four years of her life. The casual use of the name of the woman she was being left for. Tatiana. God, could she have more of a stripper name? The combination of anger and pain that mixed inside Charlie's body was bitter and awful and the tears spilled over as she watched Darcy pick up her purse, her heels clicking across the hardwood.

"That's it?" Charlie felt her blood begin to boil. *"Seriously? That's it?"*

Darcy turned around one last time with her hand on the doorknob, tipped her head slightly, and gave Charlie a small, sad smile. *"Yes. I'm afraid that's it."* She pulled the door open.

"You know what, Darcy? Fuck you."

The door shut.

Charlie sighed into the dark of the basement. There was something so horrifically degrading about being dismissed like that. She'd felt worthless. Ashamed. And so incredibly small and insignificant. She had always been pretty strong, a go-getter, someone who knew what she wanted. Trying to figure out what happened to that girl had taken a toll over the past weeks, and she seemed no closer to finding her. In a flash of anger, she picked up her phone again, scrolled to Darcy's number, and deleted it.

There. That felt better. Sort of. Maybe. A little.

With a shake of her head, she told herself she needed to try and clear her mind, get some sleep. Did her mind listen?

Oh no. Instead, it tossed her an image of Emma at the barbecue. Because apparently, that's who she needed to think about now. She sighed loudly and flipped onto her side, tucked her hands up under her pillow as she pictured Emma in her jeans and black tank. Her dark hair was pulled back, and Charlie once again noticed how long it was, how much she liked it that way. She looked terrific—not that Emma Grier ever didn't. She could dress in ratty sweats and a beat-up T-shirt and still look adorably sexy. Charlie knew this from experience, and though time had passed, some things hadn't changed.

Her eyes, though.

Emma had a great stoic face, but her eyes revealed everything.

Charlie knew that if Emma wouldn't look at her, it was because she was trying to hide the way she felt and knew Charlie would take one look in her eyes and know what that was.

That's how she knew Emma was being genuine earlier that night, near the bathroom. When she'd said she was sorry Charlie was hurting, she'd looked her in the eyes, and Charlie could see that she meant it.

Those eyes held something else, though. A sadness. A sadness that surprised Charlie. From what that girl who delivered lunch had said, Emma had no shortage of women. The date from last week. The bartender. Seemed like she did okay.

Charlie groaned and shifted positions again, pulled the covers up over her shoulder. Then she did that thing she'd learned in yoga class, where you thought about each body part individually, thought about it melting into the mattress and relaxing, so you could fall asleep. She needed to do that. She needed to sleep.

What she did not need to do was dwell on Emma, who was doing just fine and probably laughed at Charlie all the way home.

But why did her eyes seem so sad?

CHAPTER TWELVE

Charlie used her back to push open the door from the kitchen to the front of The Muffin Top, tray of almond cookies in her hand, and stopped short in surprise.

Emma stood on the other side of the display case talking to Sandy. They both looked up, and for the first time since she'd returned home, Charlie realized that Emma was not looking at her with any hint of disdain or irritation or impatience. She simply smiled in her direction and gave a nod.

"Hey," Charlie said, sliding the cookies into the display case.

"Emma has requested chocolate peanut butter pie for tonight's dessert menu," Sandy said, her smile wide as she waited for Charlie to look up from her task.

She did. In surprise. What was happening? "She has?" She asked the question as if Emma wasn't standing right there, a small smile on her face.

"I have. I was telling Sandy how good the pie was you brought to Amber's yesterday. I'd like to offer it for tonight's dessert at the restaurant. I think it would sell well." She turned to Sandy. "And I will pay." When Sandy opened her mouth to protest, Emma held up a hand. "No, if we're going to do this, I want to do it right."

Sandy turned to Charlie. "You up for it?"

"For making pie?" She snorted as if that was the silliest thing she'd ever heard. "It's what I do."

"Awesome. Bring 'em by when they're ready." Emma knocked on the counter once, smiled at Charlie again, and left.

What just happened? Charlie wondered. Sandy had a wide smile on her face and looked like she wanted to say something, but there were customers in line, and a timer was going off in the kitchen. Instead, she held out her fist and Charlie bumped it. Then she got to work.

Wanting to mix things up a bit, she decided to make four pies with two different crusts—two with graham cracker crust, and two with an Oreo crust. Sandy sent Bethany out for Oreos, and when she came back, she shyly asked Charlie if she could watch.

"Oh my God, of course," Charlie said, feeling flattered for some reason. "Chocolate peanut butter pie is actually pretty simple. There's no baking, just some mixing and some melting."

"But people love it," Bethany said.

"They do. It's the flavor combination. It's why Reese's Peanut Butter Cups are the most popular candy at Halloween. I mean, how can you go wrong with chocolate and peanut butter?"

"Right?"

She had Bethany make the Oreo crusts while she took care of the graham crackers, and they pressed each into pans, then put them in the freezer to set while Charlie worked on the filling.

"You can do these two ways," she explained to Bethany. "You can just have the chocolate crust and then the peanut butter filling, but I like putting a layer of chocolate on top as well. Makes it richer."

Bethany nodded and watched as Charlie blended a huge bowl of butter, peanut butter, powdered sugar, and vanilla. "Oh my God, that smells so good."

Charlie grinned as she stopped the mixer, retrieved the crusts, and filled them all. They went into the fridge this time. "Okay. Time for the ganache."

Bethany made a low sound in her throat that was almost a growl, and it made Charlie laugh.

"Sorry," Bethany said, her cheeks turning slightly pink. "I like chocolate."

"Totally understandable."

She melted the chocolate with heavy cream and added a bit more peanut butter. Once it was smooth, Bethany retrieved the pies, and the chocolate was layered on top.

"It's so shiny and silky looking," Bethany said, her voice quiet, as if she worried she might disturb the atmosphere.

"The sign of a good ganache," Charlie told her as she finished spreading. "There." She surveyed her work, the swish marks from the spatula, the evenness of the crust. With a nod, she said, "Into the fridge for an hour or two and they're good to go."

"I hope Sandy lets us cut one. Where is she, anyway?" Bethany stood on her toes and craned her neck to see out to the front. Her eyes went wide and she turned to Charlie and mouthed, *He's here!*

Charlie made the same opposite-of-subtle maneuver and saw the gentleman she'd noticed a while back. "The silver fox?" she whispered to Bethany, who nodded so enthusiastically, she looked like a cartoon character.

He'd been in several times since she'd started working at The Muffin Top, and he always took his time deciding. At first, she and Bethany thought he was just indecisive, but the third time? No. Much more than that. He wanted to spend as much time as he could chatting with Sandy. They'd nicknamed him the silver fox because of his gorgeous head of wavy silver hair and the fact that he was super handsome. Charlie wasn't sure if Sandy had any idea or was completely oblivious to his moves.

She and Bethany each took a spot on either side of the open area so they could hear, even if they couldn't see.

"I'd like to give the macarons a try today." The man's voice was deep, soothing. Charlie remembered his salt-and-pepper goatee and the kindness in his eyes.

"I think you'll like them," Sandy replied. Her voice held a slight and uncharacteristic tremble and Charlie looked at Bethany with a grin. *She likes him!* she mouthed, and Bethany did her crazy nod again as their question was finally answered.

Any further conversation was too muted for them to hear, until Sandy said, "Have a great day, okay?" and the gentleman said, "It's already looking so much better."

She and Bethany made tandem *OMG!* faces, complete with wide eyes and open mouths, and they waited until the bell over the door tinkled and they were sure the man was gone.

Bethany burst through the kitchen door first. "That man wants you."

Sandy's eyebrows shot up in surprise. "What?"

"We were totally eavesdropping, and that's the only possible conclusion."

Sandy turned to Charlie, who simply shrugged and grinned. "Sorry not sorry."

Sandy's blush was immediate and very, very deep.

"Oh my God, you're so cute," Charlie said as Bethany walked to Sandy, wrapped an arm around her shoulders.

"He's very handsome, isn't he?" Sandy said quietly as the bell signaled a new customer. When the three of them looked up, it was the man again, and he stopped as he realized there were now three of them behind the counter...all staring at him.

"Um..." Charlie looked at Bethany. "We'd better go check on... the stuff." She jerked her head toward the kitchen.

It took a beat before Bethany caught on. "Oh. *Oh.* Yes. The stuff. That needs checking. Yes. We should do that."

The two of them hustled into the kitchen and took their previous spots on either side of the opening.

"Hi again," Sandy said. "Did you forget something?"

"I did." Charlie fanned herself in response to his voice, and Bethany silently giggled. "Listen, um, this might be incredibly out of line. I hope not, but if it is, just tell me, okay? So, the Shaker Falls Summer Fest starts this weekend. I was wondering..." Charlie and Bethany looked at each other, fists clenched, eyebrows raised expectantly. "Is that something you'd be at all interested in going to? I mean, with me?"

"Like, on a date?" Sandy asked, and the confidence in her voice surprised Charlie, who made an impressed face and gave Bethany a thumbs-up.

"Yes. Yes. Like, on a date. Exactly like that."

"I think I would very much enjoy that."

"You would?" The man sounded so shocked that Charlie felt her heart warm for him, and she pressed a hand to her chest.

"Yeah. I would."

"Oh, that's fantastic. I'm Eric, by the way," he said, and Charlie peeked enough to see him hold out his hand over the counter.

"Sandy," Sandy replied and took his hand, shook it.

"You're open on Saturdays, right?"

Bethany burst into action then, startling Charlie so much she jumped as Bethany headed to the front. Charlie cautiously followed.

"Hey, Sandy?" Bethany stopped as Sandy's surprised face turned to her. "I almost forgot to ask you. I could really use some extra hours this week. My car needs new tires and my dad says I have to help pay for them."

"Oh," Sandy said. "Okay." She drew the word out, clearly not seeing where Bethany was going. Charlie jumped in to help.

"Didn't you say earlier that you wished you could work a longer shift on Saturday?"

Bethany looked at her with gratitude. "Yes! Yes. I said exactly that. Earlier. This morning, in fact. You may not have heard me."

Sandy was catching on, as was Eric, who smiled. "So you want to work Saturday?" she asked Bethany.

"I do." Bethany gave a nod. "All day."

"And I do, too." Charlie grinned. "And then there would be two of us here and that would mean that you could take a much-needed day off. And go do…something. Whatever."

"Exactly." Bethany pointed at Sandy. "When was the last time you had an entire weekend off?"

Sandy's smile was beautiful, her dimples prominent. "It's been a while."

"Then you're due." Bethany smiled. "Me and Charlie will take care of the shop on Saturday and you can go do…whatever." She shot a look toward Eric, turned on her heel, and headed back into the kitchen.

Charlie followed her, and they fist-bumped once Sandy could no longer see them. "Our work here is done."

❖

It had been a risk staying open on Mondays. Lots of restaurants closed Sunday and Monday to give their staff a proper two days off. And that's how things had started for EG's. Open Tuesday through Saturday, closed Sunday and Monday. Within a few months, though, Emma saw an opportunity. It seemed that most other restaurants in the area also closed on Mondays, the exceptions being fast food places and simple diners and cafés, and she wondered if it might be worth it to pick up the customers who wanted someplace nice to dine on a Monday night. So she'd experimented. And had been open on Mondays ever since.

Which, of course, made for a long week for her. She didn't expect others to work the hours she did—it was her place. So Emma manned the bar herself until four, when Sabrina would come in. She didn't mind it, but having only one day off a week could be a lot, and she was stifling a yawn behind the bar when Charlie walked in, arms full of pies.

"Wow," Charlie said. "I've been here for four seconds, and already, you're bored with me."

Emma waved a hand and chuckled. "Sorry. I didn't sleep well last night." That was the truth. Her mind had been a whirlwind of thoughts after the barbecue, and she'd tossed and turned and remembered seeing 3:27 on the clock.

"No? Well, I'm sorry to hear that." Charlie nibbled on her bottom lip and set the pies down on the bar. Then she looked around. "I really like this place, Em." Her voice was quiet and sounded genuine. "It's got a great atmosphere. It's comfortable and inviting and you want to sit and just…hang out."

"Thank you." Somehow, the compliment worked its way into Emma's heart and settled there, made her feel warm, as if it meant more than a compliment from any other person. The ice Charlie had created so long ago was starting to melt—Emma could feel it. She wasn't sure what to do with that and so did her best to shake it away. Because ignoring things always worked best. "You bring me chocolate peanut butter?"

"As requested." Charlie surprised her then by taking a seat on one of the barstools.

"Want a drink?" The question was out of her mouth before Emma could catch it.

Charlie tipped her head to one side as she said, "I would love a drink." She glanced at the stool in the corner, and Emma knew instinctively who she was looking for.

"She's at work."

Charlie flushed a pretty pink, glanced down at her hands on the bar. "How is she?" Charlie asked, and her expression said she wasn't sure if she was allowed to ask. But of all the people in Emma's life, Charlie was still the one person who knew her best, and the desire to open up and talk to her simultaneously felt like relief *and* pissed her off. Again, not sure what to do with that.

Emma lifted one shoulder as she pulled a glass out and began to make a cosmo without asking Charlie if that's what she wanted. She just knew. "She's…" Emma shook her head. How to describe her mother? "She's my mom. She's a functioning alcoholic and we both know it. She should get some help and we both know that." She closed the martini shaker, shook it over her shoulder, then strained the pink liquid into a glass. "We have some unspoken rules and do our best to follow them, but nothing will ever change until she wants it to. You know?"

Charlie nodded, her eyes filled with an understanding that Emma hadn't seen from anyone in a long time, and took a sip of her cosmo. "That's delicious," she said. "Do you still live with her?"

Emma snorted. "God, no. I have an apartment upstairs."

Charlie looked at the ceiling. "Oh, right. I think Amber mentioned you owned the building."

"Well, the bank does, but yeah. It's mine."

"Is it hard to be so close to work? Like, do you have trouble separating work life and home life?" Charlie sipped again, those eyes watching her.

"When you're the owner, I think it's almost impossible to separate, you know? They bleed into each other. But it's better than living with my mom." Emma wiped down the bar, which wasn't dirty, but she needed something to do with her hands. "I still worry about her. I still keep a close eye on her. But I just couldn't live with that anymore, you know?" Charlie nodded. She did know. Emma knew that. Charlie might be the only one who knew. Nights of finding her mother passed out on the bathroom floor, cleaning up vomit from various surfaces, worrying when she wasn't sure where her mom was. She'd had to grow up fast, and Charlie'd been there for the whole thing.

"Is that why you came back here?" Charlie's voice was soft, hesitant, again as if she wasn't quite sure she was allowed to tread this path.

Emma found she didn't mind—and that was weird. She nodded, then decided to just address the elephant in the room. "I hate that I feel comfortable talking to you about this stuff. You know that, right?"

Charlie's throat moved as she swallowed. "I know. Should I shut up?"

"God, I have hated you for so long." Emma wasn't sure she'd meant to say that out loud, but Charlie didn't look surprised. Instead, she nodded.

"I know."

"And now I'm standing here, talking to you about personal stuff over a drink, and I feel…" She looked away. Vulnerability was not her thing. She didn't do it well, didn't like the way it made her feel. Weak. Exposed.

"You feel what?" Charlie sounded shockingly calm with this discussion, but Emma knew by looking at her that she was bracing for an onslaught. One she deserved. One Emma had dreamed of hitting her with.

Instead, she blew out a breath that flapped her lips, draped the bar rag over her shoulder, and grabbed her order pad so she could count the bottles behind the bar. "I'm not sure what I feel." With her pen, she pointed at each bottle, which wasn't really necessary, as she wasn't actually counting anything, but she wanted—no, *needed*—to look like she was busy with something other than the confusion Charlie was causing her.

"I get that."

Emma entertained several different responses in her head before simply accepting Charlie's words.

They were quiet for a moment, then Charlie said, "Hey, do you know who owns that shop next to the bakery?"

A change of subject. Thank God. "The empty one?" At Charlie's nod, she told her what she knew. "It was a little boutique of some kind, then a Verizon store, I think. It's been empty for a few months now."

"But you don't know who owns it?"

"I don't. But I imagine the same person owns the whole building, right? The bakery, the hardware store, and the empty shop?"

Charlie nodded, turning to look out the window, and Emma could see the wheels turning. Her thinking face had always been very distinctive, and Emma tried—and failed—to keep a small smile off her face.

"You looking to open a store? Your own pie shop?"

Charlie grinned. "No. But Sandy has me looking into coffee for her and…" She shrugged and looked almost embarrassed. "My brain was running away for a minute there."

"You could always ask Amber. She's in real estate, after all."

Charlie's eyes went wide. "I didn't even think of that. You're brilliant." She pulled out her phone and whipped off what Emma assumed was a text to Amber.

That light in Charlie's eyes was so easily recognizable, even now.

Even after so much time. It was a creative spark, and part of Emma felt warm at seeing it again after so many years. She shook her head quickly and forced herself to focus on the bottles of alcohol, even though she wasn't actually seeing them. What was the deal with her? Why was she suddenly so much less…angry with Charlie? Questions about Charlie's past few years, her time in New York, her decision to leave everything familiar behind, began to form in Emma's head. No, that wasn't quite true. They didn't just form, because they'd been there for the past five years. But they began to glow in her mind, make themselves known, move to the forefront. She turned and opened her mouth to ask one of them, but Charlie was sliding off her stool.

"Thank you so much for this," Charlie said, indicating the glass as she left money on the bar. "I need to scoot."

Emma waved the money away. "On the house."

"You're sure?" Charlie squinted, another look Emma recognized.

She nodded as Charlie thanked her, ordered her to refrigerate the pies, and headed for the door. Her hand on the handle, she turned back, and there was a hesitation that Emma didn't expect. "Would it be okay with you if I came in for dinner sometime?" Charlie sounded so small as she added, "I've missed your cooking."

In that moment, Emma was so grateful to be far enough away that Charlie couldn't see her eyes mist. She swallowed and said, "Sure."

Charlie said nothing more, just glanced down at her feet, then pushed her way through the door.

Emma stood there, unmoving, for a long moment before giving herself a shake. Only one question was on her mind now, one she had no answers to.

What the hell is happening?

CHAPTER THIRTEEN

O kay. Hear me out."

Charlie went around the front counter into the dining area of The Muffin Top. It was midafternoon on Friday, and the tables were empty. Normally quiet. A usual time for a lull, but something that Charlie was sure would change if she could get Sandy to see her vision. Like an illusionist, she waved her hand at the pink wall that the bakery shared with the empty shop next door. "We open this up. Either completely open, or partway using, like, a fun arched doorway or something. Either would work."

Sandy stayed quiet, but Charlie could see her thinking, almost hear the wheels turning already.

"Then..." Charlie gestured for Sandy to follow her. They went out the front door, a few yards down the sidewalk, and in through the door to the empty shop, where Amber was waiting. "This is the coffee shop part of The Muffin Top. You can see it's not terribly big, so it's not like you'd be adding a huge space to deal with. We paint it to match the bakery. We trade this front door for a window and enlarge the current door at The Muffin Top so it's double. And we put the coffee counter in here." Waving her arms from left to right seemed the best way to get Sandy to see her vision. Sandy followed the movement, squinted, nodded. Looked pensive. "I ran some numbers."

The better part of the last three days had been spent putting her business education to good use. She'd researched, she'd made charts, she'd weighed pros and cons, she'd crunched numbers, done a cost analysis, calculated possible profit and loss. Now, she took out a spreadsheet she'd made last night. In fact, she'd gotten less than two hours of sleep because she'd worked well into the night and then had been so excited to share her idea with Sandy that her brain wouldn't settle.

"Here is my business forecast. I also emailed it to you." She handed the spreadsheet to Sandy and went through the whole thing, pointing out numbers, goals, and possible profit.

Charlie's nerves were jangly, like she'd had way too much caffeine. Or speed. Which was silly because there was nothing riding on her work. She was simply doing a favor for her boss, giving her an idea, showing her one possibility. But she hadn't felt so in her element since before she'd left New York, and there was something about getting back to it, about diving back into a subject she was so passionate about, that energized her. Gave her a purpose she hadn't felt in far too long. She'd finally woken up—that's what it felt like.

"This is impressive," Sandy said, her voice low, not looking up from the paper.

Amber shot a huge smile toward Charlie, gave her a thumbs-up. "Mr. Robertson likes you and was thrilled at the idea of renting this part of the building to you as well and not somebody new. He's also open to talking construction, obviously."

Sandy was nodding as she flipped through the papers. Bright, excited eyes were not what Charlie expected to see, but that's what she got when Sandy raised her head. "Can I take this to my financial guy? Get his thoughts?" Her glance darted from Charlie to Amber and back. "Do I have time?"

"Oh, of course," Amber said. "I've asked Mr. Robertson if he can hold off on any potential renters until next Wednesday, so you've got a few days."

Like a jack-in-the-box on the very last musical note was how Charlie felt, waiting to spring open and let her excited anticipation explode, and though she managed to remain calm and somewhat professional, she couldn't seem to prevent herself from bouncing slightly on the balls of her feet. Sandy noticed and laughed softly.

"You know, if we do this, I'm going to need your help, big-time."

Charlie nodded but said nothing because she hadn't thought that far ahead. Staying in Shaker Falls was not part of her plan. It never had been. She wanted to go back to New York or to Boston or Philadelphia or some other big city as soon as she could find a way to do so.

Didn't she?

Sandy looked at the space again, turned slowly in a circle, and Charlie tried to picture what she was picturing.

"I like that it's not huge," Charlie said, back in the present. "Amber told me the boutique that was here before wasn't that big."

"Right. I remember it," Sandy said, wandering slowly.

"And the small size is a good thing because it won't look or feel as empty during lulls, like it would if it was bigger." Charlie moved to the shared wall between the empty space and the bakery and slapped a palm against it. "So, we open this up." She walked over to the back. "The counter goes here, the machines and brewing stations, and I thought you could even look into roasting some of your own beans down the line, if you wanted to get into that."

"I do love good coffee," Sandy said, almost to herself.

"Right?" Amber agreed.

"There'd be a ton to learn." Sandy was still speaking softly as she slowly wandered the small, empty space, and Charlie could almost see the ideas flitting through her head, like butterflies in a field of wildflowers. They were likely the same ones that had bombarded Charlie when Amber had let her into the space two days ago.

"This could be such a cool space," she said, the thoughts that had pelted her as she researched bubbling back to the surface. "The J-Cup is the only other coffee shop in town. Their coffee sucks, and the atmosphere there isn't warm and welcoming." She glanced at Amber. "Has Bob's attitude changed since I've been gone?"

Amber snorted. "He's still the grumpiest grump that ever grumped. People want to grab their coffee and get the hell out as fast as they can."

"Not here," Charlie said, turning back to Sandy. "Here, they want to sit. On couches and comfy chairs. Chat. Work on their laptops. Meet up with friends. Hold their book club."

"Like Starbucks," Sandy said quietly, her eyes wide as she spun in a slow circle.

"But with *way* better baked goods."

"*So* much better." Sandy held Charlie's gaze for a beat as she reached out and grabbed her hand. "You've given me...a lot to think about, Charlie. So much. I can honestly say that when I asked you to look into how we could maybe, possibly sell coffee at The Muffin Top, this was not what I expected. But it's amazing. Thank you so much."

The feelings Charlie experienced right then—the excitement, the satisfaction, and, most of all, the *pride*—were part of the reason she'd gone to B-school in the first place. The rush of coming up with a new, viable, profitable idea was something she lived for. And as she stood there, Sandy gripping her hand in gratitude as the scent of possibility wafted through the air just like the aroma of her lemon cookies, she understood just how much she'd missed the feeling.

And just how much she wanted it back.

Steady. Emma couldn't ask for more than that in a Friday night dinner rush. It was the way she liked it. Yes, being mobbed was great for business, but it could be rough on her and her staff. The pace was killer, and the stress levels were high. She had worked in enough restaurants to have learned that steady was better. Which didn't mean she didn't love an occasional night where they were slammed. But steady was better.

The other benefit of things being steady was that Emma was able to find time here and there to go out into the dining area and visit tables, make sure her customers were satisfied with their meals, show her face. It was something she'd learned from Gabe in class, and then in practice when she'd been a sous chef in Burlington: customers liked to see who cooked their food. That personal touch went a long way toward keeping them coming back again and again.

It was the tail end of the dinner rush, and she put the finishing touches on a plate of grilled halibut before handing it over to the waitress. She wiped her hands and turned to Alec. "You okay if I make the rounds?"

He nodded and tried to hide his smile—she knew he loved when she left the kitchen because he was in charge. He was a fantastic sous chef, efficient, talented, organized, which meant Emma would lose him eventually, just as her chef in Burlington had lost her. Nature of the beast.

The dining area was about half full at this point in the evening and the bar was nearly at capacity. Sabrina was busy, which was good because she didn't have time to corral Emma into talking—which they really needed to do, but Emma had been avoiding it for days now. She'd sent her mother home at four. After a particularly bad evening a few months ago, they'd made a deal that her mother wouldn't hang at the bar during the restaurant's busiest times. That had been an uncomfortable conversation, but so far, her mother had abided by her wishes with only a little bit of occasional fuss.

Someone who *was* at the bar: Maddie, a girl Emma had spent a couple of nights with on and off over the past month. She had that hopeful look in her eyes as she lifted her wineglass in a subtle salute. Emma gave her a nod but looked away quickly, annoyed at herself. Having Maddie and Sabrina within ten feet of each other was surreal, and not in a good way. Her worlds colliding. She stifled a groan and headed for a table.

"Hello there, Mr. and Mrs. Jenkins," she said, smiling widely at the middle-aged couple who were rapidly becoming a weekend fixture at EG's. "Are you two here again?" She winked.

"Apparently, we cannot get enough of your food," Mr. Jenkins said, his green eyes bright.

"The osso buco was absolutely divine," Mrs. Jenkins said, closing her eyes as if in memory.

"I'm so glad you enjoyed it. Thank you for coming." Emma moved on to another table, had a very similar discussion. She looked up from those customers and her gaze landed on a table in the far corner. The Stetkos sat there, as they often did, but this time, Charlie was with them, and suddenly, Emma was whisked back a good ten years to sitting at the Stetko dinner table, joking and laughing with Charlie and her family. The warmth. The openness. The acceptance and the love. Not that Emma's mother didn't accept her sexuality, but it had taken her a much longer time to come to terms with it than it had the Stetkos with Charlie's.

Sucking in a deep breath, Emma steeled herself, then let it out slowly and headed toward the table.

"Emma," Mrs. Stetko said, her voice a bit louder than normal, probably from the glass of wine she always allowed herself at dinner. Before Emma could respond, she stood up and wrapped her in an embrace. Over her shoulder, Emma met Charlie's eyes, but her expression was unreadable. "It's so good to see you."

"You, too, Mrs. S., Mr. S." Emma bent down and kissed Charlie's father's cheek. She glanced at Charlie, met her eyes again. "Hey, Charlie."

"Hi, Emma." Charlie's smile was surprisingly tender, and she glanced down at her plate almost shyly.

"How was dinner? Everything okay?" Emma glanced at the plates to see what everybody had. "Your rib eye, as usual," she said as she pointed to Charlie's dad's plate.

"Cooked perfectly, as always," he said, then patted his stomach in satisfaction.

"The halibut special." Mrs. S. was next, and she nodded. "The asparagus?" Emma asked as her eyes moved to Charlie's appetizer plate. At Charlie's knowing nod, Emma pointed. "And the Gruyère mac and cheese." There was a healthy portion of it left in Charlie's dish, and she grimaced as they made eye contact again. "Too rich?" She had worried it might be, but during tastings, the staff said it was delicious.

"God, no, it's amazing," Charlie said, her voice adamant. "I just didn't have a lot of room left after I wolfed down the asparagus and egg." Then she did something Emma hadn't seen her do in ages: she blushed. It was so many things for Emma right then. It was cute. It was complimentary. It was infuriating. It was damn sexy. "I have never been able to fry an egg exactly right. Either the yolk isn't runny enough or the whites are too runny. I just can't manage to get it as perfect as you do." Then, as if realizing she'd said too much, her blush deepened, and she snapped her mouth closed.

"Well." Emma clasped her hands behind her back and studied her shoes for a moment. "I've had a lot of practice."

"I can imagine." Was there curiosity in Charlie's eyes just then? Or was that imagination, wishful thinking on Emma's part? *No. No, not going there.*

With a quick shake of her head, she squeezed Mrs. Stetko's shoulder. "Make sure you guys get dessert. I hear the strawberry rhubarb pie is to die for." Did she wink at Charlie just then? Seriously? What was wrong with her? Emma clenched her jaw and headed off to another table, needing to get away from Charlie and those eyes as quickly as possible.

What the hell is this about?

Emma didn't understand it.

She made the rounds, greeting customers, smiling, listening to their comments about their meals. All the while, in the back of her mind, sat Charlie. Just sitting there. Just waiting. And she was so conflicted about that. Half of her hated it. Charlie had torn her heart from her chest, tossed it on the floor, and stomped on it. The other half of her, though, settled right in to the familiarity that Charlie represented, because—surprisingly—Charlie hadn't seemed to have changed that much. She had a little bit of a big city air about her. But mostly, from what Emma had seen so far, she was just…Charlie. More grown-up, but still her Charlie.

And that was the problem, wasn't it?

The relief she felt when she was back in her kitchen wasn't lost on her. With Charlie, Maddie, and Sabrina all in the dining room, the kitchen was her safest bet. Plus, she could throw herself into work and not have to think about anything else but steak and chicken and fish and seasonings and herbs and presentation. So that's what she did for the next two and a half hours. The kitchen stopped serving food at nine. The bar stayed open until eleven.

At ten thirty, she ventured back out. The dining room was empty, but the bar still had a handful of customers. Jazz played softly over the hidden speakers, and not for the first time, Emma wondered if she shouldn't try live music. Not anything big and loud, but maybe a pianist. Or a duo. It was something she'd been bouncing around for a while now.

Maddie still sat on her barstool, the glass of white wine in front of her half empty, the print from her lipstick clearly visible. She was very pretty—blond, petite, tan. She looked at Emma with expectation in her big green eyes.

They'd been together three times. Never at Emma's. Always at Maddie's place. Emma didn't bring women to her place. Too complicated. But she was pretty sure that's why Maddie had been sitting at the bar nursing a single glass of wine for the majority of the evening. Emma nibbled the inside of her cheek for a moment, then walked over to stand next to her.

"Hey, listen," she said, her voice low. "I still have some stuff to take care of in the kitchen and I'm *really* tired."

"That's okay." Maddie smiled, but there was a hesitancy in it that was unmistakable, and Emma's guilt seeped in slowly because Maddie deserved better. "I can be quiet and not bother you. I'll just lounge on your couch."

Sabrina was subtle enough not to come stand right near them, but not subtle enough that Emma didn't notice her eavesdropping.

"Yeah, I don't think so. I really have a lot to do."

Maddie blinked at her. Emma could almost hear the wheels turning in her head, and she watched as the pieces clicked into place. "I see."

Emma hated this part. She was always very clear up front that she wasn't looking for something long-term, just some temporary company. And they always seemed to understand, but then sometimes this happened. And Emma always felt like an asshole.

Maddie downed the rest of her wine in one large gulp and set the glass on the bar. Then she retrieved her purse from the hook near her knees and slid off the stool. "Have a nice life, Emma." She turned on her heel and was gone.

Sabrina was wiping a glass with a white rag as her gaze followed Maddie out the front door. Then she turned to look at Emma, and the judgment on her face was clearer than if she'd had a neon sign flashing above her. Then she just shook her head slowly, but Emma could see a ghost of a satisfied smile on her face.

"Goddamn it," Emma muttered, then fled back to the safety of her kitchen.

❖

When Charlie and her parents returned to the house, Sherry was there, home from a long day at work, apparently.

"We gonna do this fire pit thing?" her father said, clapping his hands and then rubbing them together.

Sherry held up a bag of marshmallows.

"You remembered," her mother said, taking the bag from her daughter.

"There's a fire pit?" Charlie said, unable to hide the surprise in her voice.

"Has been for three years now," came Sherry's reply, the ever-present tinge of irritation obvious.

"Okay, everybody go get their fire clothes on, and I'll get things started." Her dad went out the back door, and it slammed behind him.

"Just put on something ratty," her mom said with a grin, then headed upstairs, presumably to change.

Sherry opened the fridge and pulled out several bottles of beer. She moved them to a small cooler on the table and arranged them to fit as she asked, "Do they even have ratty clothes in the big city?"

That was it for Charlie. She had had a couple glasses of wine at the restaurant, and seeing Emma, having Emma wink at her the way she did, it had nudged Charlie off-balance, and she hadn't been able to right herself since, felt off her axis. Sherry's ire just felt like more pushing, and she'd had just about enough of it.

"What is your problem?" Charlie snapped the words in a hissed whisper, and they came out harsher than she'd intended.

Sherry had the good sense to look surprised for a split second before her eyes darkened. "*My* problem? *Mine?* What is *your* problem, Charlie? You leave and don't come home for, what? Two fucking years?" She lowered her voice on the curse and then joined Charlie in the angry whispering. "Do you know how hard it was on Mom and Dad to never see you? And suddenly you're back, but only because your rich girlfriend dumped you? And what do our parents do? They make you a fucking apartment in the basement and welcome you back like you're the princess returning home from a long trip. As if I haven't been here the whole fucking time." She scooped some ice from the tray in the pull-out freezer and tossed it on top of the beer bottles.

Charlie didn't know what to say, so she stood there, blinking and absorbing her sister's words, as she watched her snap the cooler shut, grab the handle, and head out the back door. Shock. Anger. Hurt. Regret. Guilt. So many emotions rolled through her then. Her eyes welled up and a lump formed in her throat as she stood there, but when she heard her mother coming down the stairs, she turned quickly and headed down to the basement, her steps slow as if she wore cement shoes.

Once down there, she tried to busy herself by finding clothes suitable for sitting around a fire, but the lump stayed, uncomfortable and almost painful, as did the almost-tears. Sherry's voice, her eyes, had held such…venom.

She sat down on the bed, an old T-shirt in her hands, and stared at nothing. For the first time in months and months, she had no choice but to think hard about the choices she'd made, and who she'd hurt with them. The list was long, and it sucked, and she didn't like the way it made her feel. But she sat there and forced herself to deal with it all. She cried quietly, guilt and shame pouring over her.

She hadn't wanted to come home. She didn't want to be here.

But that was part of the problem, wasn't it? She *was* here. And—dare she say it?—she was happy. Ish.

The plan had always been to go back to the city, to find a way. A job, a place to live, some extra cash, and she'd go. That was the only goal she'd had her eye on since her return. Everything here was temporary. Her job at the bakery. The friends she'd reconnected with. Seeing Emma. All temporary, right? She didn't want to be here, had no intention of staying. All she'd wanted after school was to see this town in her rearview mirror. She hated Shaker Falls. Hated it with a passion.

Didn't she?

CHAPTER FOURTEEN

Another Sunday, and Emma felt like she always did, like she was supposed to be doing something. She'd had to make a rule for herself: she wasn't even allowed to enter the restaurant on Sundays because if she did, she would inevitably find some work to do and would end up there for hours. Danielle had come by one Sunday and literally grabbed her arm and dragged her out the door to keep her from working anymore.

So on this particular Sunday, getting herself a latte and heading over to the Summer Fest in the park sounded absolutely divine, the perfect way to spend the morning. She had her Kindle and a blanket tucked into her small backpack, and she was going to find a nice shady spot under a tree where she could relax and read until the live music started up in the afternoon. Then she'd find some wine or a beer and just chill to the tunes. The weather was forecast to be the perfect end-of-June day: low eighties, sunny with a light breeze.

The J-Cup was mildly busy, the two college-age kids behind the counter taking their sweet time filling orders, probably wishing they were anywhere else. The coffee shop was no Starbucks, and its menu was pretty limited. Coffee or tea, lattes, cappuccino. That was about it. Emma tucked her phone into her back pocket as she stepped up to the counter and placed her order with a bored-looking young man.

"You drink lattes now, huh?" The voice came from behind Emma, soft and familiar, like fingertips tickling down her spine. She turned to face Charlie, those hazel eyes sparkling with something Emma couldn't put her finger on.

"I do."

"You never used to like coffee. This is unexpected."

"People change. I do a lot of unexpected things now."

"True, and I'm sure you do." A definite sizzle passed between them as they stood there, face-to-face.

"Can I take your order?" the barista asked, his voice uncertain, as if he could see the strange connection and was hesitant to break it.

Emma stepped aside wordlessly, but her eyes stayed locked on Charlie's for another moment until Charlie looked away to place her order.

Charlie looked good. Emma gave her a subtle scan. Better than the first time she'd seen her back in Shaker Falls. She'd put a little weight back on, so her face was no longer gaunt. Her cheeks had a healthy pink in them, and her eyes were bright. The ponytail was super cute, and she was dressed casually in denim capris and a black-and-white-striped tank, flip-flops on her feet. Mirrored sunglasses were perched on top of her head, and when she finished placing her order, Emma quickly took her phone back out and pretended to be engrossed. Couldn't have Charlie thinking she was staring.

"I'm not used to seeing you out of your clothes."

She looked up from the nothing she was doing on her phone and squinted at Charlie, whose eyes went suddenly wide, apparently hearing what she'd said.

"Oh my God. *Chef's* clothes. Your chef's clothes. That's what I meant." She looked away, clearly embarrassed, muttered, "God."

"You saw me in regular clothes at Amber's."

Charlie nodded. "That's true. Still, when I picture you now, it's in your white chef's coat." She seemed to study Emma's face for a few seconds before adding, "It looks really good on you. Not that what you're wearing now doesn't look good on you, because it does. Really good. I just meant that the chef's coat also looks really great, gives you an air of authority or something. Oh my God, stop talking, Charlie."

Emma couldn't help but grin. She didn't want to. She was trying hard to hold on to the distance she was attempting to keep between them. But nervous rambling was one of Charlie's more endearing qualities, along with the deep blush that had colored her cheeks from a healthy pink to a deeper almost-red, and for a second or two, she let herself be transported back to the past, before *that woman* had swooped in, before Charlie had sprinted to New York and left Emma and her shattered heart behind.

"I think somewhere in there were a couple of compliments," Emma said. "So thank you."

Relief washed over Charlie's face, and they stood there in silence until the barista slid Emma's latte toward her. She thanked him, then whispered to Charlie, "One mediocre latte for Emma."

Charlie laughed softly. "Can you keep a secret?"

Emma tilted her head. "Is that a real question?"

"Ha. Sorry. I know you can." Charlie glanced around as if to see who was in earshot. The answer to that was nobody. Still, Charlie stepped closer, into Emma's space, close enough for her to smell the cherry almond body lotion Charlie had always used. The familiarity put a small lump in her throat that she tried to swallow down while Charlie spoke. "The J-Cup might have some competition soon."

"Really?" She felt her eyebrows rise up toward her hairline. "Explain."

The barista slid Charlie's coffee across the counter, and then they walked to the door together, just as if they'd planned to the whole time. They turned right and strolled down the sidewalk toward the park as Charlie talked.

"So, when I first interviewed at The Muffin Top, Sandy mentioned that she was interested in selling coffee because she thought she'd get a bigger early morning crowd that way. She knew I had business experience, and I guess my mom did a little cheerleading for me, so she asked me if I could look into it when I had a chance, just do some research for her."

Emma listened as Charlie relayed the research she'd done, the ideas she'd come up with, the empty shop next door. Again, it was as if she was transported back in time, like the door of the J-Cup had been a portal, and now she and Charlie were actually walking down the sidewalk eight or ten years ago. It simultaneously warmed her and freaked her the hell out.

"She liked what I showed her, she's got my numbers, and she's going to talk to her finance person. So we'll see."

"That's amazing," Emma said, and she meant it. Seeing Charlie so excited about an idea was a familiar sight that she'd always loved, and she decided in that moment not to overanalyze it. Charlie looked happy, and Emma could admit that it made her happy to see it.

"I can promise you this: we will have *way* better coffee than the J-Cup. Way better."

"Well, the bar isn't really all that high, is it?"

"Ha! Right?" Charlie talked some more as they strolled, spoke about the possibility of roasting their own coffee beans, creating different specialty drinks.

It occurred to Emma then that the way Charlie spoke made it sound like she planned on sticking around. And she wanted to ask about it. She really did. But fear kept the question locked inside her head. And that confused her. Because what was she afraid of? She was long past the days of shielding herself from Charlie, right? Long past.

"I can't help but notice, the more people we see, that we're headed in the direction of Summer Fest." Charlie smiled and turned sideways to allow a couple to pass. "Was that your plan?"

Emma nodded. "I was just going to find a spot to chill out and read." Why was it so easy to tell Charlie her plans?

At Charlie's light chuckle, she turned to regard her, watched as Charlie pulled a Kindle out of her bag and held it up. "Great minds."

What happened next was so strange and so *not* strange at all. Emma barely thought about it. They walked into the park, into Summer Fest. It was still midmorning, so the crowd was small, people milling around here and there, vendors opening their tents and tables for business, food trucks propping open windows and getting their kitchens up and running. Lots of strollers and people walking dogs. She and Charlie slowed their pace, strolling along, pointing things out to each other, until they found the perfect spot. A large oak tree stood tall on the edge of the park, far enough away from the main pathway of the festival, but close enough to people watch. Emma unzipped her backpack, pulled out the navy-blue and white blanket, and spread it out at the base of the wide trunk. She and Charlie sat down, and there was enough room for each of them to lean comfortably against the tree.

Emma reached into her bag again, pulled out a baggie just as Charlie did the same thing. They looked at each other and laughed and Charlie's eyes widened. "Are those your famous homemade granola bites?" She sounded like a little kid looking at her favorite candy and Emma grinned at her.

"They are." She squinted at the bag Charlie held. "And are those dried cherries, your favorite snack in all the land?" Some things you just didn't unlearn about each other.

"They are. And you know what they go really well with?"

"My famous homemade granola bites?"

"Ding, ding, ding!" Charlie pointed at her, smile wide.

Baggies were unzipped and set on the blanket between them. They each reached into the one belonging to the other, tossed the snack into their mouths, then pulled out their books.

Emma was surprised—but not at all, really—at how easy it was to fall into a routine with Charlie. How comfortable it was to just sit next to her and read. The silence wasn't awkward. Charlie's proximity wasn't weird. In fact, this was the most relaxed Emma had been in a very, very long time.

That got her attention.

But when she turned to Charlie and opened her mouth, Charlie was gazing off in the distance and spoke first.

"How do you decide what the special's going to be?"

Emma felt her brow furrow at the shift in subject—at least for her. "What?"

"At the restaurant. How do you decide that tonight's special will be, I don't know, eggplant Parmesan or something." Charlie turned to Emma then, eyes filled with curiosity. Open.

Her mouth went dry. *Goddamn it.* "Been giving this a lot of thought, have you?" *Good job, Em. Keep things light.*

"Maybe." Charlie popped another granola bite and waited.

Emma took a breath. "Well, there are a lot of factors. If one of my vendors has, say, eggplants on sale, then I might decide to make eggplant Parmesan as a special for a night or two because I can make more money. Or if I find a new recipe I want to try and it comes out good in testing, I'll do that."

"In testing?"

"Yeah. I make it ahead of time, try it out on my staff. On Sandy and her staff." She tilted her head toward Charlie. "And I see what the consensus is."

"Have you ever made something that didn't go over well?"

Emma squinted, honestly thought about the question. "You know what? I don't think so."

"Well, that doesn't surprise me." Charlie reached in for more granola.

"No? It surprises me."

"Why? You're fantastic at what you do. You always have been. You're the only person I've ever met who found their calling as a kid." The way Charlie spoke was almost dreamy. Filled with admiration. It made Emma feel warm.

"Really?"

Charlie scoffed. "Name somebody else who did."

She wrinkled her nose, racked her brain. She had many friends who were happy in their careers, but she couldn't think of one who'd discovered their passion in junior high. "You may be right."

"It happens once in a great while." A faraway look parked itself on Charlie's face then.

"What happened, Charlie?" The question was out of Emma's mouth before she even realized she was thinking it, but her voice was soft, gentle. Hurting Charlie didn't even cross her mind, nor did reveling in her pain. She simply wanted to know.

Charlie turned to her, and suddenly, her eyes clouded, shadowing the curiosity and the openness from earlier. So many alarmingly clear emotions: sadness, pain, regret. She took her time inhaling, then let it out just as slowly. "You really want to know? I'm sure it'll make your day."

The words weren't exactly sarcastic, but they held an element of embarrassment. Of shame. Part of Emma took a sliver of pleasure in that, she could admit it, but only for a moment. A larger part was sympathetic, and that shameful expression on Charlie's face made her feel bad that she'd even asked. She lifted one shoulder. "I mean, you don't have to tell me. It's really none of my business."

"No." Charlie laid a hand on her forearm. "No. I don't mind."

Their gazes held, and Emma saw so many things whip across Charlie's face then, most of them too fast for her to identify, but that connection was there. Again. That same damn connection they'd always had from the very first time they'd met. The one Emma loved when they were together and despised when they'd split, because it felt so permanent, like a tattoo, a part of her she could never get rid of. She'd fought with it. Ignored it. Cursed it. And she realized right then that, while she'd been able to tamp it down, to put it in a box on a high,

high shelf, it was still there. It was always there, and it probably always would be there.

"You were right." Charlie said it factually, with a shrug, doing her best to be nonchalant about something that Emma could see she felt anything but nonchalant about.

"About what?"

"About Darcy. She just wanted to get in my pants." Holding up one finger, she continued. "I did last longer than any of the past girls, so I do think she had feelings for me, but…" Again with the nonchalant shrug. "Somebody better came along."

Emma's first reaction, her instinct again, was sympathy for Charlie. Empathy. Sorrow. "Oh, Charlie. I'm sorry."

"You are?"

"Of course I am."

Charlie popped some granola into her mouth, chewed thoughtfully as she watched a woman pushing a double stroller. "I was waiting for you to say I told you so."

"Well." Emma playfully bumped her with a shoulder. "I mean, I *did* tell you so."

"There it is." But Charlie laughed and the sound was achingly familiar. And wonderful. And Emma felt herself being tugged in a direction she'd refused to even look in for years now.

What the hell?

Before she could analyze—or try to avoid analyzing—any further, she heard her name called and could see Danielle walking toward them. She wore denim shorts and a white sleeveless top, and her red curls were pulled back from her face. To her credit, her smile only faltered slightly when she saw who was sitting next to Emma. If Emma didn't know her so well, she'd have missed it.

"Hey," Danielle said, standing in front of them with her hands parked on her hips. "What's up?"

Emma shook her head. "Not much. Just hanging. You remember Charlie?" She turned to Charlie. "This is Dani. You met her at Amber's."

"Right, right. Of course." Charlie smiled up Dani. "Good to see you again."

"Same." Danielle set down her bag and sat on the edge of the blanket facing them. "I thought you were just hanging alone this morning."

She didn't hide the implication very well, and Emma felt the air around Charlie shift just slightly.

"I was," she said, injecting her voice with as much cheer as she could. "We ran into each other at the J-Cup and just ended up sort of wandering in the same direction. We had the same idea." She pointed to Charlie's Kindle where it sat on the blanket as if to say, *See? I speak the truth.*

Dani nodded, then stretched her arms out behind her to brace her weight and crossed her legs at the ankles. It was a pretty clear *I'm going to hang right here*, and it irritated Emma, though she didn't want to analyze why.

And then, in true Danielle Schwartz extroverted fashion, she started talking. "Remember the dude from that bar in Clifton I was telling you about?" She launched into a story about a man Emma was vaguely familiar with, a man Charlie would have no clue about. Then she told another story, then another, always adding something like *Remember when we went there?* or *We had the best time.*

To her credit, Charlie stuck around for a good fifteen minutes before, during a lull, she began gathering her things. "I think I'm going to wander a bit. It's been a while since I hit Summer Fest." She stood up and smiled down at Emma. The smile was uncertain. "Thanks for sharing your blanket and your granola." She turned to Dani. "It was good to see you again." She shouldered her bag and walked away, Emma's gaze following her, watching the familiar gait, the gentle sway of her hips.

She turned back to Dani, spoke a tiny bit more harshly than she'd intended. "What the hell was that?"

Dani's eyes widened, seemingly in innocence, but Emma knew better. "What was what?"

"What you just did. Sitting down, chatting away to me about people and inside jokes that Charlie would have zero knowledge of. You purposely left her out of any and all conversation."

Dani opened her mouth to speak and must have thought better of it. She closed it again and looked down at her hands.

"You made her feel like an outsider."

"She *is* an outsider," Dani snapped. "And she broke your fucking heart, yet here you are, all cozied up on a blanket under a tree sharing coffee and breakfast."

Emma flinched at the tone. Dani didn't yell, didn't even raise her voice, but her tone was almost harsh. She simply blinked at her in surprise.

Dani sighed. "I'm sorry. That was...a lot."

"You think? Jesus."

Dani's position shifted so she was sitting next to Emma and leaning against the tree. Dani put her hand on Emma's knee, squeezed it. "Look, it's just..." She stared off into the distance as if searching for the right words. "You've told me so much about what you went through with her, how hard it was when she moved to New York and left you and your relationship behind. How she didn't answer your texts or calls. How heartbroken you were. I know I wasn't around then, but I am now. And she's here, and I don't want to see all of that happen to you again. You know?"

Emma saw the sincerity in her blue eyes, heard the gentleness in her voice, and knew that one of her besties was simply looking out for her. While she didn't like the approach, Emma understood the point.

"I know. I get it. I do."

"Yeah?"

"Yes. And it's fine. Really." She glanced down to grab some granola, noticed that Charlie had tucked her dried cherries next to the bag, couldn't help but grin. "We were just hanging out. It wasn't planned. We ran into each other and just ended up walking in the same direction. It was no big deal. I promise. I have no desire to get sucked into anything with Charlie Stetko again. Trust me."

But even as she said it, her brain was remembering how familiar, how natural, how comfortable it had been to stroll along the sidewalk listening to Charlie talk about her new business venture, how much Emma had always loved the excitement, the sparkle Charlie got in her eyes when she was pumped about something new. And as Dani began to talk about a new vodka her company was selling, Emma kept picturing Charlie in her enthusiasm. Dani's voice faded a bit until all Emma could hear were her own thoughts.

Well, just one thought.

I'm gonna be in trouble here, aren't I?

CHAPTER FIFTEEN

Morning had morphed into afternoon, and that was hurtling toward evening. Charlie hadn't planned on staying at Summer Fest so long. Not even close. She was going to read for a bit, drink her coffee, do some people watching, check out some of the vendors, and then head home to spend the rest of her Sunday either in the backyard or vegging out with Netflix. Like she was middle-aged. God, her life was riveting.

Instead, though, she kept running into people she knew. Old school classmates. Friends of her parents. Her aunt and uncle. A couple cousins. Three different bakery customers who wanted to chat and give her suggestions for pie flavors. Her brother—one of only two full-time, paid firefighters in an otherwise volunteer station—was manning the beer table to raise money for the firehouse and kept refilling her plastic cup and introducing her to his volunteer firefighter buddies as "my big sister Sharlie."

By four in the afternoon, she was a little bit tipsy, which hadn't been part of her plan. But the day was beautiful, sunny and gorgeous, and it put everybody in a great mood. Charlie could remember more Summer Fests than she could count growing up that had ended up rainy or windy or both.

"No, no more," she said vehemently now and pulled her cup away as Shane tried to grab it and fill it. She glanced across to the other side of the walkway, and her gaze was snagged by Emma standing in front of a booth that was selling pottery. She was still at Summer Fest, too, and Charlie smiled at the thought. Emma looked super cute in her denim Bermuda shorts and white tank top, and Charlie tried not to stare at her legs—Emma had always had spectacular legs, long and toned and smooth. The lightweight hoodie she'd had on earlier was now tied around her waist, her backpack still slung over one shoulder. Her mass of dark curls was still pulled back, and Charlie realized, oddly, that since she'd been back, she had yet to see Emma with her hair down. As she squinted, Emma's eyes locked with hers, and Shane laid a heavy hand on her shoulder.

"What are you doing, big sister of mine?" He asked it quietly and without any sort of judgmental tone, but it was definitely knowing.

Charlie swallowed and felt like she'd been caught doing something wrong. "Nothing."

"Go easy. Okay?" When Charlie turned to look at him, look into his kind blue eyes, she saw love. She also saw warning. She nodded, and he squeezed her shoulder, then gave a shout of greeting over her head and went back to pouring beer.

Emma was still looking her way, though the distance was too great for Charlie to read her expression. With a toss of her cup into the trash can, Charlie smoothed her hands over her hips, cleared her throat, and crossed through the flow of people to the booth where Emma stood.

"You're still here." Perfect. Awesome opening line. *Way to go, Captain Obvious.*

"So are you." Emma's smile was easy, soft, and Charlie recognized it.

"Have you also been slightly overserved?"

Emma scrunched up her nose in an adorable show of thinking really hard. "I believe…yes. Yes, I have."

"I was going to go home about"—Charlie looked at her watch—"like, four hours ago?"

"Same," Emma said, and they both laughed. "You want to walk me?" The question must have surprised her because her eyes widened in an almost comical way, and Charlie chuckled lightly at the sight.

"Walk you where?"

"Home."

"I do. Absolutely." The words were out before Charlie could review them, think about them, edit them. And it was probably the beer, but she was fine with that. "I can get an Uber from your place."

"Perfect." Emma held out her elbow, and Charlie hooked her hand through it without question. "It'll be Tom."

"Tom?"

"He's pretty much the only Uber guy. He and I go way back."

They were tipsy, but they weren't drunk. Not enough to not understand what they were doing or how they were feeling. At least, that's how Charlie felt. As they strolled, smiled, and said hi to people they knew, she was ultra-aware, not only of how they must look to other people, but how she felt walking side by side with Emma this way.

It felt familiar.

It felt comfortable.

It felt like home.

She tried to shake those thoughts out of her head. Tried to scrub them away. Tried to ignore them. But they kept coming back, especially that last one. How was it possible? How, after everything she'd done, after all the decisions she'd make differently, after how vehemently she didn't want to come back here, how was it possible that walking next to Emma, arm in arm, felt like home? How?

And what the hell was she supposed to do with it?

❖

"You got quiet," Emma said as they reached EG's and she led Charlie around back to the door to her upstairs apartment. "You okay?"

It was weird being this close to Charlie, and it was also good. It was frustrating and it was comfortable. It fanned an angry spark in the pit of Emma's stomach, but it also warmed her heart.

She had no idea what to do about any of it.

"Yeah." Charlie smiled. "Just coming down from the day, I think."

"I get that." Emma slid her key into the door, pushed it open, and headed up the stairs.

"Is it a blessing or a curse that you live above your workplace?" Charlie asked as she followed Emma up.

"It's both."

"I bet."

At the top of the stairs was another door that she knew she should lock but rarely bothered to, and she pushed it open. "Welcome to my humble abode," she said, holding out an arm like a model on *The Price Is Right*.

Charlie walked in, walked past Emma, and strolled into the wide-open space.

Taking a look around, Emma tried to see her place through Charlie's eyes. It was open-concept and very bright—two things that had been nonnegotiable when she had it fixed up. Working in a dim restaurant and windowless kitchen made her long for natural light during the times she was home. The hardwood floors had been buffed and polished to a pristine shine. Her furniture was simple but classy, and halfway between modern and traditional.

Charlie walked slowly, dragged the tips of her fingers over shelves, picked up knickknacks, then set them down, seemed to take it all in.

Emma set her bag down near the coat closet, unknotted her hoodie, and tossed it onto a chair as she watched Charlie out of the corner of her eye. There was a small table in the far corner of the living space that held several framed photos, and Charlie reached it before Emma could steer her away from it.

Crap.

Charlie stopped, picked up different photos, studied them, set them back down. She finally found the one way in the back. The one Emma hid but couldn't bring herself to toss in the garbage or pack away forever.

Charlie turned to her, held up the framed photo of the two of them on graduation day, and raised her eyebrows.

Emma knew the photo by heart, knew every line, every color. Their arms wrapped tightly around each other, their smiles enormous and giddy. She gave Charlie a sad smile and a shrug.

No words were spoken about it.

"Want some water?" she asked, needing to do something other than stand there and fidget as Charlie examined her apartment.

"Love some."

The kitchen looked out into the living area, but Emma opened the fridge with her back to Charlie and bent toward the water bottles. A moment. She just needed a moment to steady herself. To breathe. To get her pounding heart to shut the hell up. Why did she feel so weird all of a sudden? Was it the alcohol? She wasn't drunk, just a little buzzed, but was getting more sober by the second. What was her problem?

Back out around the counter and into the living room, she handed a bottle of water to Charlie, who was holding another frame. The photo in it showed three people nearly twenty-five years ago. A white woman, a black man, and their light-skinned three-year-old daughter. All of them smiled widely, and if there was a happier family photo in existence, Emma had never seen it. Less than six months later, her father had left her and her mother. Fled. Abandoned them. Never looked back.

Charlie looked at her, and Emma could read the question on her face; they'd always been able to do that, and it was so bizarre that they still could.

"I know where he is. I found him on Facebook a year ago."

"You finally looked."

"I had a weak moment." Emma gave a bitter laugh. Charlie had tried to get her to look for her absentee father for years, but she'd always had an excuse why she didn't want to.

"Where is he?"

"Nashville."

"Huh. Did you contact him?"

Emma shook her head. "He's got a new family."

"What do you mean?" Charlie set the photo down and cracked her water open.

"I mean just that. He's got a new family. Wife. Twin sons. I think they're, like, ten? Twelve?"

"Okay. So?"

Emma flopped onto the gray microfiber couch and blew out a long breath. Charlie had always been an advocate for Emma finding and reaching out to her dad. "So it's been almost twenty-five years since he left. I haven't heard from him at all. That's a pretty clear message, don't you think?"

Charlie sat down next to her. "I mean, it's been a really, really long time. People change."

Something in Charlie's tone made Emma turn to her. "Do they?" Their gazes were locked, and Emma couldn't have turned away if she tried.

Charlie's swallow was audible, and her voice was just above a whisper when she said, "They do. And they have regrets. And they wish they could go back and do things differently."

"But they can't." She kept her voice just as low.

"No." It was Charlie who looked away, down at her hands fiddling with the water bottle. "And that's the hardest part."

"Do you have regrets, Charlie?" The alcohol in her system was making her bold. Emma knew that but couldn't stop herself from asking the question she wasn't sure she wanted the answer to.

Charlie kept her eyes on her bottle, let go of a sarcastic smile. "More than I can count."

Emma wanted to delve into that. And she didn't. She wanted to know more about Charlie's regrets, what she would've changed or done differently. But she also didn't. Because it was too late, wasn't it? The damage had been done. Charlie had left her behind for something better, just as her father had left her and her mother behind.

"Does your mom know you found him?" Charlie asked, then took a slug from her bottle.

Emma shook her head. "I debated telling her, but…" She shrugged. "I'm really not sure how she'd take it. She's never offered to help find him. She's never said anything nice about him since he left. You know how she got." Charlie was the only one who knew. She'd spent so much time at Emma's house that she'd witnessed more than her share of her mother's meltdowns.

"I remember. What were we, thirteen? Fourteen? And you told her you wanted to know more about your dad, asked her if she knew where he was, and then she went on and on for, like, an hour, just ripping him to shreds and telling you how much it would hurt her if you looked for him. So. Yeah. I get it."

It had been hard on Emma, the bashing of her father that her mother did. Charlie knew that, too, was one of the few who did. While Emma understood her mother's devastation at being left that way—she felt it, too—the fact remained that half of her was her father. So any bad things her mother said about her father, she was also, in a way, saying about Emma. As a teenage girl, that had been hard to reconcile. *Am I like him? Would I do something horrible to the people I love?* Questions like that plagued her off and on her entire life.

"Anyway." It was time to change the subject. "How's the pie baking going?"

Charlie's demeanor changed a bit at the question, and again, Emma felt something inside her warm at the sight. "It's pretty great. Unexpectedly so."

"What do you mean?"

"Well…" Charlie hesitated, as if she was trying to find the right way to say something. "I mean, I didn't come back here to make pie. You know?"

"Why did you come back?" It was the question that had been on Emma's mind since the moment she'd stepped out of the kitchen at EG's and seen her ex standing there after years of no contact. She'd been afraid to ask it. But why? Afraid of what? The answer?

Charlie pursed her lips, chewed one, then the other, as if contemplating her response. "I came back because I didn't have a choice."

Emma waited silently for more.

And Charlie blew out a breath of what seemed like defeat. Of resignation. "When I moved to New York, I worked at Darcy's firm and shared a place with six other girls. It was crowded and small and hot and I hated it. But I loved the job." She looked Emma in the eye, then looked away quickly as she said, "When things started to…develop with Darcy, she moved me into her penthouse apartment. It was stunning, which I'm sure doesn't come as a surprise. It was a whirlwind at first."

Emma was proud of herself for sitting there and listening and actually being okay with it. She had no desire to run, to clamp her hands over her ears and shout *La, la, la!* like a toddler so she couldn't hear. She found herself completely interested in Charlie's story, and when Charlie ventured a tentative glance up at her, Emma simply nodded for her to go on.

"It was only a couple months in when Darcy claimed me as her personal assistant. I got to do so much. It was amazing. Her company is very active in several charities and works with some nonprofits, and she asked me to take that over, so she could focus on growing the commercial side of the business."

"So you did."

"So I did. And I really loved it, both things. I loved the advertising work more, but I was just happy to be so busy, and at first, it didn't matter to me that all the work I did didn't actually pay. But after a while, I was *too* busy."

Emma was starting to get the picture. "So you were doing what Darcy wanted you to do, but at the expense of your own career, your own independence, and your own joy."

"It didn't feel that way at first." A smidgeon of defensiveness slipped into Charlie's voice, which Emma was actually happy to hear. "I enjoyed it for a while."

"You were happy."

"For a while."

"And then?" If you had asked Emma a year ago if she had any interest in hearing about Charlie's glamorous life in the Big Apple, she'd have waved a dismissive hand and walked away. Somehow, somewhere along the line, that had changed. Seeing Charlie had changed her opinion, and not because she wanted to revel in Charlie's failure, but because she was unexpectedly okay having her back in town, and she simply wanted to know why she was.

"And then…her hours got long. I saw her less and less. I didn't love what I was doing, and I missed the excitement I'd experienced working with paying clients. I hated not having much of my own money. I mean, as it was, I started to feel dependent on Darcy."

"Because you were. She made it that way."

Charlie sighed. "Yeah. And then she met Tatiana." She rolled her eyes with such exaggeration that Emma burst out laughing. "Right?" Charlie grinned at her. "Doesn't that just *sound* like somebody who's about to wreck your relationship?"

"It kinda does, not gonna lie." They laughed some more.

"So, when she finally told me she wanted to be with the home wrecker, I had none of my own money and no way to afford finding another place to live."

"Ouch."

"Right? Darcy offered to pay for something, but at that point, my ego was too bruised. I look back now and think I should've taken some money and run with it, but…"

"That's not who you are."

"No. It's not. And I was so incredibly embarrassed because I'm pretty sure everybody knew something was going on except me."

Emma grimaced.

"So my only option was to come running home to my parents with my tail between my legs. Their big city executive daughter was a miserable failure, in business and in love."

"I'm sure they don't see you as a failure."

"Well, I do."

The shame that colored Charlie's expression was hard to see, so Emma said softly, "I'm really sorry you went through all of that."

Charlie barked a laugh and bumped against Emma with her shoulder. "Oh, please. You are not. You're loving this story."

"Well…" Emma held her thumb and forefinger millimeters apart. "Maybe a *tiny* bit." Charlie looked at her then, met her gaze, held it. There was that sizzle again, and Emma felt a wash of something that made her clear her throat.

"It's okay," Charlie said. "You're allowed to find joy in my catastrophe. Absolutely. That's called karma." A beat went by, then another, as the eye contact held. Finally, Charlie whispered, "I'm so sorry, Em. I'm so, so sorry for what I did, for how I hurt you. I wish I could go back and do things differently. I really do."

Of all the things that might have happened, of all the variations of how the day could have gone, this one was the very last one Emma ever would have predicted. Sitting on her couch, now completely and instantly sober, listening to Charlie apologize for devastating her was… *unexpected* seemed too weak of a word to describe it.

She looked down at her hands, fiddled with a string hanging off the hem of her shirt. "We were young."

"We weren't that young," Charlie said. Then she sighed, gave Emma a sad half grin.

Emma chuckled and reached for Charlie's hand. They entwined their fingers—which was so perfectly familiar, it made Emma's chest ache—and sat there quietly for several minutes. Finally, Emma turned to Charlie and asked, "Hey, are you hungry?"

"Oh my God, it's about damn time. Why the hell do you think I followed a chef home?"

Emma's laughter bubbled up from deep in her body, a big belly laugh that she hadn't let loose in longer than she could remember. With a push and a groan, she stood up and went into the kitchen to find something to whip up for the two of them. Charlie stayed on the couch, and as Emma worked, she made little glances in Charlie's direction, watched as she looked at the stack of books on Emma's coffee table, as she thumbed through the cooking magazines there, and the realization hit her out of nowhere, though it wasn't unexpected.

Things were different now.

They'd turned a corner or come full circle or one of those clichés. And while Emma had no idea what it meant or what she was supposed to do next, she didn't mind. She felt like this was the beginning of not just a new chapter in her book, but of a whole new part. *Emma's Life, Part Two.* She could see it as clear as day. She could feel it.

And much to her own astonishment, she was ready to turn the page.

❖

Charlie hadn't expected to be so comfortable at Emma's place. In fact, she'd second-guessed her decision to walk her home the entire way here, even on the way up the stairs. But once inside, that had changed. Her nerves melted away. Her uncertainty evaporated like fog on a sunny summer morning. Emma's place felt inviting. Welcoming. Happy to have her there—which was silly, she knew, but that's how it felt.

It was weird, right?

She and Emma hadn't exactly ended on good terms. No, scratch that. They'd ended on very, very bad terms. Totally Charlie's doing and she knew it. And Emma knew it. Yet here they sat, in astonishingly easy silence, eating side by side on Emma's couch.

Emma had sautéed sliced zucchini and cherry tomatoes in butter, garlic, and fresh basil from the tiny herb garden on her windowsill. Then she'd topped it with fresh mozzarella cheese and served Charlie a heaping portion. Charlie scraped her plate and did her best to resist actually licking it clean, which was beyond tempting. This was obviously a talent of Emma's that she'd not only not lost, but had improved on immensely: whipping up a meal using whatever ingredients were handy.

"My God, that was good." Charlie stood from the couch—not without a bit of a struggle from being full—and reached for Emma's plate.

"Yeah? I'm glad. Super easy to do. I could show you."

Charlie took the dishes into Emma's kitchen and rinsed them both. "I don't need to learn. I have you." The implication of the words hung in the air between them. Charlie felt herself flush and did her best to focus on the dishes rather than looking at Emma's face to see her reaction.

"You'll just have to keep me supplied with pie, then."

"Seems like a reasonable trade."

What were they doing? What the hell were they doing?

Charlie finished rinsing the plates and put them into the dishwasher. "This is a great kitchen. Not at all what I was expecting from an upstairs apartment." *Yes, Charlie. Change the subject. Smooth.*

"I did some work, had some things rearranged." Emma was stretched out, her legs crossed at the ankle on the coffee table, looking casual and comfortable. "I can go downstairs and experiment in the restaurant kitchen easily enough, but sometimes, I just want to be home. You know?"

"Makes perfect sense." Charlie gave a nod, then glanced at her watch. She didn't really want to leave, and that was a strange thing to come to grips with. "Well, I have to get up super early—life of a bakery employee—so I should probably head home."

"I'd offer to drive you, but I'm still a tiny bit buzzed." Emma grimaced but sounded sincere as she stood up.

"No, no. No worries. I can call…what was his name? Tom?" At Emma's nod, she said, "I can call Uber Tom." Charlie hit the right buttons and called for a ride. "Three minutes away. Wow."

"Faster than catching a cab in New York, I bet." There was a playful twinkle in Emma's dark eyes that took away any sarcasm Charlie might've assumed. Or fully expected.

"Definitely, especially if it's raining." Still struck by the feeling of not wanting to leave, she found her bag and slung it over her shoulder. Emma met her at the door and opened it for her. "This was…" Charlie let the sentence dangle, not sure of the right words, but only because there were so many.

"Unexpected?"

"Yeah. That. And nice."

"It was." Emma looked down at her feet, and when she brought her gaze back up, she scrunched up her nose. "Is that weird?"

"So weird!" Charlie said immediately and they both laughed. Then, before she could second-guess herself, Charlie reached out and wrapped Emma in a hug.

Oh my God.

How could this be? How could hugging Emma feel so incredibly perfect? After all they'd been through. After so much time apart, so much time with other people, how could Emma still feel this exactly right in her arms?

Charlie wondered if Emma was feeling the same thing because her arms tightened around Charlie's form, held her close. Emma's nose was in Charlie's hair. She could hear her breath near her ear. Emma's body beneath Charlie's hands was solid but soft, familiar, comforting.

They pulled apart very, very slowly. Barely apart. Stayed close enough that the tips of their noses almost touched. Emma's eyes had gone even darker, and the heat Charlie felt simmering in her core was the only thing she was aware of. Well. That and Emma's mouth so close to hers.

Were they both breathing hard?

Charlie was, that was for sure, and when she wet her lips with her tongue, Emma made a soft sound—a combination groan-whimper— and that was it.

Their mouths crashed together, and suddenly, they were kissing. No, they were full-on making out. Right there in Emma's doorway, and Charlie couldn't remember when anything had felt so exactly perfect in her life before that. Lips parted, tongues danced. Emma's mouth was soft and hot and wet, and she tasted like the past and the future and home.

Before she could analyze any of it, especially that last bit, her phone pinged.

Startled, Charlie jolted back a step. Her chest was heaving, as was Emma's, and they stood there. Blinking. Staring. Emma's cheeks were flushed, her eyes still dark and heavy-lidded. Charlie swallowed.

"My ride's here," she whispered.

Emma nodded.

"Okay." Charlie lifted a hand in a weak wave. "I'll see you."

Emma nodded again. Apparently, words had left her completely.

Charlie turned and fled down the stairs.

That really was the best way to describe it: She fled. Almost ran. She couldn't remember ever feeling this torn between staying put and running away at top speed, and she burst out of the first-floor door like she was crashing through the finish line of a race. She quickly checked the license plate of the car, then hopped in and collapsed against the seat. As the Uber pulled away, she ventured a glance up at the second floor of the building.

Emma was standing in the window, and Charlie couldn't look away.

What the hell just happened?

CHAPTER SIXTEEN

One advantage to making pies for the bakery was that, while it gave Charlie the chance to experiment and try new things, she also didn't have to be creative when she wasn't feeling it. She could make a coconut cream pie with her eyes closed, and that Monday, that felt like exactly what she was doing.

Not only had her little tryst with Emma kept her awake all night, but she'd also gotten a text later from Lily Bricker, who had a line on a job for her in Boston and wanted to talk to her about it. Charlie had the end of the text memorized.

I know this guy really well, talked you up, you're pretty much in for an interview. See? It's what you've been hoping for!

And it was. It was exactly what she'd been hoping for. What she'd been waiting for since she pulled into her parents' driveway several weeks ago. To find a way to go back—Boston wasn't New York, but it would do—and survive on her own. *On her own.* No help from anybody.

Push, knead, fold, repeat...

She worked the dough for the piecrust with her hands, not thinking about it at all because her mind was on other things. So many other things. Lily's text had given her something to focus on besides Emma—besides Emma's mouth, Emma's eyes, Emma's hands—but it hadn't eased her stress, only added to it.

She'd loved working in a big, bustling marketing firm. The breakneck pace, the competition, the working at all hours. It had been exhilarating...hadn't it? She hadn't done it for longer than a year before Darcy pulled her away to do other things. But she was living under Darcy's roof, Darcy paid for pretty much everything, so doing what she asked of Charlie seemed not only reasonable, but right. It was a way to contribute…the only way Charlie had.

If she got this job, she would be redeemed. She'd show Darcy that she really didn't need her, hadn't needed her at all to make her own way in the business world. Darcy used the city, the success of her company, the pace, the money, she used all of it to lure Charlie. To woo her. And it had worked like a charm. Charlie hadn't been the first, and she could admit now that there was some part of her that had always known she probably wouldn't be the last. Getting a job at another company and succeeding all on her own would give her some serious satisfaction. It would be a giant middle finger raised in Darcy's direction. Not that Darcy would notice.

Charlie hadn't told anybody about the text, and she hadn't responded yet. Her brain had been too full of Emma last night, and this morning, she was too damn tired.

As she rolled out the dough, Sandy came through the doors from the front, humming softly, and got started on her famous—well, in Shaker Falls—brownie batter. Sandy'd been humming since Charlie had arrived over an hour ago, her face sporting a gentle smile.

"So…" Charlie drew the word out. Bethany was coming in late today, and she and Sandy were alone in the kitchen. "How was your date with Mr. Silver Fox?"

Sandy's face flushed in an instant, her cheeks tinting to match the pink apron she'd put on, and she blinked several times, not looking up at Charlie.

"That's quite the blush you've got going there, Ms. McCarthy. So good, then?" She grinned at Sandy because it made her heart warm to see her so obviously happy. "Care to share?"

Sandy added flour to the mixing bowl, cocoa powder, vanilla, and seemed to contemplate what she wanted to say. When she lifted her eyes to Charlie, her expression was contemplative, brow furrowed. "So… my marriage wasn't great," she began, cracking an egg on the counter and adding it to the bowl. "It wasn't horrible, but it was very…" She pursed her lips for a second. "Stale. Stagnant."

She hadn't expected this glimpse into Sandy's personal past, but she nodded in understanding. She'd never experienced that exactly, but she could imagine.

"We never had kids because neither of us really wanted them, so you'd think that would've made us tighter, you know? Do more stuff together. Be the envy of our friends who were tied down both timewise and financially because of their children. But it didn't. We just got boring." She turned off the mixer and poured half the batter into a large pan. Then she put the bowl back under the mixer and added walnuts to the remaining batter. "No, correction. My *husband* got boring. I wanted to do stuff and he just didn't. We were in our early forties and I was starting to feel seventy. We'd go to dinner once in a while, but we mostly stayed home, watched TV. I could literally feel myself getting old before my time." Sandy glanced up at Charlie and waved a dismissive hand. "Sorry. You didn't ask for all that."

"No, no, please," she said with a smile. "It's nice to actually talk. You know?"

Sandy's dimples appeared as she smiled back. "It *is* nice, isn't it? Anyway, my point in giving you the History of Sandy McCarthy's Love Life is simply to highlight how different Eric is than my ex. He wants to do stuff. Go places. Have fun." Her eyes were bright. "*Live*. I haven't had that in a long time. We talked a lot about it. His ex-wife is very similar to my ex-husband."

"Maybe you should hook *them* up. I mean, I didn't spend much time with him, but he seems really nice."

"Oh, he is. A complete gentleman. Wicked sense of humor. I can't remember the last time I laughed like that."

"Somebody who can make you laugh is *huge*." She thought about Emma, her sense of humor, how she knew just how to crack her up.

"Right? You don't realize how important that is until you meet it."

"I take it you'll see him again?"

"He's making me dinner tonight."

"And he cooks? Score!"

"I know, right? Is he too good to be true?" Sandy's eyes went comically wide. "What if he's a serial killer?"

"I mean, it's possible, right?" she asked with concern, playing along. "You could be an episode of *Dateline* in a heartbeat."

"That'd be just my luck."

Talking to Sandy about her love life did a great job of occupying Charlie's mind, and before she knew it, it was after noon, and Jules had popped by with a lunch delivery of turkey avocado wraps from EG's.

"Not tonight's special, but Emma said it's a beautiful day out and she wanted everybody to eat wraps for lunch. Or some such weirdness." Jules snorted a laugh and shrugged. "I just do what she tells me."

"Let her know that Charlie will be over with coconut cream pie in a little while," Sandy said, picking up the bag to take into the back.

"Will do." Jules bounced out of the bakery and was gone.

In the kitchen area, Sandy pulled out three foil-wrapped tubes. Each had a little Post-it stuck to it.

Bethany, who had just arrived, put hers in the big refrigerator to eat later, then went out front to handle customers. Sandy handed Charlie her wrap.

Her Post-it read: *Charlie—mayo instead of Italian dressing* :-)

"How does Emma know you don't like Italian dressing on yours?"

Totally innocent question, but she felt herself panic just slightly, then chastise herself, because why? Why the panic? She had nothing to be embarrassed about, and Sandy had poured her heart out earlier. Maybe it was time to do a little opening up herself.

"Emma and I have a history." She could feel more than see Sandy's brows rise.

"A history? What does that mean? You went to school together? You were friends? You dated?" Sandy chuckled as she unwrapped the foil on her lunch.

"Yes, yes, and yes." Charlie swallowed hard, unwrapping her own lunch and carefully not looking at Sandy. Internally, she shook her head in dismay. Twenty-seven years old and still hesitant to come out to people. She exhaled and forced herself to take a bite of the wrap even though she was suddenly not all that hungry.

"You guys dated?" Sandy's voice registered incredulity, which she immediately corrected with an upheld hand. "No, no. That came out wrong. God." She covered her eyes and flushed, and her embarrassment was clear. "What I meant was it's just that the idea of you guys together is kind of perfect. I've thought more than once that you'd make such a hot couple." She laughed nervously, as if unsure whether she was fixing things or digging herself a deeper hole.

"Really?" Charlie smiled at that.

"Oh God, yes. You're both so gorgeous. Her with all that beautiful hair and you with your unique eyes and terrific smile. You two would have beautiful babies."

"Ha. If only it worked that way, right?"

Sandy nodded as she took a bite of her wrap and furrowed her brow like she was contemplating the Universe as she chewed. "So," she ventured after swallowing, "tell me about the history. I know nothing."

Charlie acknowledged the relief she felt knowing that neither her mother nor Emma had gossiped about this aspect of her life and sent up a silent word of gratitude.

"It's a long story, but we've known each other since we were little kids. We were BFFs in school, did everything together, realized our sexuality together, and it was only natural that we'd become girlfriends."

"You were each other's firsts?" Sandy asked, and there was a slightly dreamy quality to her voice that made Charlie grin.

"We were. We were together through much of college, but we had started to drift. Being at different schools took its toll, and it's hard to expand and learn and grow with somebody when you're hours apart." This part still made her sad, and she felt that old familiar veil of melancholy gently fall down over her story. "I guess I felt a little lost. Unsure of myself." It was the first time Charlie had admitted that out loud, and she felt a little twinge of surprise. She took a breath and continued. "There was a businesswoman, an entrepreneur, who spoke at my college a few times while I was there and she...took a liking to me." Ugh.

"In a business-y way or a personal way?" Sandy asked, and Charlie was amused.

"Both."

"I see. Go on." Sandy took another bite of her wrap and listened, looking enraptured by the story.

"Her name was Darcy Wells. She's smart and beautiful and sexy and is a major success story, and she offered me a job at her marketing firm in Manhattan."

"How do you not grab that, right?" Man, it sure seemed like Sandy got her. More gratitude.

"Exactly. But Emma was cautious. She was sure Darcy only wanted to get into my pants. Which was insulting, but because we'd already drifted so much—and I realize now, partly *because* I was insulted—I went ahead and took the job."

"And?"

"And it was great, for a short time."

Sandy held her gaze for a beat before asking her question. "Was Emma right?"

Charlie sighed. Chewed. Thought. "Yes and no is my answer to that."

Sandy squinted. "Explain."

The bell above the door tinkled, and Bethany glanced back at them as several customers filed in.

"Saved by the bell," Sandy said and pointed at her. "Finish your lunch and my pies. We'll revisit this another time."

Was she relieved? She couldn't tell. In the moment, it had felt good to talk about the whole thing. She hadn't really told anybody the entire story since she'd gotten home. Not her mother. Not Amber. Everybody had snippets. Nobody had all the details, and part of her had been ready to finally supply them.

Ah, well.

Her turkey wrap was frigging delicious, and she allowed herself a moment she hadn't taken earlier—a moment to think about the fact that Emma had made hers especially for her, the way she liked it.

Also, Emma had kissed her.

No. No, let's be honest here.

She had kissed *Emma*. She couldn't help herself. Hadn't even tried to help herself. It was Emma, for God's sake. The one who'd always been her rock. And she'd been standing there, looking beautiful and open, and Charlie had let instinct take over, and apparently, her instinct was to push her tongue into Emma's mouth.

And Emma had sent her lunch, made it just the way she liked it.

What should she do with that?

The buzzer to the oven sounded, and Charlie shook herself back to the present. *I guess now's not the time. The pies need me.*

❖

Emma was in a good mood on Monday, which was new. Not that she was ever in a horrible mood, but Monday was Monday, and she was most commonly neutral as far as her Monday mood.

Not today, though. Today, she hummed along to Taylor Swift as she prepped. The turkey wraps she'd made and sent across the street were like food of the gods, if she said so herself, and she popped the last bite of the extra one she'd made into her mouth, chewed slowly, savored.

Tonight's special was cedar-plank salmon, and the soup was gazpacho. Alec was already working on that, chopping and dicing and blending. He worked quietly at his end of the kitchen, and Jules got salad stuff ready, while Emma gathered her info for the bar. Danielle was coming in any time now to take her liquor order.

Until she'd owned her own restaurant, Emma hadn't experienced the full impact of pride that always swept through her at this time of day in the dining room. There was only her, Jules, and Alec, and with them in the kitchen working, Emma would simply wander among the chairs and tables, listening to the quiet, inhaling the scents of food left from the most recent meals. She'd straighten the photos on the walls, make sure the bud vases and tea lights were centered on the tables. Run her fingertips over the backs of the wooden chairs.

EG's was hers. Hers alone. She owned it. She'd even venture to call it a success. Granted, she had a significant loan she was paying, and there were definite lulls. She sat down with her business advisor twice a year to go over marketing and ideas to keep things fresh, and she felt pretty good about that.

She was the head chef and owner-operator of her own successful restaurant before she hit thirty. She took a moment and allowed herself to be impressed. Not for long, though. She didn't want to get too big for her britches, as her mom would say.

A moment of standing proudly with her hands on her hips was all she needed, and then she moved to the front door just as Danielle pulled up out front.

"Hey, bitch," Danielle said as she slammed her car door shut.

"I love when you wear a suit and pretend to be all businesslike and important."

"Hey, there is no pretending here." Danielle circled the car and stood next to her, briefcase in hand. "Ready to buy all the alcohol? Make me the number one sales rep for my company so I can win the Caribbean cruise I'm so close to, I can taste it?"

Danielle's job took her all over the state, and some of her clients were major restaurants, bars, and grocery stores. EG's was a teeny, tiny blip on her radar, but Emma appreciated when she made her sound like a big deal.

"Yes, absolutely. Come in so I can buy twenty-seven cases of everything you have."

"Excellent! Jamaica, here I come!"

They laughed together as she held the door open for Danielle, and they moved behind the bar where Danielle immediately started to examine each bottle of alcohol, each liquor, the wine rack and wine fridge, jotting notes on a pad of paper.

Emma loved watching her work. She wasn't sure why, unless it was the sheer organization. Danielle kept a record of all her sales and knew how well each brand and variety sold, or didn't, at EG's. She came by at least once a month, sometimes more frequently, depending on her schedule or new products, and offered Emma suggestions for buying some or avoiding others. She knew what was hot, what was on the way out, what would never sell. She was a veritable wealth of cocktail info. A fun friend to have.

"You're blowing through the Fireball," Danielle said, almost to herself.

"Sabrina keeps inventing new shots and drinks that include it."

Danielle nodded. "It's very hot right now."

The front door opened, and the blast of sunlight made them both squint. As soon as Emma saw who it was, she felt her heart rate kick up a notch or two. Or twelve. She couldn't help but smile.

"I come bearing gifts," Charlie said as she stepped into the restaurant and let the door shut behind her. She took a beat, blinking, three stacked boxes in her arms. "Help. I can't see."

Emma scooted around the bar and took the boxes gently out of Charlie's hands, their fingers grazing as she did so. A jolt of energy seemed to shoot between them, but Emma didn't know from which of them it originated.

"I heard a rumor today was coconut cream day. Truth?"

Charlie grinned. "Yes, ma'am. They came out pretty good, if I say so myself."

"I'm not surprised. That always was one of your best."

"You think? I feel like I've always had trouble with the texture."

"Not that I can remember." Emma set the boxes on the bar, caught the expression on Danielle's face. Concern? Warning? Disapproval? All of the above? She turned away from her quickly, as if the look was burning her retinas.

"Thanks for lunch," Charlie was saying.

"You liked it?"

"Oh my God, *so* good. Sandy and I ate ours in, like, four bites each." Charlie held her gaze for a moment before adding, a bit quieter, "Thanks for making mine without dressing. I can't believe you remembered."

Emma tapped her finger against her temple. "Steel trap."

"Always was."

Danielle cleared her throat. Emma rolled her lips in.

"Hey, Danielle," Charlie said as she leaned to the side and gave a little wave in Danielle's direction. "Good to see you."

"You, too," Danielle said. "Hey, Em, can you help me with this?"

She stifled a sigh. "Sure." She grimaced at Charlie. "Duty calls."

"Oh, sure. Sure. Go."

"Thanks for the pie. I'll let you know how it goes."

Charlie's smile was bright, and Emma somehow felt it in the pit of her stomach. That might have had something to do with the fact that she was now flashing back to those same lips on hers the night before. That same face in her hands. That tongue pressing against hers. She swallowed hard as she watched Charlie leave, stood there until the door closed softly.

"Seriously?" At least Danielle waited until the door had completely closed before she spoke.

Emma turned to face her. "What?"

Danielle's notepad was down by her side, her head tipped one way, one brow arched in obvious disapproval. "You know what."

Emma shook her head, feigned confusion as she opened one of the boxes and inhaled the heavenly scent of coconut. The pie was gorgeous, all light-colored custard, bright white whipped cream, and the earthy brown of toasted coconut sprinkled on top. "I'm going to try this out. Want a slice?"

Danielle gave a little groan of obvious frustration as she took a couple steps so she was exactly opposite Emma, the bar between them. "Em, listen. You've told—" She stopped and inhaled. "God, that smells divine," she whispered. "Yes, I want a bite, but we're not finished."

Emma sighed loudly. "What, Dani?"

"Don't get all snarky with me," Dani scolded, rightfully so. They had a quick stare down before Emma looked away in defeat. "I saw you two leave Summer Fest together yesterday. What happened?"

She felt her face flush, and she shrugged, knowing she probably looked like a teenager caught doing something she shouldn't and pretending it was no big deal. "I was a little tipsy and Charlie walked me home. I made us some food." She shrugged again, then instantly wished she hadn't because Dani snorted.

"Overplaying your hand a bit with the shrugging, don't you think?" Dani's gaze was like a laser beam, and Emma found herself squirming internally. "You sleep with her?"

"What? No. Of course not."

Dani stared. Simply stared. It was like she was reading her mind, like she could see right in and knew everything Emma had done, and Emma hated it.

"Stop that."

"You kissed her, though."

Emma's eyes went wide. "How the *hell* do you know that?"

It was Dani's turn to shrug like things were no big deal, keeping her eyes on her notes. "It's all over your face."

Was it? She made some noncommittal sound, hoping to end this conversation.

"Listen." Apparently Dani wasn't done. She set her pad down, then her pen, leaned her forearms on the bar, folded her hands, and stared at Emma until she got around to making eye contact. "All I'm doing is looking out for you. You've told me all about Charlie. All about how badly she hurt you. Hell, you haven't had a healthy relationship since. Do you want me to list the qualities she has that you told me about?"

"Not really."

"Okay, good. I will. She's selfish." Dani ticked off each word on a finger. "She's unreliable. She doesn't understand what love is. She's blinded by material things. She doesn't have your back. She's not who you thought she was." Each statement felt like a slice from a razor, death by a thousand cuts, and Emma swallowed hard. "These are all things *you* told me, things *you* said about her. Shall I go on?"

She shook her head, the shame and embarrassment nearly unbearable, the solid lump in her throat making words hard.

Danielle's shoulders dropped and her expression relaxed, as if realizing she'd been a little harsh. She reached across and grabbed Emma's forearm. "I just worry about you." Danielle's voice was gentle. "I love you, and I worry about that tender heart of yours."

"I know." She really didn't want to talk about this, so she told Dani she'd be right back with pie, and she fled to the kitchen.

Didn't matter what was going on in life, no place in the world made her feel better than the kitchen. It was as if there was extra oxygen secretly being pumped in through the vents because Emma felt like she could breathe again. She put two boxes into the big fridge, then carefully lifted the third pie out and set it on the counter. She cut two slices and plated them, grabbed forks, but needed another minute to pull herself together. Danielle wasn't wrong. All those negative qualities she'd ticked off on her fingers out there? Yeah, she'd said every one of them about Charlie. And how the hell did she know Charlie wasn't still just like that? It was a few hours at the park and one kiss. One hot, steamy, dynamic kiss, yes. But just one kiss. It wasn't hard to look back and call up all the pain, all the devastation she had felt. It hadn't *really* been all that long ago.

Maybe Danielle was right. Maybe she needed to take a step back, dig out her armor, and put it on. Maybe she needed to be more careful around Charlie, the one person in the world who had hurt her more than anybody else ever had. Because maybe people didn't change.

She sliced her fork through the tip of one piece of coconut cream pie, put the bite in her mouth, and her eyes closed all on their own, the thick, sweet creaminess coating her tongue and pulling a hum of delight from her throat.

"Oh my God," she said quietly, so nobody else heard. "Well, her pie hasn't changed."

That only solidified her earlier thought: *People don't change.*

Did they?

CHAPTER SEVENTEEN

"Thank you so much for your time and consideration," Charlie said as she smiled into the webcam on her laptop. She'd been forcing that smile for much of the half-hour Skype interview and wondered if she was coming across as creepy or maybe slightly deranged. "I hope to hear from you."

She hit the red *End* button and the smile dropped as if yanked right off her face. Her shoulders drooped and she let out a huge breath.

"That was awesome, honey!" Her mother suddenly trooped down the basement stairs like she was being chased, and Charlie couldn't help but laugh.

"Geez, Mom, were you standing there with your ear pressed to the door?"

"Pretty much, yeah." Her mom took a seat on the bottom step as Charlie closed out of Skype and put her laptop away. "Nice outfit," she commented when Charlie stood to reveal she was wearing a very professional-looking shirt and blazer on top...and leggings on the bottom.

"Why, thank you." She padded across the basement in bare feet and set her laptop bag in a corner.

"So? How'd it go?" Her mother's eyes were bright, her brows raised expectantly, her excitement palpable. It really was kind of adorable.

A casual shrug. "Pretty well, I think. He seemed impressed with my résumé." She didn't add that she'd had to fudge a bit to explain why she'd been a junior account executive for such a short time. Luckily, she'd been part of a couple of very successful marketing campaigns, so she was able to talk those up.

"That's great." Her mom clapped her hands together and grinned so widely that Charlie squinted at her.

"You okay, Mom?"

"Of course I am." Her mother tipped her head to one side, her eyes watering slightly. "I'm just getting used to having you back home is all."

Ah. She understood then. "I'm not going anywhere just yet. I promise."

"I know." There was an unspoken *But you will* beneath her words, and they both knew it. There was a beat of silence before her mom slapped her thighs and stood. "Okay. Gotta get dinner ready." She took a couple steps up before turning back. "I do hope you get the job, sweetie. You know that, right?"

She met her mother's gaze, saw the uncertainty and the tinge of guilt, and had the immediate need to fix it. "I know, Mom."

Her mom looked at her tenderly for a moment longer before heading up the stairs and disappearing from sight.

Charlie picked up her phone and texted Lily, thanked her for setting up the interview, and reported how it went. Lily sent several smiling emojis, said she was in a meeting, but she'd call later to get all the deets.

She should've been excited. Charlie knew she should. In the grand scheme of interviews, hers had been a good one. Definitely. She'd been articulate. Insightful. She'd come across as intelligent. Knowledgeable. No questions had stumped her, not even the standard *What would you say is your biggest weakness?* She had that one down—trying to predict people's reactions to things, often incorrectly. If they didn't call her for a second interview in the next week, she'd be very, very surprised.

So why wasn't she flying high right now? Why wasn't she researching Boston? Neighborhoods and housing prices and rental properties? Why wasn't she doing more research on the company and trying to learn all she could about each senior account executive, so she could hit the ground running when she got there?

She didn't want to think about the answers, and that was the honest-to-God truth. Avoidance. She was becoming a pro.

❖

Friday morning was crazy at The Muffin Top. People coming in and out. Four preorders for cookies and muffins. Charlie had baked five different made-to-order pies first thing for a rec center event in Clifton, which Sandy had been thrilled about.

"News of your pies is spreading," Sandy'd said to her with the excitement of a toddler at a playground as she wiped her hands on her pink apron and hurried by to pull a tray of macarons from the oven. They were a soft pink and looked like little desserts made of cartoon clouds.

"Those are gorgeous," Charlie commented as she pushed another apple onto the peeler-corer for slicing. She'd decided to go with good old-fashioned apple pie to honor the upcoming July Fourth holiday. Since she'd started at The Muffin Top, she'd gone from making two pies in the mornings to three to five to sometimes seven or eight. Three automatically went across to EG's. Business had picked up steadily, both for whole pies and by the slice—which was a great sign, as Charlie would've expected things like pies and cookies to sell better over the fall and winter holidays than through the summer.

"I want to talk to you for a minute before you take pies over to Emma this afternoon, okay?" Sandy took a second tray out of the oven, this time loaded with mint-green macarons. "Don't leave until you see me."

"Got it."

Sandy's mention of Emma sent Charlie's mind there, to that place she'd been trying not to dwell in, and she ended up there for the remainder of her shift. Through pie-making and ringing out customers and cleanup, her brain rolled it all around. She hadn't spent any time with Emma since last Sunday and that kiss. That magical, familiar-but-new, amazing kiss they'd shared. She'd seen Emma a few times when delivering pie, but conversation had been sparse, Emma claiming to be super busy. Tuesday, she came out, said a quick thanks, and scooted right back into the kitchen. Wednesday, she'd come out from the kitchen with her phone to her ear, obviously on a business call, and she'd given Charlie a wave, scooped up the pies, and disappeared back into the kitchen. Yesterday, she hadn't come out at all, and Charlie left the pies with Jules. Charlie certainly understood that Emma had a job that kept her very busy, but this seemed odd.

Maybe she was reading into things too much. After all, it wasn't like she really *knew* Emma any longer, right? Years had passed. They were different people now. Still. She'd felt a sense of distance from Emma since Monday, and it was beginning to frustrate her. It was probably time to call her on it. *I mean, maybe? Is that even allowed?*

Things finally died down enough in the early afternoon that Sandy stopped running around like a madwoman and Bethany was able to give her fingers a rest from the constant pressing of buttons on the cash register. Charlie came out of the kitchen with her pie boxes stacked and set them on the counter. They looked at each other and exhaled loudly all at once, then burst into laughter.

"What a day," Bethany said. "That was insane. I don't think there was a point since we opened this morning that there hasn't been at least one person in here."

"That's a good thing," Charlie said.

"That's a very good thing," Sandy added, her dimples made prominent by her relieved smile.

"I'm ready to take these over," Charlie said, indicating the boxes. "You wanted to see me first?"

"Oh!" Sandy said, as if just remembering. "Yes. Come with me." Sandy led her through the kitchen and into the very back of the store. Sandy called it her office, but really it was just an old metal desk pushed into a corner with a laptop on the surface and papers scattered around. "Have a seat." Sandy indicated the desk chair, then leaned her butt against the edge of the desk.

Charlie sat down, crossed her legs, and looked expectantly at Sandy. The look on her face was hard to read, a mix of hesitation, concern, excitement. "Is everything okay?" she asked. "Did I do something wrong?"

"Oh God, no. Not at all. The opposite, actually."

Charlie narrowed her eyes. "Okay." She drew the word out.

Sandy took a deep breath and blew it out in a loud puff. "I've decided to move forward with the addition of the coffee. I'm going to rent the rest of the building and expand."

Charlie jumped out of her chair. "Oh my God! That's amazing! When?"

"Well, I'm going to take the weekend to let it all sink in and make sure I don't panic, and then I thought I'd get the ball rolling next week. That's why I wanted to talk to you."

Charlie nodded. "Sure. What can I help with?"

"So." Sandy found a metal folding chair leaning against the wall and opened it, and they both took a seat so they were eye to eye. "I can do this. It's what I've wanted for a long time now, and I think the expansion is only going to help The Muffin Top be more successful. I mean, Shaker Falls isn't that big, so being successful has its limits here." She made air quotes around the word *successful*. "I'm also in my midforties. Which means I'm no spring chicken."

Charlie waved a dismissive hand. "Please. You have more energy than some of the twentysomethings I know."

Sandy grinned. "True. But my point is, I'm going to need some help. I'd love it if that help came from you."

She was not expecting this. "Me?"

"It's your business plan. Who knows it better than you? You're young and you're hip and you know how to reach a wider demographic than I do. And if you come on board with me permanently, we would talk down the line about you partnering with me. Becoming part owner."

Charlie sat back in her chair, thoroughly astonished. "Wow. I…I don't know what to say." She had not seen any of this coming. At all. Stunned didn't begin to describe how she was feeling in that moment. Proud. Nervous. Excited. Worried. All.

As if sensing her shock, Sandy put a hand on Charlie's knee. "Listen, you don't have to say anything right now. I know it's a lot to take in. Just think about it. Take the weekend. Take all next week. I'm going to take the next steps anyway, but I'd love it if you'd be my wingwoman of sorts. You know?" Her smile was gentle, slightly tentative, like she didn't want to push Charlie, but also definitely wanted to push her. "Mull it over."

Charlie nodded slowly. "I will. I promise."

"Good." Sandy patted Charlie's knee, then stood. "Now get those pies across to Emma and go home. It's Friday. Go do something fun."

With a smile and another nod, Charlie stood and headed out into the bakery where she scooped up her pies and walked them slowly across the street.

In front of EG's, she turned and looked at The Muffin Top along with the empty shop next to it, and she pictured it expanded, taking up both storefronts. All pink and new and filled with people, the scents of fresh muffins and roasting coffee beans wafting down the street, drawing customers in by their noses and their growling tummies.

Charlie laughed softly at the image, and as she stood there, it occurred to her what she was actually seeing: another possible future for herself. A possible future she'd never even considered before.

What to do about that?

❖

Friday's special was prime rib. Emma didn't serve it often because it was a lot of prep to get it just right, but it always brought in a crowd and sold well, so it was worth the extra work. It was midafternoon, and Alec already had some of the meat slow-roasting; the kitchen smelled like heaven. Most people preferred their prime rib medium, but Emma wanted to make sure there was enough rare, for those with a more discerning palate, and a bit that was more well done, for those outliers who had no idea how to enjoy beef, so she'd helped Alec with the prep and now checked it regularly.

She'd hired three extra staff members for the weekends over the summer—two waitstaff and one cook—and they were due in by three o'clock. The bar was already abuzz with happy hour folks who'd bailed out of work a little early, and the atmosphere at EG's was one of fun and relief and weekend anticipation. For Emma, Fridays were all of those things, along with a higher level of stress, but she didn't mind. She fed off it—it energized her.

It also helped her focus on things that were not the super cute girl across the street baking pie. That girl had been taking up way too much of her headspace, and she'd take any distraction she could because Dani's words had hit her hard and hadn't left. In fact, they'd taken up residence in her brain. Pitched a tent. Started a campfire. Brought the makings for s'mores.

That kiss, though.

Right next to the camp where Dani's words had moved in was The Kiss. Side by side, they sat there in her mind and poked at each other, first one, then the other. *Think about me! No, me!* It made her edgy. Touchy. She'd snarked at Alec earlier in the week for no good reason.

She'd returned Dani's texts, but only with abrupt, one- or two-word responses. Her patience with her mother was in the toilet, as proven by the fact that there were six unanswered texts from her on her phone at that very moment.

Emma felt like she was going a little mad.

Which was probably why, when she pushed through the swinging door to the dining room and saw Charlie coming into the restaurant with three pie boxes in her arms and that hesitant smile on her face—the hesitation Emma had put there, she knew, from her avoidance of Charlie all week—her coping skills completely bottomed out, and she was unable to keep the frustration at bay.

That hesitant smile melted right off Charlie's face. Emma watched it happen, felt a twinge in her gut at the sight, as Charlie sort of stutter-stepped toward the bar. Like she was afraid.

"Hey," Charlie said, bowing her head a bit. "Brought you pie."

"Great." Emma slid her palms down the sides of her chef's coat. "Listen, tell Sandy it's time to write up a proper order form. I want to pay for these."

A small glimmer appeared in Charlie's hazel eyes, but the hesitation was still there. "I can do that. She'll be happy." She put the boxes on the bar. "Today was blueberry day. They're in season, so very fresh. Also, one apple. I mixed it up for you."

"Great. Thanks." She wished she had something to do, but she couldn't remember why she'd come out of the kitchen in the first place.

They stood there awkwardly, until Charlie seemed to find some strength. She sighed and smiled, this time not so hesitantly. "I haven't been able to stop thinking about Sunday." And there was that blush again.

Emma wanted to grin back. Wanted to tell Charlie the truth, which was she hadn't stopped thinking about Sunday either. But then Dani's voice started shouting things in her head. *Selfish! Unreliable! She broke your heart!* And Emma just couldn't. She just couldn't. Instead of smiling, she shook her head.

"I can't do this with you, Charlie. Not again. Sunday shouldn't have happened." She was careful not to look at Charlie because she knew exactly what she'd see: that grin melting away again, only to be replaced by pain, sadness, disappointment. She didn't want to see it. She couldn't.

As usual, Sabrina had impeccable timing and came through the kitchen into the bar right at that moment. Sabrina stopped, looked from Charlie to her, and Emma could almost feel her demeanor change. While she hadn't told Sabrina about her past with Charlie, it was glaringly obvious that she now knew there had been *something*. Perils of living in a small town. News traveled like lightning. Emma closed her eyes, knowing she'd get an earful at some point.

"Well," Charlie said, straightening her stance, obviously trying to find the tiniest shred of dignity with which to walk out the door, and Emma felt a zap of guilt. "Good to know." With that, she turned and left, the blast of sunlight as the door opened making Emma squint until it shut again. Even then, she just stood there feeling depleted.

"Trouble in paradise?" Sabrina asked snidely as she tied a black apron around her waist and then turned on the water to fill up the under-bar sink.

Emma shot her a look, then escaped back to her sanctuary, to her kitchen, with only one question on her mind.

Why the hell did Charlie have to come back to Shaker Falls?

CHAPTER EIGHTEEN

Sunday was July Fourth, but the annual Shaker Falls fireworks display was on Saturday night. Everybody was down at the park again for the closing night of Summer Fest, which would be capped off by the fireworks, but Charlie was in no mood for the crowd. She'd been feeling slowly deflated. Like a balloon with a tiny pinhole, losing air over the course of hours, days. Since her talk with Emma on Friday— hell, could one back-and-forth even be considered a talk?—she'd felt that way. Like she was just losing air, little by little, until she'd be nothing more than a flat and empty bag on the ground.

Sherry apparently didn't want anything to do with crowds that night either, and Charlie was surprised to run into her in the kitchen. She was even more surprised when Sherry not only looked her in the eye, but spoke to her just like she'd speak to any other person in the world. *What is happening?*

"Hey," Sherry said, pulling two beers out of the fridge. She held one out to Charlie. "Not going to the fireworks?"

She took the beer and shook her head. "Not in the mood."

"Same. Wanna start a fire and sit with me? We should be able to see some of them from the backyard."

"You know what? That sounds perfect." And it did. It had been so long since she'd spent time alone with her sister, and despite the snark-fests they'd had the previous weeks, Charlie still missed her.

They worked silently together as dusk fell, moving a decent supply of wood from behind the garage to near the fire pit. Sherry got some newspaper and kindling and got things going in an impressive manner.

"Wow. When did you become Queen of Fire?" Charlie asked as

she watched the flames spread from beneath the teepee of wood Sherry had designed.

A half shrug. "When Mom and Dad got the fire pit, I just kind of took it upon myself to be the fire tender. I got good at it."

"I guess so. I'm so impressed with you right now."

"Oh, thank God. I live to impress you." Sherry caught her eye and gave her a grin to take away any sting the words might have carried.

"As well you should," Charlie said, playing along. "Me being the big sister and all."

Fire stoked, beers opened, and bodies stretched out on chairs, they relaxed in the quiet of the summer evening. Behind their house was a copse of trees that separated their street from the next one over, and in those trees, Charlie could see the occasional blink of a firefly. She took a sip of her beer, sat there quietly, and simply watched, letting herself be transported back to her childhood.

"Remember when we used to spend hours chasing fireflies?" she asked.

A quiet chuckle came from Sherry. "And we'd put them in a jar in our room and never understand why they were dead in the morning?"

"Who knew the concept of air holes was so important?"

"Right? Why didn't Mom know that?"

"We must have killed hundreds of the poor things in our child-hood."

"We are mass murderers." Sherry was laughing openly now, and Charlie joined her.

"God, it feels good to laugh with you."

Sherry's laughter died down and she sipped her beer. She kept her eyes on the flames as she said quietly, "I missed you, you know."

"I missed you, too."

"No." Sherry did look at her then, and Charlie saw so many things in her sister's eyes, despite the darkness and the flickering of the fire: pain, sadness, confusion. "I mean, I *missed* you. I felt like you just left me." Sherry held up a hand when Charlie opened her mouth to speak. "Not literally. I know that's what happens, that that's the next step in life. But you left in every way. I mean..." She sighed and seemed to struggle with finding the right words.

"I want to jump in and say something, but"—Charlie swallowed, felt an uncomfortable wave in her stomach—"I think I need to let you talk." She wasn't sure why or where that had come from, but it was like a feeling on some psychic level, as if the Universe was talking to her. Telling her to shut the hell up and listen. So she did.

Sherry's eyes welled up and Charlie swallowed down her alarm. Sherry was not a crier. She didn't cry. It was so rare, she could count on one hand how many times she'd seen it from their teenage years on. The epitome of stoic, that was her little sister.

With a clear of her throat, Sherry said, "I needed my sister." She shifted her gaze so she was looking directly at Charlie. "I *needed* my sister. When you left, it was like..." She tapped her chest with a finger. "Like there was this hole, and like I said, I knew it was part of life, that you were starting your life, but you hardly ever came back. And you invited me to come, like, once. It took you hours or sometimes even days to respond to my texts. You were so caught up in New York, and your big high-powered job, and *Darcy*." She didn't sneer the name, but it was close. Close enough for Charlie to clearly understand how her little sister had felt about her girlfriend. "And then there was Emma. You wrecked her. You know that, right?"

The question wasn't the least bit accusatory, just matter of fact, and maybe that made it worse. Charlie felt her own eyes fill and she nodded silently.

"Emma was like another sister to me, but after you broke up with her, she felt like she couldn't be part of our family anymore. Which makes sense now, I guess, but then? I lost *two* sisters, thanks to you. That's what it felt like. And you know what?"

She looked at Sherry, unable to swallow down the lump in her throat. "What?"

"I really could have used one." Again, Sherry's voice was quiet and calm, no blame, no snottiness.

"I'm sorry, Sherry." Her voice was ragged.

"You were so selfish. You just did what you wanted to do, so you could have what you wanted to have."

Charlie gave a rueful laugh. "I mean, don't sugarcoat it or anything."

Sherry shrugged and said nothing. Which shouldn't have been a surprise, as Sherry didn't sugarcoat anything. Charlie knew that. She just spoke the truth, and if it stung you, too damn bad.

Besides, what Sherry said was true, and Charlie knew it. Granted, she could defend herself by calling on her own youth or her confusion about being desired by somebody as glamorous as Darcy Wells or her fascination with the big city and wanting to get out of Small Town, USA. All of those were valid excuses. But none of them really exonerated her from what Sherry said. She *had* been selfish. She had wanted to see what it was like to be wooed by a woman like Darcy. She had wanted to feel the energy and fast pace of New York City. She had felt like her family, Shaker Falls, Emma all held her back. And now her sister had called her on it. On the selfishness she'd displayed, and it slapped her right in the face. Finally, she got it. *Finally.* She felt herself crack open.

"You're right," she said, nodding. She tipped the bottle up and finished her beer.

Sherry turned to her and it looked as though she was trying to cover her surprise at Charlie's words.

"I mean it. You're right." She felt a tear spill over and roll down her cheek she absorbed her sister's words. Then another, and soon they were flowing steadily. She sniffed. "I'm so sorry."

Sherry blinked at her a few times in silence before getting out of her chair, walking over, and wrapping her arms around her. "Well, Jesus, you don't have to cry about it." Sherry's voice cracked as she said in Charlie's ear, "I missed you, goddamn it. I just missed you."

She wrapped her arms around Sherry, held her tightly.

It didn't last terribly long, as emotional displays were not Sherry's thing. She let go of Charlie, went into the house to retrieve two more beers, and stoked up the fire before sitting back down.

There was a moment of silence before Sherry asked, "So, what's going on with you and Emma?" She stared into the fire, never looking at her.

"What do you mean?"

At that, Sherry did look at her. Tilted her head. "I saw you at Summer Fest. Everybody did."

Ugh. Small fucking towns.

Charlie gave up on the innocent act and sighed. "I don't know. I thought something might be happening. It's so weird, Sherry."

"What is?"

And just like that, she found herself spilling her guts to her little sister. "Getting sucked back in. It's so *easy* with her." She told Sherry about meeting at the J-Cup. How they'd wandered together to the park like it was the most natural thing. How Emma's friend had sort of scared her off, but then they'd found each other again and walked back to Emma's place. How Emma had cooked for her. "It was like no time at all had passed. It felt perfectly natural to be there on the couch with her, talking about life."

Sherry watched her face the whole time, said nothing, but nodded here and there, and seemed to listen carefully.

"And when I left..." Charlie hesitated. She'd never really talked this openly about her sex life with Sherry—it had always seemed off limits, as if their age gap made it a taboo subject.

"You kissed her."

Charlie glanced at her sister.

"What? It's not a surprise. Sounds like the whole day was leading up to it."

Shaking her head with a smile, Charlie felt a small sliver of shame crawl through her at the thought of not giving her sister enough credit. "Yeah."

"And? Then what happened?"

"Nothing. I came home and we barely spoke all week. I realized that she was avoiding me, so yesterday when I brought pies over, I called her on it."

"What did she say?"

"She shut me right down. Said she couldn't do this with me again and that kissing me had been a mistake." She did her best to sound nonchalant and unaffected, even lifted a shoulder in a half shrug. *See? Doesn't matter. Didn't hurt at all.* But she felt her heart squeeze simply at the memory. Emma's face, the determination in her expression, the hardness of her dark eyes.

"Can't say I blame her."

"Gee, thanks."

Sherry sat up, slid to the edge of her chair. "Charlie. Did you hear the part about how you broke her when you left?" A few seconds passed, and then Charlie looked at her, swallowed hard, and nodded. Sherry sat back again. "If I was her BFF, I'd tell her to run as fast and as far away from you as she could."

Wow.

Charlie swallowed again as all the words flew out of her head. She turned her gaze to the fire and said nothing, even though her head—and her heart—were full. But not of good. No, they were full of awful things. Regret, shame, sorrow, regret, sadness, depression, regret.

So much shame. So much regret. So much wishing that she could go back, do things differently.

My kingdom for a time machine.

"Did that dough do something to make you mad?" Bethany gestured to the ball Charlie was kneading—way too firmly—as she walked by with a tray of scones.

"Damn it." Charlie scooped the dough up and tossed it in the trash where it joined that last ball she'd worked too hard and melted all the butter in. Sandy was going to fire her ass if she kept wasting ingredients like that. With a loud groan born of frustration, she started over again.

Anger and self-deprecation had simmered within Charlie since the fireside chat she'd had with Sherry on Saturday night. It was now Wednesday, and those feelings hadn't dissipated at all. Instead, they had bubbled steadily, simmered, reminding her of the awful things she'd done, continually telling her that she was selfish. It wasn't healthy—she knew that. She should probably find a therapist to help her deal with the self-loathing that now seemed to color every thought she had. She knew that, too. But for now, she beat pie dough into submission. Hey, it was something.

She wouldn't call herself an overly confident person, but she did okay. She tried new things. She knew what she was capable of and was willing to step out of her comfort zone if need be, but her conversation with Sherry had stuck with her like no other in her life. She could be standing in the shower, minding her own business, and something Sherry said would suddenly echo through her skull as if she was in a cave.

I lost two sisters, thanks to you.

She'd have no choice but to sit with that for a while until she'd be blow-drying her hair and it would happen again.

And then there was Emma. You wrecked her. You know that, right?

Tipping the mixing bowl over for the third time, she rolled the dough up and began to knead, being very careful to go slowly, gently. She didn't want to ruin this batch.

You were so selfish. You just did what you wanted to do, so you could have what you wanted to have.

She swallowed hard as her eyes welled up.

"I'm loving the idea of a flavor of the month," Sandy said, her voice light and cheerful as she entered the kitchen. "Don't you?"

Charlie nodded, pasted on a smile, and hoped she looked excited about Sandy's new idea to feature one particular kind of pie every month.

"Apple was a good call for July. I'm thinking key lime for August. Something fresh and light for those humid days, yeah?"

She nodded some more, not trusting herself to actually speak words. The lump still sat lodged in her throat.

"Awesome." Sandy squeezed Charlie's upper arm and was off to the other side of the kitchen to make a batch of snickerdoodles. Thank God, because Charlie wasn't sure how long she'd have been able to hold it together if she'd been forced to actually use her voice. She caught herself just before overkneading this third batch of dough, split it up, wrapped it in plastic, and tossed it in the fridge to chill while she started on the apples. Her jaw ached from clenching it, but she couldn't seem to make herself stop. Sherry's voice still spoke to her, and every time she said that one, devastating line, her head dropped a little more.

If I was her BFF, I'd tell her to run as fast and as far away from you as she could.

Charlie cleared her throat, blinked away tears, and focused on the apples.

CHAPTER NINETEEN

I can't, Sabrina. For the third time." Emma tried hard to hold on to her temper, but Sabrina had changed tacks. Now, instead of being constantly snide, she pivoted to the opposite approach and asked Emma on a date. Emma had politely declined, but Sabrina kept asking, and at this point, the continued attempts to spend time with her were starting to grate. And when she thought about that, she knew how selfishly cruel she sounded, but she couldn't seem to pull herself away from that attitude. She didn't need this today. She was already completely stressed out.

"Why not?" It was just before three in the afternoon and they were behind the bar. Thankfully, no customers were there yet. Sabrina tossed her bar rag down on the surface and folded her arms over her chest in a stance of determination.

"Because I can't," Emma snapped.

"Can't or won't?"

"Does it matter?"

"It does to me."

"Look." Emma set down the pad of paper she'd been using to keep track of her liquor order, even though Dani was out of town this week, and parked her hands on her hips. "I told you *from the beginning* that I didn't want anything serious. I stressed the word *casual*. You said you were okay with that."

"I did. I know. I was." Sabrina's expression softened just the smallest bit.

"Then what do you want from me?" Emma held her arms out to the sides, palms up.

Sabrina looked at her for a long time before tearing her gaze away, reaching behind her back, and untying her apron. "I didn't think it was that much," she said quietly. "But it's obviously more than you're willing to give." She set her apron on the bar and gave Emma a sad smile. "Take care of yourself, Emma."

"Wait." Emma watched as Sabrina rounded the bar and walked across the floor toward the door. "Sabrina. Come on."

But Sabrina didn't look back as she pushed the door open and left EG's, her job, and Emma behind.

The door was stopped from closing all the way by a white-sneakered foot, and then it was hauled open again, and Charlie stood there with three pie boxes in her arms, her gaze following Sabrina's retreating form.

Oh, perfect. Just what I need.

Emma sighed, took the rag Sabrina had tossed onto the bar, and began wiping down the surface. After a moment, Charlie came in. Her approach was a little bit tentative now, Emma noticed. It had been for the past week. She used to come strolling right in. Now, it was as if she was hesitant. Unsure. Navigating a field of land mines between the door and the bar. Not quite bracing for a blow, but almost.

She had done that to Charlie.

Dani had gotten in her head, and it was a good thing, really. Right? She couldn't risk letting Charlie in again, not after the last time. No, Dani was right. Charlie was unreliable and would just hurt her again. That comfort? That familiarity and warmth she felt with her? The desire to talk to her, to share her day, her ideas? She just had to ignore those things. They would get her nowhere. And they'd go away eventually. Wouldn't they?

"Everything okay?" Charlie asked, her voice quiet, as if she was afraid she'd disturb something.

Emma sighed loudly, scrubbing at a nonexistent spot on the bar, not looking up. "Well, my produce order came in all wrong, my landline is on the fritz, as is my internet connection, so reservations are a mess. I don't know where the hell the phone company is. And my bartender just quit. It's a banner day so far."

Charlie set the pies down on the bar. "Well, that all sucks. I'm sorry."

She lifted her head, and it registered immediately how cute

Charlie looked. She wore worn denim shorts with a frayed hem, a hole near the pocket, and what was likely a smear of batter on one leg. Her white T-shirt also had a smudge, this one on the shoulder and light blue, so Emma guessed frosting. Her hair was pulled into a ponytail, and it seemed like the day had fought with it because several strands had escaped and now skimmed along Charlie's face or hung in tiny blond ringlets at the nape of her neck.

Another sigh and Emma stopped wiping as she felt her phone buzz in her back pocket. "I'm sorry. None of this is your problem." She pulled the phone out, hit the notification on her Facebook Messenger, and squinted at the words.

It felt like everything stopped moving then.

Her lungs stopped.

Her heart stopped.

A lump formed in her throat, but she couldn't swallow it down because her body wouldn't move. There was no air. No sound. What the hell was she reading?

"Emma?" Charlie's voice sounded far away, as if Emma was underwater and Charlie was calling her name from the surface. She blinked rapidly and Charlie called her name again. "Emma?"

The world came back in a rush, a whooshing sound filling Emma's head. She was surprised to find Charlie standing right next to her behind the bar, hand on her back, eyes wide with concern.

Blinking rapidly seemed to be the only thing she was capable of in that moment, so that's what she did. Turning her head, she met Charlie's eyes and blinked some more, still no words, still nothing solid to hold on to. Was she drifting? Floating away, untethered? It sure felt like it. Was she a balloon?

"Sweetie? Let me see."

She felt Charlie taking the phone out of her hand, knew she was reading the message, watched Charlie's beautiful hazel eyes widen in…what? Shock? Disbelief? She read it a second time through, and Emma kept watching her, waiting for Charlie to explain it. To make some sense out of it. Charlie read it through one more time, then gave a nod.

"Okay. Here, come with me." Charlie took her arm and led her out from behind the bar, through the kitchen doors. Alec looked up and his concern was instant. Same for Jules, who had just arrived, apparently, and was tying her apron around her waist. Charlie held up a hand with one finger at them, silently telling them to give her a second. They reached a small desk area in the back corner. "Sit down right here for just a second, okay? I'll be right back."

Emma watched as Charlie crossed the kitchen to Alec, gestured for Jules to join them. Her hands moved. Up, down, point, around. Charlie was an animated talker, talked with her hands. She always had. Emma couldn't hear everything Charlie said. Her head still felt fuzzy, like it was stuffed with cotton. Alec nodded. Jules nodded. Alec pointed, gestured, nodded some more. Then Charlie pulled out her phone, did some typing, handed it to Alec. Alec did some typing, handed it back. Then Charlie surprised Emma—and Alec, judging by the look on his face—and hugged him.

"All right. Come on." Charlie was back, gently pulling her to her feet. She led her out through the back door and to the steps that went up to her apartment. Emma turned to look at her, and what she saw on Charlie's face stole what little breath remained in her lungs. Reached right in and pulled it out, that expression.

Concern.

Determination.

Love.

"Come on, baby. I've got you."

She let herself be led upstairs.

Charlie had never seen Emma paralyzed before. Not as kids. Not as teenagers. Not even as college girls. Emma was always the stronger of the two of them. The one who never froze. The one who could put her emotions aside and act logically. Be practical. She'd always been the lead. Charlie was the emotion. Emma was the logic.

But paralyzed was exactly what Emma was now. She sat on the bed, a small carry-on bag on the floor at her feet, exactly where Charlie had left her twenty minutes ago when she'd run home to throw her own stuff in an overnight bag and then had sped back. Emma hadn't moved an inch.

She had Emma's Facebook Messenger message memorized, she'd read it so many times.

Dear Emma—

> *I'm so sorry to send this in a message, but I don't have your personal phone number and I couldn't get through on your restaurant's number. My name is Zaya Grier and I am married to James Grier. Your father.*

Charlie had gasped the first time she read it.

> *It breaks my heart to tell you that he passed away yesterday of a massive heart attack. I know you haven't had any contact with him, but not a day went by when you didn't cross his mind. He thought of you so often and he loved you very much. I have no idea if any of this matters to you. I know you have a business to run and a life, but I thought you should know. He would want you to know.*

Zaya had left her number, along with the time, date, and location of the services, which were tomorrow afternoon, and Charlie knew instantly that Emma needed to go. Not just that she needed to, but that she wanted to. She had no idea how she knew this, but she did. She felt it in her heart more solidly than almost anything else. Emma needed to do this. If she didn't, she'd regret it for the rest of her life.

Emma hadn't fought her on it. Yet. She was still in some kind of emotional shock.

"Hey," Charlie said softly as she touched Emma's arm. "You ready?"

"Is this a good idea?" Emma's voice held no accusation, no anger. It just seemed like an honest question.

She took a seat on the bed next to Emma and studied Emma's hands as she talked. God, those hands—she'd loved them so much at one time. "I think it is a good idea, yes. Because I think if you don't go, you're going to have so many questions and so many regrets. It's going to be tough. That's a given, and that's why I'm going with you. We'll face it together, okay?"

Charlie hadn't taken any time at all to think about it. It never occurred to her to wonder if she was the right person to accompany Emma on this trip because she knew—somehow, some way, she just *knew*—that she was. Didn't matter that she was the ex. Didn't matter that they hadn't parted amicably. Didn't matter that she'd shattered Emma's world and left her to pick up the pieces all by herself. None of that factored in. All she thought was that Emma needed to do this and she, Charlie, still knew her better than anybody.

They'd do it together.

Emma swallowed audibly, then inhaled slowly and deeply. She blinked several times as she exhaled, then turned, held her gaze, those dark, dark eyes of hers boring into Charlie's as if searching for... something. Then Emma gave one subtle nod and said simply, "Okay."

"Good. Uber Tom is waiting. Come on."

They picked up their bags, locked Emma's apartment, and headed down the stairs. Emma did a little stutter-step at the door to EG's, but Charlie touched her on the arm.

"It's okay. Alec has everything under control, and he has my number in case he needs anything."

"He's a good guy," Emma said but hesitated still, before finally managing to pull herself away from the door and toward their waiting ride.

"He stepped right up," Charlie said, remembering the sadness in his eyes when she'd told him what had happened and how it made her wonder if he'd lost his own father at some point. She recalled how eager the sous chef had been to help and what a relief that had been. Once ensconced in the back seat and on their way to the airport, she turned to Emma. "I told Sandy what happened so I could take a couple days off, and I told my mother when I ran home." She paused. "I didn't contact your mom. I thought it should come from you. When you're ready. I wasn't sure what to say to her." She lifted one shoulder.

Instead of freaking out, though, Emma simply nodded. "Okay. I'll call her at some point."

She thought Emma should call sooner rather than later, given they were headed out of town with zero warning, but she kept that to herself. Emma had enough on her plate at the moment.

They were quiet for much of the drive, looking out the window at the summer lushness of the passing green, trees in full bloom, electric blue sky, and bright, cheerful sun. It certainly didn't feel like a death had occurred. A woodchuck sat up on the side of the road as they passed. A hawk circled overhead. And then Charlie felt it.

Emma's hand on hers.

She turned her own hand over and entwined her fingers with Emma's, looked at her, smiled.

"Thank you," Emma said softly, her eyes wet.

"You're welcome," she said back.

CHAPTER TWENTY

I don't know how you managed all of this," Emma commented as she tossed her bag onto one of the queen beds in a hotel room in downtown Nashville. It was late, as their flight had not been a direct one, and they were both tired. "You had, like, zero time. Do you have magic powers I don't know about?"

Charlie smiled. "Well, it has been a few years since you've seen me, and New York does change people…" She let the sentence dangle, glad to be at least the tiniest bit lighthearted.

"True." Emma yawned widely, stretched her arms above her head, which made her shirt ride up just enough for Charlie to see a peek of skin.

"When I was in New York, I had to set up a lot of travel for people. It was part of my job there initially. I got good at it."

"I will pay you back. Just give me a total."

"We can worry about that later." Charlie fell back onto her bed. "Right now, I'm exhausted." A beat went by. "This may have been ill-advised," she said, pursing her lips.

"Don't want to get back up, do you?"

"Really, really not."

"I guess that means the bathroom is mine." Emma gave her a small smile, grabbed her toiletry case, and disappeared through the doorway.

Meanwhile, she lay on her bed, alarmingly comfortable in more ways than one, and searched her brain to try to figure out why, despite somebody being dead and her spending time on a trip with the ex she'd devastated, everything felt perfectly, exactly right.

❖

Charlie wasn't sure what woke her up, but her eyes popped open, and when she glanced at the clock, she was surprised to see that it read 3:23 a.m. It felt like she'd barely been asleep for an hour. As she lay there, still, blinking in the dark until her eyes adjusted, she heard a soft sniffle.

"Em?" she whispered. "You okay?"

A sigh came from the direction of Emma's bed. "Did I wake you up? I'm sorry. I was trying to be quiet."

"No worries."

"I don't know why I'm upset." Emma sniffled again.

Charlie sat up, now able to make Emma out in the night. Her dark hair was splayed out over the white pillow, her arms visible on top of the white hotel bedspread. "Your father died," she said with emphasis. "Of course you're upset."

"But I didn't even know him." Emma's voice cracked, and she lifted her arms and let them drop over her eyes in obvious frustration. "I'm so stupid. This is so stupid."

"Hey." Charlie didn't even think. She simply slid out of her bed, made a scooting gesture to Emma, who moved over, and crawled into bed next to her. She lay on her side and propped her head in her hand, elbow on the pillow. "You are *not* stupid. There is nothing stupid about you."

"Well, I feel stupid."

"*That's* the part that's stupid. You feeling stupid is stupid."

Emma squinted at her before a small grin peeked through. "Funny."

"Thank you."

They were quiet for several minutes before Emma turned to look at her again. Their gazes held. Even in the darkness, Charlie could feel the weight of it, the intensity. Even in the darkness, she could see Emma's eyes well with tears.

"My father's dead," Emma whispered.

"I know," she said, just as softly and with a slow nod.

A tiny sob escaped from Emma's lips. Again, Charlie didn't think, she just acted. With a small cry of sympathy, she gathered Emma in her arms and wrapped her up, pulled her close.

"I'm so sorry, sweetheart." She pressed a kiss to Emma's forehead, and Emma buried her face in the crook of Charlie's neck. "I'm so sorry." She tightened her arms, held Emma tightly, felt Emma's arm go around her midsection, Emma's leg slide over hers, as Emma simply cried. It was quiet crying. Soft, as if she didn't want to disturb anybody with her emotions, but it was crying, and it was significant because Emma didn't cry easily. That was Charlie's job. Charlie was the crier. Emma was stoic.

But not tonight.

Charlie lost track of how long they lay wrapped up in each other, but she felt Emma's breathing even out, deepen, and knew Emma'd finally given in to sleep. Out the window of their hotel room, she saw the horizon slowly go from black to indigo to deep purple before she finally followed Emma into slumber.

❖

"Ready?" Charlie's voice was quiet. Gentle. Not at all pushy. Charlie stood next to Emma in the very full parking lot of Germano's Funeral Home, waiting as their Uber drove away.

Emma inhaled slowly and deeply and smoothed a hand over the hip of her all-purpose little black dress, the one she basically wore to weddings and funerals. Her shoes had a modest heel, and she'd pulled her hair back off her face. She gave her neck a stretch, one of her vertebrae popping loudly, and took another deep breath before glancing at Charlie.

Her dress was nothing short of stunning. Chic. Simple, yet elegant. Also black, but with capped sleeves and a layer of black lace that gave it texture and interest. Her heels were not modest—they were strappy sandals that put her eye-to-eye with Emma, and she wore her sandy hair down and wavy and skimming her shoulders. Very Manhattan. Charlie was the epitome of patience, not rushing her, simply standing next to her like a supportive pillar, waiting until she was ready.

With a nod, they walked forward together.

Emma wasn't sure she'd quite absorbed what had happened over the past twenty-four hours. Part of her felt like she was functioning on autopilot, which she supposed was normal for people dealing with a sudden death. But why was it affecting her in such a weird way?

She hadn't seen her father since he left when she was a toddler. She barely remembered anything about him. She hadn't spoken to him. Hadn't tried. And yet, her heart felt like it was cracking in her chest with something that must be sadness or sorrow, right? She was smart enough to understand that there was also a whole lot of anger, but she was doing her best to keep that in a box for now.

There were a lot of people filing in for the calling hours. A lot. Were they friends? Family? She had no idea, and as they got closer to the front door, she felt her steps falter. Charlie looked up at her with concern evident in her hazel eyes, eyebrows raised as if silently asking if she was okay.

She swallowed, glanced down, and held out her hand. Charlie took it without question, entwined their fingers, and squeezed. Emma could hear the unspoken words in her head. *I've got you.*

They walked through the big wooden double doors.

The scent of the place tickled Emma's nose, an odd combination of sterile and floral. The decor was typical funeral home generic. Uncomfortable-looking upholstered chairs, a matching love seat, and several metal folding chairs—the extras, Emma thought. There was a line. A long one. Apparently, James Grier had touched a lot of people. She and Charlie took their place, dropped their hands.

"Doing okay?" Charlie asked.

"I think so," she replied. "It just all feels so...weird." She punctuated that with a shrug because she had no other way to explain it. She noticed a few framed photos and a large piece of poster board with snapshots taped to it, but she yanked her gaze away, not feeling strong enough to study them.

Charlie gave her a sad smile and they took another step forward.

The soft buzz of conversation was all around them, like flies or bees, people trying to be polite by keeping the volume at a minimum, but also wanting to talk, reminisce, hug each other. The general wardrobe was split—some folks in suits and dresses like her and Charlie, others in jeans or shorts, maybe coming right from work. Her nerves rattled in her body as if they were made of chain and somebody was shaking them by the ends, banging them against her bones, her skin. She swallowed hard as she realized the line was actually moving along fairly quickly, and she looked to Charlie for reassurance. Charlie grasped her hand again, held it, and Emma felt it like an anchor, holding her steady, keeping her from being cast off into oblivion by the bizarreness of the situation.

They inched closer until Emma could make out the people standing in the reception line. An older woman, both distinguished and beautiful, her snowy hair cropped short stark against her mahogany skin, her stance tall and proud—though it did nothing to disguise the sorrow in her deep brown eyes that were red-rimmed. Next to her was a younger woman, in her early forties, maybe, her sepia complexion pale with grief. She was tall and lean, attractive in an effortless way, her dark hair combed to the side and off her face, about shoulder-length, tucked behind both ears. Her eyes were red-rimmed, too, and puffy, and she looked like a woman doing her best to stand tall for the two young boys on either side of her, as she shook hands with a gentleman three people in front of Emma and Charlie.

Zaya. Her stepmother.

Her heart began to pound, and her hands became clammy. Still, Charlie held on, and they took another step. Zaya turned and met Emma's gaze. Zaya's eyes went so wide it was almost comical, and Emma would've laughed if she wasn't on the verge of a nerve-induced meltdown.

"Emma," Zaya said softly, and next to her, the older woman jerked her focus in their direction. Zaya reached a hand out to Emma even as her eyes filled with unshed tears. "Oh my God, you look just like him."

"She really does," the older woman said, and she too seemed on the verge of tears. Also reaching for Emma, she laid a hand gently on her upper arm. "I'm Mary, James's mother."

My grandmother, Emma thought but couldn't seem to make the words leave her throat, which had closed up unexpectedly. She felt tears spill over and course down her cheeks, and she squeezed Charlie's hand so tightly, it had to hurt. But Charlie didn't let go. She squeezed back.

"I'm Zaya. James's wife." She slid her hand down Emma's arm, grasped the hand Charlie hadn't laid claim to. "I am so glad to finally meet you."

"I'm Emma. And this is my...friend, Charlie Stetko."

"Charlie. Hey." Zaya smiled warmly at Charlie but didn't let go of Emma's hand.

"I'm so sorry for your loss," Charlie said, and Emma felt the tears well up again.

Good God, where had all this emotion come from? She felt like she might explode into horrifying sobs at any moment, so she clenched her jaw tightly to keep that from happening. Which meant she couldn't say a thing.

Zaya must have felt it, the emotional precariousness, and pulled things together, took charge. Emma got the instant impression that was what she did. Zaya closed her other hand over Emma's so she was holding Emma's hand in both of hers. "Listen, can you stay for a while? Please? I'd really like to be able to sit and talk with you, but I have to…" She gestured subtly at the people still waiting in line.

Emma nodded and finally found some words. Words that surprised her. "Sure. Okay."

"Great. Do you have a phone? I'll give you my number and then I can text you my address. We'll be there after the services, and we have a ton of food. We could use help eating it." She voiced the last line as a question, as if she'd realized she was giving orders and tried to lighten that up a little bit.

Emma pulled her phone out of her purse, ignored the three missed calls and nine texts from her mother, and pulled up the keypad screen. Zaya punched in her number.

"Text me and I'll send you the details, okay?"

Emma did so right then. "Done."

Zaya took a deep breath and her eye contact was so intense that Emma felt trapped, held like a butterfly pinned to a board. "I'm so glad you came."

With a nod, Emma moved forward, realizing she was holding up the line. Behind her, she heard Zaya tell somebody they meant a lot to James. When she glanced back, one of the boys was looking at her. He was at that lanky, awkward stage boys go through as they approach their teens, all gangly limbs. She gave him a small smile, then turned back toward Charlie.

"You want to do this?" Charlie asked quietly, and she knew Charlie was referring to the casket that lay at the front of the room. The one that contained the body of the father she'd never known.

"No?" Emma inhaled deeply. "But I think I need to."

Charlie still held her hand, and Emma was almost startled to realize it. More startling was that she had no desire to let go. Charlie had been like a lifeline since they walked in the door. A tether of sorts, grounding her, keeping her steady.

They walked up to the casket together.

Emma didn't kneel on the little cushioned bench provided. She just stood and looked down at the face that, even in repose, looked remarkably like hers. The slight almond shape of his eyes. The placement of his cheekbones. His square jaw. Even the long fingers clasped over his chest were shockingly similar to Emma's.

She didn't know what to feel. That was the hardest part. There were so many emotions rolling through her in that moment that she couldn't focus on any certain one. There was sorrow and anger and confusion and so many questions…and also the knowledge that she'd never, ever get to talk to this man. Her dad. Never.

Emma swallowed, the lump in her throat so big it was painful, and she felt like her lungs wouldn't hold enough air. Another tear spilled down her cheek.

"You okay?" Charlie whispered.

"I can't breathe."

"What do you need?"

"Can we go?"

"Absolutely." Charlie tugged her away from the casket and past all the people—so many people!—toward the front door.

Once outside, away from the fog of sorrow and death and regret, Emma inhaled deeply, took in as much fresh air as she could, then bent forward with her hands on her knees. She felt Charlie's warm hand on her back, rubbing in slow circles. After what could have been two minutes or two weeks, she had no idea, she stood up. Felt the tiniest bit better.

"Well. That was fun." She turned to Charlie, whose eyes were filled with warmth and worry. Emma smiled at her. "I'm okay."

"You sure?"

"Just needed some air."

They stood quietly for a moment as people milled past them, in and out of the funeral home. Emma watched. Wondered who they were, how they knew James. Her eyes scanned the bodies as they moved by, but then her gaze stopped on Charlie.

No longer holding her hand, but right there next to her. Again, the word *anchor* popped into her head, and she had the sudden thought that she didn't know how she'd have done this without Charlie. Hand still on her back, still rubbing gently, Charlie was also people watching, and as she studied Charlie's profile, Dani's words echoed through her head.

She's unreliable. She doesn't understand what love is. She's blinded by material things. She doesn't have your back. She's not who you thought she was.

Emma blinked rapidly. Dani hadn't been wrong—she'd simply been repeating the things Emma herself had said about Charlie over the years. But as she stood there now, she felt herself rewinding, reexamining, rethinking.

Because today? Charlie fit none of those descriptors.

Today? Charlie was their opposite.

CHAPTER TWENTY-ONE

Emma was doing shockingly well. At least, up until now. Charlie had been watching her carefully, paying close attention to her eyes. Everything you ever needed to know about how Emma was feeling was always right there in her eyes, clear as could be. You just had to know how to look, and Charlie did. Even after all this time, she still knew how to read Emma. It was bizarre and comforting at the same time.

James Grier had a small family, but a lot of friends. He'd been a high school math teacher. A popular one, judging by the number of teenagers and young adults that had passed through the funeral home just in the short time she and Emma had been there. Now, at the Grier home, they sat quietly at the kitchen table, most people gone, the twins having been taken up to their rooms by Mary, who was just returning downstairs, and Zaya looking utterly exhausted.

Zaya poured four glasses of white wine without asking and carried two at a time to the table. Mary plopped down in one of the two remaining chairs as Zaya set the second two glasses down, then fell into her own chair with a sigh.

"What a fucking day," Zaya said softly.

Mary shot her a look but seemed to think better of scolding her daughter-in-law for her language on a day like today. Instead, she held up her wineglass and said, "To James."

Charlie picked hers up and glanced at Emma, who did the same, and the four glasses clinked softly, the only sound in a house that had buzzed with activity for the past three hours. Both Mary and Zaya looked weepy, but Charlie imagined the two of them must've been so tired of crying at that point, though there would be plenty more tears, she was sure.

"So, you own your own restaurant," Zaya said, her deep brown gaze settling onto Emma. "That's impressive, especially given your age."

Emma opened her mouth to talk, closed it again, and Charlie could see her brain sifting through her thoughts, trying to decide what to say first. "How…" Her dark brows met in a V above her nose. "How did you find me? When? Was he looking for me?" Charlie knew the tone. It was Emma's *I want to stay calm and in control, but this is driving me crazy* tone. She'd used it on Charlie many, many times over the course of their friendship-turned-relationship.

Zaya exchanged glances with Mary. Then she inhaled deeply and let it out slowly, and it was as if she had known Emma's questions were coming, had expected them. "Oh, sweetie, he's followed your life for years."

Emma's eyes went wide, and she grappled under the table for Charlie's hand, for stability, Charlie knew, and grasped it tightly. "What?"

Again, Zaya looked to Mary.

"Tell her," Mary said with a nod.

Zaya took a sip of her wine as if hoping to garner strength from it. "Your father regretted ever leaving you behind. As you know, he was very young, and if he was here now, he'd tell you he was also stupid and selfish, as young people often are." She folded her hands on the table and leaned slightly forward. "Look, I don't know your mother other than what James told me about her, and it sounds like their relationship was volatile. She wanted to get married—he thought they were too young." Zaya nibbled the inside of her cheek for a moment as she studied Emma's face, like she was trying to decide how to say what she needed to say. Charlie could see the indecision playing across her face. The hesitation. "He and your mom were like oil and water, and when he wanted to split up with her, she made things very difficult for him."

Charlie turned to look at Emma, and though her expression remained neutral, there was a pain in her eyes that she wanted to take away. She squeezed Emma's hand tighter as Zaya went on.

"When he got settled here"—Zaya glanced at Mary—"back with

his mother, he tried to contact your mom to let her know where he was, but she'd moved. Taken you and moved, and she hadn't told him."

Emma swallowed audibly.

Zaya sipped her wine, set the glass down and turned it slowly in her fingers. "He decided maybe it was better for you not to have two parents in two different states fighting over you." She glanced up at Emma, a hand raised like a traffic cop. "But like I said, he was young and stupid, and he regretted that decision deeply as he got older. Years later, after we'd gotten married, had the boys, he did some searching and found you'd ended up in Shaker Falls."

"He never even called…" Emma's voice was gravelly.

"No." Zaya sighed. "You were doing so well. He watched your social media accounts and read the school bulletins. He worried about disrupting your life." Emma shot her a look and Zaya had the good sense to look chagrined. "I know. I didn't say it was the right decision. We argued about it more than once."

"It would've been nice to have a dad around."

"I know."

There was silence for a moment as Emma absorbed what had been said. Charlie still held her hand. Emma's grip had not loosened, and she could tell there was a ton of emotion coursing through her, swore she could feel it pumping just below her skin, but she sensed Emma didn't want to let it loose in front of these two people who were virtual strangers, and also Emma's family. It was so hard for Charlie to watch, and in that moment, she knew the only thing she should be doing was getting Emma out of there.

"Look," she said. She kept her voice calm and even. "This is a lot. A lot." She softened that with a gentle smile. "It's kind of like Emma found and lost her father in less than forty-eight hours, so she's going to need some time. And you guys need to grieve your loss without having this situation added to the mix, so…" She glanced at Emma, who was watching her with crystal clear gratitude in her eyes. It warmed her from the inside, reassured her that this was what Emma needed. "Let's do that, okay? Let's all take some time, do some absorbing, some thinking, and revisit all of this"—she waved her palms over the table—"when we've all had a chance to breathe. Is that okay?"

She wasn't a hundred percent sure, but Zaya seemed relieved by the suggestion, and she nodded, gave them a weak smile.

"It's a lot," Zaya said, looking at Emma. "I know. I'm so sorry."

Emma attempted a smile, but Charlie knew that expression as well, and it meant Emma's emotions were way too close to the surface. She stood and pulled Emma up with her, and the other two women stood as well. "Thank you so much for inviting us to your home." Was that weird? Charlie hoped not, but she couldn't think of anything else to say.

Emma nodded, her eyes darting. Yeah, it was time to get her out of there. Charlie pulled out her phone and quickly ordered a ride.

"Come on, baby," she said quietly as they walked slowly toward the door, ignoring the pet name that had slipped out. Both Zaya and Mary followed behind them. "I've got you."

Their good-byes were awkward, but how could they not be? Neither Zaya nor Mary attempted to hug Emma, even though it was obvious to Charlie that they wanted to—she was another, albeit distant, connection to the man they'd lost—and she was grateful for that. Emma was barely hanging on to herself right now. She sent up a silent thanks when their Uber pulled up, and with one more wave and a thank you, they turned away from James Grier's house.

Once safely in the back seat and moving, silence fell. She took Emma's hand in hers, realizing how many times they'd held hands today and how completely natural and normal it had felt every time.

Emma gazed out the window, said nothing, and held on.

❖

They were both so tired. Bone weary. Mentally exhausted. They didn't speak for the entire ride, nor in the elevator on the way up, nor when they got into their room. By unspoken agreement, Charlie used the bathroom first.

In the full-length mirror on the back of the bathroom door, she studied herself. In a weak attempt to gain a teeny tiny bit of satisfaction when she left New York—and Darcy's Upper West Side apartment—she'd taken as many of the pricey clothes Darcy had purchased for her during their time together as she could fit in her car. Today's black dress was one of them and she loved it. It was simple but looked great on her, hugged her body in all the right places, and probably cost more than her father made in six months. Maybe one day, she'd be able to wear it for Emma *not* at a funeral.

Squinting at herself in the mirror, she wondered where that thought had come from. Wearing something for Emma. *Don't be silly. Emma doesn't care what you wear. She made that clear.* Emma's voice from the other day reverberated through her head. *I can't do this with you, Charlie. Not again.*

Charlie sighed. She knew why her thoughts had gone there: because she'd felt close to Emma all day. The way Emma had leaned on her for support, the way Emma'd clung to her hand, it only made sense she was feeling this way. Anybody would in her shoes. Didn't mean anything. Didn't mean anything at all.

Consciously banning those thoughts from her head, she stripped out of the dress, put on shorts and a tank top. Then she brushed her teeth, removed her makeup, washed her face, and handed off the bathroom to Emma.

"I'm gonna take a quick bath," Emma said, tossing down her phone in seeming frustration. "I need to wash this day off me."

"Sure." Charlie got in bed as she heard the water start up, made herself comfortable, took out her Kindle. There was something soothing about the sound of the bathwater running. Emma had always been a bath girl. She loved to soak off the day. She said it relaxed her and helped her sleep, warmed her up if she was chilly. And she recalled how great Emma always smelled when she came out of the bathroom. She let herself sink into the pillow and just listened to the rhythm of the water through the closed bathroom door.

When she next opened her eyes, the hotel room lights were off, but the blinds were wide open and light from the view bathed everything in a soft, bluish glow. She had no recollection of falling asleep, but she must have dozed. She watched as Emma let go of the blinds' mechanism, then turned to look at her, and her gaze was intense, even in the low light. Clad in only a T-shirt and underwear, Emma crossed the room to Charlie's bed, pulled the covers aside without any warning, without any words, baring Charlie. Stood there. Staring. She would swear to all the gods and everything that was holy that she could feel Emma's eyes on her. Literally feel them as they raked over her body, took in her pajama-clad form.

"Emma?" Her voice was a dry and ragged whisper. Where had all the moisture in her mouth gone?

Emma didn't answer, but she moved then, got in bed with Charlie, who instinctively moved over to make room. But Emma apparently didn't want room as she shifted her body so she was half on top of Charlie, looking down at her as Emma slid one leg over her thigh.

Their eye contact held, and even in the dark it was deliciously powerful. It had always been like that for them, and Charlie couldn't look away. Then, she didn't have to, as Emma, without uttering a word, brought her mouth down on hers. Not harshly, but not gently, a kiss that was both giving and demanding, both hard and soft.

Thoughts raced through her brain like cars on a track, and she had trouble grabbing on to any particular one because, God, Emma used to be an amazing kisser, but had she gotten even better? That same push-pull that had always been a hallmark of making out with her had intensified, and her body was already responding. Her blood was hot, rushing through her veins and heading south, her center had become instantly wet, her body preparing itself for Emma before she even had a chance to think.

Emma's hand cradled Charlie's face as they kissed, then slid down her neck to her breast. It stopped there, and Charlie caught her breath in a light gasp as Emma ran a thumb over her nipple, and it poked at the fabric of her tank top.

"Em," she whispered. "I don't...do you think...what...?" Sentences were hard.

"Please," Emma said quietly. She stilled her hand and gazed down at Charlie with those dark, dark eyes so filled with...anguish? Desire? Desperation? She couldn't tell for sure. "I just need something solid. I feel like I'm adrift, you know? I need something familiar. I need an anchor." She paused, and her voice went even softer when she said, "Please, Charlie."

This is a terrible idea. You should put a stop to it. Tell her no!

The words blared through Charlie's head like a foghorn, but she couldn't bring herself to say anything, let alone that. Instead, time seemed to stop. The world came to a halt. Nothing moved. Nothing breathed as they lay there in suspended animation. She searched Emma's face, looked deep into her eyes. This was Emma. *Emma*. And though they'd had some awful times, Charlie *knew* her. She felt safe with her, which was saying a lot, as she realized in that exact moment that she'd never felt completely safe with Darcy.

Well. That's a sobering thought.

But one to be dealt with later. Because to hell with all that. To hell with everything. The here and now, that's what mattered. Decision made, Charlie slipped her hand around the back of Emma's neck and pulled her down into an absolutely soul-searing kiss.

And then something weird—and beautiful—happened. They fell into sync. Easily. Sensually. Once Charlie gave in, the feel of Emma's body on top of hers was so many things: sexy, hot, achingly familiar, perfect. They full-on made out, Emma's tongue deep in her mouth as she ran her hands under Emma's shirt and raked her nails down Emma's bare back. The groan that move elicited from Emma, deep and throaty, sent a surge of arousal through Charlie that almost made her cry out, and she opened her legs to make room for Emma's hips.

They rocked. They always had. It was a move that was truly theirs. Emma's hips between her thighs, her legs wrapped around Emma's body as Emma moved slowly, rhythmically, against her, center to center. It would never get her all the way there, but there was something erotic and intimate about it, and doing it now brought back so many memories, so many feelings. Charlie dipped her head, snagged Emma's gaze and held it. That was the best part of the rocking—that's what created the intimacy of it: the eye contact.

Emma moved against her, their breathing increased, and Charlie's arousal skyrocketed. She was ready for more. She *needed* more.

As if reading her mind, Emma grasped the hem of Charlie's tank and yanked it up, lowered her head to close her mouth over her bare breast.

That did it.

Charlie surprised herself as well as Emma when she sat up. With Emma straddling her lap, she yanked her tank off and tossed it to the floor, then did the same with Emma's T-shirt. Their position was perfect, and she took her time using her mouth on Emma's breasts, pulling sounds from her that she never realized she'd missed until right then.

It was intoxicating.

She took over. It was unlike her. She'd let Darcy take the lead in bed almost always. But tonight, she felt different somehow. Confident.

Certain. Any hesitation she'd had when Emma had first gotten into her bed was long gone. Now? All she had on her mind was anchoring Emma as she requested. Bringing her to release. More than once if she'd let her. She spun them around so she was on top. Then she slowly tugged off Emma's panties, tossed them aside, and followed them up with her own shorts.

And then they were both completely naked, and Charlie took a moment to just look. She hadn't been naked with Emma in years, but it felt like no time had passed at all. It felt astonishingly, achingly perfect, and she had to force herself not to dwell on that.

Emma beneath her was a gorgeous sight. Her skin glowed, that glorious, impossibly soft skin of hers, and Charlie ran her palms over it, up Emma's arms, down her sides, then up her stomach, across her chest, and cupped both breasts in her hands, kneaded slowly, took time to feel the weight, the shape of each one, how perfectly they fit in her hands. When she zeroed in on the nipples, Emma arched her back, pushed her head into the pillow, exposing her neck, which Charlie took as an invitation, and she bent forward to run her tongue from shoulder to ear.

Emma whimpered. Charlie grasped her face and kissed her. This time, it *was* hard. Authoritative. Bossy. She wanted more. *More, more, more.* She felt Emma's hands on her hips, gripping tightly as she straddled her, on all fours over Emma's body.

Kissing Emma had always been one of the most sensuous and invigorating things in Charlie's life. They joked all the time how well they kissed together, but they were also both aware that they'd only ever kissed each other at the time. In the back of her mind, she had wondered if she thought kissing Emma was incredible simply because Emma was the only person she'd kissed back then. She remembered distinctly the first time Darcy had kissed her. Charlie had waited for months, had anticipated it, and when it finally happened, it was good. Not great. Not fireworks or time standing still. But it was good. Kissing Emma? The earth moved under Charlie's feet. She was sure of it, and that apparently hadn't changed, because right now? The ground was shaking, and she wanted to kiss Emma for the rest of her life.

Charlie lost herself in that kiss, on her hands and knees over Emma, tongues gliding against each other. Everything else faded until she felt Emma's fingers slip between her legs, stroking through what

Charlie knew was a ton of hot wetness. She could feel it. A sound came from deep in her throat as she broke the kiss and looked into Emma's eyes just as Emma pushed into her.

Charlie gasped.

Emma's grip tightened on her hip as Emma began to move the fingers of her other hand slowly inside her.

Pushing herself up so she was on her knees and straddling Emma, Charlie began to move with her, sliding herself up and then down, slowly, setting up a lazy rhythm.

Emma bent her knees, and that extra support was just what Charlie needed. She put a hand on each of Emma's knees and let her head fall back as she increased the pace of her movements, letting her hips do the work, as erotic pleasure began to sizzle through her thighs and tickle the pit of her stomach. Her climax was rushing toward her much more quickly than she'd expected, and she lifted her head, looked at Emma in surprise. She pitched forward onto her hands, back to her original position on hands and knees above Emma, as her orgasm tore through her body, almost unexpectedly. She let out a cry, never one to be quiet in bed, and rode out the waves, still moving against Emma's fingers, gripping the pillow on either side of Emma's head, every muscle in her body tightening.

Her face tucked snugly in the crook of Emma's neck, she breathed heavily, waited for her body to begin to relax. She felt Emma's fingers at the back of her head, playing with her hair, while the fingers of Emma's other hand were trapped inside Charlie, pinned between their bodies as her breathing finally began to ease.

"That was…" Emma let the sentence dangle, and Charlie wasn't sure if she didn't know what she wanted to say or if she knew exactly what she wanted to say, but decided not to.

She lifted her head and gave Emma her best sexy look as she said, "Oh, we're not done yet."

Before Emma had time to respond, Charlie had repositioned herself between Emma's thighs. She took a moment to glance up, and her line of sight—along Emma's naked body, between her breasts, on to Emma's eyes—was the most erotic thing she had ever seen, and it sent another surge of arousal shooting through her, something she didn't think was possible.

Without preamble, she lowered her head and ran the flat of her tongue over every inch of Emma's center. She flattened her palms on Emma's hips to keep them from rising off the bed and went to work.

How had she forgotten how good Emma tasted? How she was salty and sweet and tangy all at once? How could she have forgotten the little sounds she could get Emma to make? The ones Emma wasn't even aware of and that made her blush later when Charlie told her about them? How could she forget the velvety softness of Emma's inner walls when she slowly slid her fingers inside, how they tightened around her as she picked up the pace of her tongue?

It didn't take long. She knew it wouldn't, and Emma came almost before either of them was ready, her hips rising, her gentle grip on Charlie's hair tightening, a long, deep groan emanating from her throat as she arched her neck back.

It was immensely beautiful to witness, and it was so very sexy, and it brought tears to Charlie's eyes. She did her best to hide them, cleared her throat quietly, leaned her cheek against Emma's warm thigh, and waited, her fingers still tucked snugly inside. Emma's eyes were still closed when she reached down and gently tugged at Charlie's hand, her silent directive for Charlie to remove her fingers now. She did, and Emma's body twitched. Charlie grinned. Another memory.

A moment went by before she felt it—the gentle movement of Emma's body—and heard it—the soft sniffle. Emma was crying.

"Oh, honey," Charlie said softly.

Eyes still closed, Emma gestured for her. "Come up here," Emma whispered, and she obeyed, tucking herself into Emma's body, looking down at her, at her soft eyes and wet cheeks.

Charlie said nothing, simply stroked the tears from Emma's face with her thumb. When Emma's gaze met hers, she could literally see all her resolve, all her strength, everything she'd been using to hold herself together all day simply crumble, like a dam that just couldn't hold the water at bay any longer. A sob ripped out of her and she looked so incredibly lost that Charlie's eyes filled as well.

"Oh, baby, come here." She wrapped Emma in her arms and was surprised when Emma let her. She bundled her up and rocked her, pressing kisses to her forehead, promising her in gentle whispers that everything was going to be okay.

The strangest part of that moment in time? She felt instinctively—

felt it right down into her bone marrow—that this had been predetermined. That she was exactly where she was supposed to be and doing exactly what she was supposed to be doing.

It was weird and comforting and confusing and terrifying all at once.

They should probably talk.

Charlie knew it, but this was not the time. She knew that, too. Emma's sobs had eased. She'd wiped her eyes, blown her nose with the Kleenex Charlie had snagged from the nightstand, and now she was just breathing. Emma seemed relaxed, in no hurry to leave her embrace, and Charlie refused to examine her gratitude for that. They were warm, and she was sure Emma was as exhausted as she was. Probably more so. It seemed like only seconds had gone by before her eyelids became too heavy to keep open.

Emma's deep and even breathing was the last thing she remembered.

CHAPTER TWENTY-TWO

It was 3:46 a.m. according to the clock on the nightstand that sat between the two beds. Emma had slept for a little while after crying herself to sleep, but just now had simply opened her eyes for no apparent reason.

Of course there's a reason. About a dozen of them, if I'm gonna be real with myself here.

Real. Ugh. Did she have to be?

How had so much happened over the course of less than three days? How was it even possible? She'd been going along, living her life, minding her own business, and what? The Universe decided she didn't have enough chaos? The gods got bored? A butterfly flapped its wings in New Zealand? What the hell had happened? And what was she supposed to do with it all?

She wasn't a person who dwelled on regret. The past was something you couldn't change. Yes, you did something stupid or rude or hurtful, but you couldn't change that. Until somebody invented a working time machine, the past would always stay what it was and your stupid or rude or hurtful actions would always also be things that stayed. She had learned to let things go, to focus on moving forward. Once in a while, she'd get dragged backward—by her mother, usually—but she handled it. She didn't let regrets become a thing. She recalled asking Charlie if she had regrets, and her emphatic *yes*, the pain and guilt so obvious on her face. Emma had been glad then that regret wasn't something she focused on. She kept her eyes looking ahead, not back. She wasn't going backward.

But now? Today? In this moment?

My God, do I have regrets.

The thought wedged in her throat and filled her eyes with tears. She'd known where her father was for a year now. A whole entire year, and she'd done nothing to contact him. And now, she never could. She could never yell at him, never tell him how hard it had been sometimes when she'd had to take care of her mother, or what a coward she thought he was for not trying to contact her. She could never look in his eyes or see the physical resemblance for herself that seemed to be a consensus. She could never hear his voice or know what he smelled like or learn what he liked to eat and cook it for him or hug him.

Regrets.

Charlie made a small sound in her sleep, and it pulled Emma back to the present. She took a deep breath, did her best to shelve the whole regrets thing until later, and smiled softly as she let herself remember two things specifically. One was that Charlie always murmured in her sleep. She didn't talk. Didn't snore. But she murmured little sounds, and once, she'd laughed. It had taken her nearly an hour to convince Charlie it had actually happened, vowing to try and record it next time.

Emma didn't remember them shifting positions. She was pretty sure she'd fallen asleep in Charlie's arms, but now their spots were reversed, Charlie's head tucked into her, under her chin. She tightened her arm as best she could, given that it had gone almost completely numb, and pressed a gentle kiss to Charlie's forehead. Charlie tightened her arm across Emma's midsection, stirred and pressed her knee into Emma's center ever so slightly even though her eyes stayed closed. That was the second thing: Charlie slept all over her, clinging to her like a spider monkey. It had taken some getting used to, but soon her discomfort at having Charlie so wrapped around her became fake, a kind of performance. After all, they'd been young and not living together. Their time together was so limited. So she would sigh dramatically, pretend to be all annoyed, but Charlie knew it was an act, and she'd just cling to her tighter and tighter until they were both laughing.

Charlie.

What in the actual fuck was she going to do about Charlie?

She breathed in deeply, then let it out slowly. Charlie had been beyond surprising. She reflected back, could still hear Dani's voice in her head, see her ticking off on her fingers all the issues Emma had had with Charlie. She was unreliable. She wasn't who Emma thought she was. She didn't have Emma's back. She didn't know what love was. Emma felt her brow furrow as she thought about that list. Charlie had been none of those things over the past two days. Not one of them. She'd been beyond reliable and had absolutely had her back, taking over, setting everything up, staying right next to her the entire time. If that wasn't an example of love, she didn't know what was.

Love? Seriously?

No. She was absolutely in no condition to explore anything like that right now. Or even to take a tiny peek. Besides, Charlie would head back to New York the first chance she got, and Emma would be in Shaker Falls alone again. Which was fine. It had been fine for the past couple of years and it would be fine again.

Unexpected emotion threatened to close up her throat, and she had to force it back down. She would not—could not—let Charlie back in. Not into her brain. Not into her heart. Not into her life.

Except it's too late, isn't it?

❖

"Where the hell are you? Are you okay? Not in that order." Dani's voice was a combination of worried, terrified, and pissed off, and she had every right to be. Emma knew that. She'd been texting and calling since yesterday and Emma had been ridiculously abrupt, sending nothing but emojis.

"I'm fine. I'm in Nashville." Charlie was in the shower and she had taken the window of time to call Dani, whose texts had become more and more frantic. She'd even left voice mails, angry ones, which Dani rarely ever did. *Voice mail is for people who don't know how to text*, she'd say.

"What the fuck is in Nashville and why didn't you—*ooh*." Dani's sudden understanding was clear. She knew that Emma's father and his family were in Nashville but had no other details. "Did you finally decide to visit him? Why didn't you tell me? I'd have come with."

"He died." It was blunt. Blunter than it should've been, but she didn't have time to get into the details. She didn't want to be on the phone with Dani when Charlie came out. "He died. I got a message from his wife, and Charlie got me on a flight."

"I…oh my God. Wow. I'm so sorry, Em." Danielle's voice softened by a lot. "Are you okay? Do you need me to come there? I totally can."

"I'm good. Charlie's here." She could almost feel the ice crackle across the phone lines. "I appreciate it, though. Thank you so much."

"Charlie's there?"

"Yes, and I'm sorry, but I really have to go. I'll give you all the details when I get home, but please don't worry. I'm fine." She ended the call, feeling horribly guilty because she'd essentially hung up on her best friend, and she'd never done that before unless they were screwing around. She waited for the angry text to come, and when it didn't, she knew it was worse than she'd thought. She would have ground to make up with her when she got home, but honestly, there was no room in her brain right now for any more stress. She set Dani aside and texted Alec to make sure things were running okay at EG's.

Steam filled the room when Charlie opened the bathroom door, and another familiar habit of hers lodged itself in Emma's brain and made her smile. "Still haven't learned to turn on the fan, I see."

"It makes me cold and I don't like the sound," Charlie replied, her standard response. Her hair was combed back from her face, and she was in her shorts and tank again as she wiped a towel across the fogged-up mirror. Charlie'd been a bit distant this morning, and Emma was sure it was because of last night. They really needed to talk about it, but she was so low on emotional energy as it was…

Looking at Emma's reflection, Charlie asked, "Dani mad at you?"

"Yup."

"I'm sorry."

"No reason to be. Dani's a big girl. She'll get over it."

"She's just looking out for you." Charlie unzipped her toiletry case and took out her moisturizer. "Check in with your mom?"

"I don't think I can go to the funeral," she said instead of answering the question. She sat on the edge of the bed as Charlie turned.

"No?"

She'd been thinking about it since she'd popped awake just before four. Eyes closed now, she shook her head slowly. She exhaled little by little, and when she opened her eyes again, Charlie was leaning against the doorjamb of the bathroom, just looking at her.

"You don't *have* to go, you know."

Emma absorbed the words.

"Nobody says you do."

"Maybe…" She squinted, searching for something she couldn't identify. "Maybe we could just, like, go get something to eat? And I can think about it?"

Charlie nodded. "We can absolutely do that." The certainty in her voice was almost tangible, and Emma felt like she could hold it.

"Good. I'm starving."

❖

Emma wasn't kidding when she said she was starving. Charlie watched her go to town on her western omelet, alternating bites with sourdough toast and extra crispy bacon.

They'd texted their mothers, assured each that they were both alive and fine and would be home soon. Emma had avoided any details with her mom, told Charlie it was something they'd need to discuss in person, and her anger was palpable.

Now they sat in a red vinyl booth at a place called Jed's, a small diner on the edge of the city that they'd found using Yelp. Charlie hadn't been in a diner in…she couldn't remember the last time. The crowd wasn't big, but it wasn't small, and it was easy to pick out the regulars just by the way they conversed with the waitstaff. *Darcy wouldn't be caught dead in here.* The thought flew through Charlie's mind, but she shoved it away and focused on other things, like the smell of Jed's that was an oddly pleasing mix of old grease, coffee, and bacon. The air was warm, the waitress friendly and plump and looked like she'd happily give you a hug if you needed one.

"There is nothing like diner food," Emma said as she chewed.

"Seriously?" Charlie took a sip of her coffee, which was strong and rich and gave her a little kick in the pants. Which she needed after getting so little sleep the night before, something that needed to be addressed, but she was…What? Waiting for the right time? *I guess?*

"Absolutely. Short-order cooks are amazing. They're incredibly fast, have most recipes in their heads, and some put their own spin on traditional things." She pointed to her omelet with her fork. "Like this. A western omelet has ham, but this has sausage crumbles instead.

Chorizo. Combined with the peppers? Gives it a whole new flavor profile." She took another bite and gazed out the window.

Charlie, on the other hand, had little appetite. She'd ordered scrambled eggs and hash browns, but had only taken a few bites, and they sat in her stomach like stones. The coffee was the only thing going down without a problem.

"I don't think I can take facing them again," Emma said, and it took Charlie a second or two to realize she was talking about the Grier family. "It's just so much. You know?" Emma turned to face her, and her eyes held a sorrow Charlie hadn't seen there before. "I mean, I've got two brothers and I didn't even talk to them. I didn't introduce myself. Say hi. Let them know they have a big sister if they ever need anything." Her eyes went wide, as if she was hit with a realization. "Do you think they even want a big sister? Do you think they hate me?"

"Why would they hate you?" Charlie asked, trying logic. "They don't even know you."

"But would they want to?"

With a shrug, she said, "There's only one way to find out, really."

"Right." Emma finished the last bite of her omelet, picked up a slice of bacon, and took a bite, returning her gaze to the window, to the cars in the parking lot coming and going. She watched her chew, watched the thoughts play across her beautiful features. "I had so much to say to him." She said it quietly, almost to herself, and the sorrow in her voice was so thick, Charlie felt like she could reach out and touch it, actually hold it in her hands. "It's like I didn't even realize it until I lost my chance."

"You can still say it." It sounded so weak to Charlie's ears, and she shrugged, half grimaced, sipped her coffee.

Emma turned then, studied her face, seemed to take that in, roll it around in her head. She nodded, sort of absently, like you did when you're thinking about something. "Yeah."

"It's okay if you need time. You get that, right?" Charlie squinted and studied Emma's face, because in all honesty, she wasn't actually sure if Emma *did* get that. Judging by the way Emma's eyebrows rose just a bit, she was right.

Emma blinked at her. "Like, I don't *have* to do *anything* right now, do I?"

"Nope." She snagged a slice of bacon off Emma's plate.

"Huh." Emma said the one word as if she'd never thought of that option. They ate quietly for several more minutes, the silence not at all uncomfortable. Finally, Emma seemed to make a decision. "Okay. Let's go home, then."

"Yeah?"

"Yeah. I'm tired. I miss my restaurant, and I need some time to absorb all of this."

Charlie knew she was likely talking about more than just her father's death but didn't press. She agreed, and they took their time paying the bill, then figured out a schedule.

A lot of things were left unfinished, but Charlie suddenly felt just as bone weary as Emma seemed to be, and one thing was clear. She, too, was ready to go home.

CHAPTER TWENTY-THREE

O kay, I'm afraid I have to ask." Sandy's voice surprised Charlie, as she hadn't seen her come in. Her tone was low, almost conspiratorial, and Charlie barely heard her over the pounding that came from next door where a crew of guys was working on what would eventually be the rest of The Muffin Top. They'd only just begun, so all they were doing was demoing, really, but God, it was loud. Bracing herself for Sandy wanting an answer about their working relationship, she looked at her.

"Ask me what?"

"What did that dough ever do to you? Again?"

She blinked at Sandy, then looked down at the pie dough she'd kneaded way too hard and for way too long and remembered, not so long ago, when Bethany had asked her the same thing. Just like then, she was on the verge of ruining a batch. It would be dense and unpleasant, and she sighed in frustration. "I'm sorry. I've got a lot on my mind, but I shouldn't let it affect my work." She felt the heat rise to her cheeks, embarrassed to have messed up something she could do in her sleep.

It was Tuesday. She and Emma had gotten home Friday evening, but Emma had run right to the restaurant to relieve Alec and make sure things had gone okay, and Charlie had barely seen her since. They'd both conked out on the flight home, so no talking had happened. Not about Emma continuing to struggle over her father, not how she was going to approach her mother and her part in keeping her dad from her, not about their night together. That was the hardest part for Charlie. She didn't know where they stood. If anywhere. Did they stand anywhere? Had that been a simple night of comfort and that was it? Did Emma want more? Did she? But she couldn't ask any of these things right now because Emma's issues around her father took precedence.

So she stayed quiet and, essentially, waited her turn.

Which was frustrating as hell.

And apparently added up to ruined pie dough.

Balling it up, she then tossed it into the trash and started over again, internally sighing at how her emotions seemed to be directly proportional to her pie crust handling.

"Wanna talk about it?" Sandy asked. She was at the next counter over, mixing ingredients for an order of lemon bars for a retirement community's midsummer picnic.

Charlie lifted one shoulder. She did. She did want to talk about it. With Emma.

"Is it you and Emma?"

Charlie glanced at her, surprised.

It was Sandy's turn to shrug. "I hear the way you talk about her. I saw you at Summer Fest together, the way you look at her. The way she looks at you."

"Really?"

"Honey, I've got about twenty years on you. I know stuff." She tapped her temple with a finger and winked.

It was like a dam suddenly broke inside Charlie. She spilled it all to Sandy. Every detail as if it had been clawing at her skull to be set free. She kept her voice down, as Bethany was out front waiting on customers. Because of that and the construction crew, Sandy turned off her mixer and came to stand closer. Charlie told her about the make-out session after the Summer Fest, how Emma had regretted it and told Charlie so, how Charlie had taken over when Emma found out about her dad because she'd seemed paralyzed. The pace of her words picked up as she talked about meeting Zaya and the rest of the Grier family and how hard and confusing it had been for Emma, how helpless she'd felt because she couldn't make it easier for her. And she told Sandy about the hotel—how wonderful it had been, how comfortable and perfect, and how they hadn't touched on it since.

Sandy listened carefully, nodded here and there, but made no comments until Charlie finished completely. By that time, she was almost breathless, on the verge of tears, her voice cracking. She'd gotten more emotional over the story than she'd intended, and she'd shared way more detail than she should have, and now she felt the heat rise in her face. "I'm sorry. That was a lot. That was too much." She covered her eyes with one flour-dusted hand.

Sandy laid a hand on her arm, gently tugged Charlie's hand away. "Hey." Sandy waited until she looked at her. "Don't apologize. There's no need. We're friends, right?"

Charlie nodded.

"It's gonna be okay. Take a breath. Just breathe."

"This is not what I expected when I came home, you know?" A tear spilled over and coursed down Charlie's cheek. "I was going to take a few weeks, lick my wounds, get myself situated, and go back to New York. But now…" She shrugged in a gesture of not knowing what to do because she really *did not know* what to do. She sniffled, then looked at Sandy and wondered if the horror she suddenly felt was visible on her face. "I haven't thought about my ex in days."

"Isn't that a good thing?"

"I don't know!" It was almost a wail, and she thought she saw a ghost of a smile pass across Sandy's face.

"All right. First things first, take a break." Sandy took the butter Charlie needed for the pie crust and put it back in the fridge. "Go back to my office in the corner. Take a seat. Have some water. Like I said, just breathe. Okay? Give yourself some time. Bethany and I have got this. When you come back out, we'll talk some more. Or we won't." Her gentle smile brought out her dimples, and Charlie was suddenly so grateful for this new friend in her life. Sandy touched Charlie's cheek. "Everything will be okay. I promise."

Though she didn't necessarily believe that, she nodded, wiped her hands, and headed back to the corner where the desk was. She dropped into the chair like she'd been carrying boulders all morning and blew out an enormous breath.

"Just breathe," she whispered to herself.

She actually did feel the slightest bit better. Maybe she'd needed to get some of that stuff off her chest, out of her head. Though she harbored some guilt about spilling Emma's private life and details about her father, it wasn't enough to make her feel awful. Instead, she felt a sense of relief.

As she sat back in the chair and forced herself to relax her shoulders, which felt like they'd been up by her ears for days now, her phone buzzed in her back pocket. Lily. She must've been texting rather than calling because it was the middle of the workday.

They loved you! Talked to my friend and they will want to do a second interview soon, in person, but he said it's really just a formality! They'll likely offer you the job! Way to go!

Charlie blinked at the phone. At all the exclamation points. Read the text again.

How the hell was she going to get a job offer? From a big marketing firm in Boston? Yes, the interview had gone well, but she'd been sure once they called Darcy's company for a reference, she'd end up on the reject pile. This was huge. Really huge. It was awesome. It was exactly what she'd been waiting for.

So why wasn't she thrilled? Why wasn't she jumping up from the chair and flossing a victory dance? What the hell was the matter with her?

❖

It was her mother's lunch out with the girls, as she called her little group of friends, and everybody else was working. Looking forward to having the house to herself for a little while, Charlie was surprised to see her father's truck in the driveway and even more surprised when she walked into the kitchen and saw him standing at the stove, spatula in hand.

"Hey, Dad," Charlie said, dropping her bag.

"Hey, sweetheart," her father answered. He wore his usual summer work clothes: jeans, a T-shirt, and work boots.

"Are you trying to get murdered by your wife?" she asked playfully with a pointed glance at his boots. The ones he wasn't allowed to wear in the house and *tromp dirt and sawdust all over my kitchen*, according to her mom.

He gave her a wink, flipped what looked to be a grilled cheese sandwich, and Charlie approached him, nose in the air.

"How come you're home already?"

"Just taking a quick late lunch–early dinner break. We have to finish up a job today, so might be working late."

"Oh my God," Charlie said when she got close enough to notice the fresh tomatoes from her mother's garden, one on the counter already sliced. "Grilled cheese *and* tomato? Can you make me one, too? I'll pay you. I swear to God."

"Keep your mouth shut about the boots, and you've got a deal." Charlie laughed and her father slid the finished sandwich onto a plate and handed it to her. Then he picked up a knife and sliced more tomato, constructed a second sandwich. "How was pie?"

Charlie sat down at the table, the sudden realization that she had her father all to herself warming her heart. It hadn't happened often when she lived here before she'd left for New York, and it hadn't happened at all since she'd been home. It was a strange feeling to unexpectedly miss somebody who was standing right in front of you, but she missed her dad deeply right then and decided to embrace the moment. "Pie was hard."

Her father didn't turn to her, kept his eyes on the frying pan. "How come?"

"Because my brain wants to focus on everything *except* pie lately." Charlie took a bite of the sandwich and closed her eyes. The blend of melty cheese and tangy tomato was like a symphony in her mouth, and she was pretty sure she could hear sweet baby angels singing.

Her father plated his own sandwich, grabbed a Diet Coke out of the fridge, and sat down at the table across from Charlie. "You want to talk it out? I've got another forty-five minutes before I need to get back to the job site."

The look on her dad's face then—open, loving, ready to listen—filled Charlie with emotion that tapped gently at what remained of her resolve to keep everything in, knocking the final bricks away one by one. Between Sandy that morning and her father in that moment, she felt like a dam had crumbled and her story would pour out continually. Endlessly. To everybody. As if she had no control.

And she felt like she didn't anyway, so…

She chewed her sandwich as she collected her thoughts.

"Is it about Emma?" Her father's question wasn't accusatory. It wasn't snarky. It was simple, matter-of-fact. And took Charlie by surprise.

"Why does everybody ask me that?" she asked.

He simply shrugged, bit into his sandwich, and waited her out.

She gave in. "Some, yes. Some about work. Some about my future." She hadn't told anybody—not her family, not Emma, not her friends—everything that had happened. Now that she thought about it, everybody knew bits and pieces. Sandy knew about Emma, yes—and apparently, so did her father—but she didn't know about the other job offer that was coming. Her family didn't know about Sandy's offer to her or about the incoming Boston job offer, though they knew she'd done the Skype interview. Not surprisingly, she was starting to feel a bit scattered, and as she sat there trying to sort through things in her mind, looking for a good place to begin, something stopped her. She looked up at her father and asked quietly, "Do you think people can change, Dad?"

"Change? What do you mean? Like, their opinions? Their values? Or just as a person in general?"

Charlie picked up the second half of her sandwich and bit off a corner, thinking as she chewed. "As a person in general. Like, do you think a person can make mistakes or poor decisions and then come back from them? Have people look at them the way they did before they made the bad decisions?" It felt like her bite of sandwich had decided to park itself halfway down her throat, and she set the rest down, fiddled with her napkin as she held herself in check. When she finally dared to look up, her father's expression was gentle. Sympathetic, even.

"Yeah," he said with a slow nod. "Absolutely, I do."

"You do? Oh, good." The relief that washed through Charlie right then was inexplicably strong. She'd had no idea this was something that had bothered her so much, but she felt like a weight had been lifted, just from her dad giving her a little encouragement. "That's good."

"Look," her dad said, picking up his can of soda, dwarfing it in his enormous hand. "I don't know all the details here. You've never been a share-the-details kind of girl, especially with your parents, and I get that about you. I respect it. We don't all have to know every little thing about each other. But I know you, Charlotte. I know *you*. You're my daughter. My firstborn child. And you're struggling. I can see that."

So much for keeping herself in check. The tears began to flow, and she realized right then that she'd been holding them in for days now. It was simultaneously awful and wonderful to finally let them go.

"What would your mother tell you to do?"

Charlie met her father's gaze, puzzled, not following.

"When you were confused about your sexuality. When you

weren't sure which college to attend. When you were undecided about New York, what did she tell you to do?"

It was clear then, and she answered with a smile. "She told me to follow my heart. Every time."

"Exactly. *Follow your heart and things will work out the way they're supposed to.*"

"My mother is Mary Poppins, isn't she?"

Her father's laugh boomed through the kitchen. "I'm not allowed to comment on her secret identity. But she's usually right."

"She is."

"I mean, you followed your heart to New York." He used the last bite of his sandwich to hide his grin. "And look how well that went for you."

"Hey!" Charlie grabbed a dish towel and threw it at him, laughing while half faking a pout. "Don't make fun of me. Can't you see I'm a mess over here?"

Her dad caught the towel and when their laughter died down, he said quietly, "No, you're not. You're great. You're amazing. You always know exactly what to do. You grab life by the balls. You're kind of my hero, you know."

What? Had her father just said she was his hero? She sat there. Blinking. Speechless. Her heart swelling with love and gratitude for both of her parents. She'd left them behind a few years ago and now, strangely, felt like she had them back, as if she'd lost them at some point. "Thanks, Daddy."

He lifted a shoulder and half shrugged like it was no big deal. "You'll figure it out, sweetheart. You always do. It's one of your best qualities." He stood, gathered their plates, and put them in the sink. Then, as he walked past her, he dropped a kiss onto her head. "Back to work for me. Love you, kiddo."

"I love you, too." She watched as he grabbed his keys and plaid flannel shirt and left the house. She stayed sitting at the table until she heard his truck start, back up, drive away, and his words echoed through the empty kitchen.

You always know exactly what to do.

Maybe he was right. Because right then, she did know. She knew without a doubt. She had to talk to Emma. No more waiting for Emma to come to her. No more being okay with the excuses of being too busy. No more. They'd had sex, for God's sake. They'd spent an amazing, very intimate night together, and she finally let herself admit what she'd been keeping inside for a week.

That it meant something.

She inhaled, let the breath out slowly. Yes, it was well past time to talk to Emma. If nothing else, she needed to know where she stood. It was more than likely that Emma still didn't trust her, was keeping herself protected against her. And Charlie hated that, but also understood it. So if Emma said it was a one-time thing and nothing more, she would have to find a way to deal with it.

But she didn't believe that. She couldn't make herself believe that. Time might have passed and people might change, but she still knew Emma, and Emma was the same person she'd known and loved since high school.

The question was, did Emma think Charlie was the same person, too? Because the fact of the matter? She was not.

She was pretty sure she'd shown Emma that, but maybe she needed to come right out and say it. Talk about it. Communication was good, right? It was something she'd decided she needed to work on right after Darcy left her because she and Darcy obviously hadn't done it well. At all.

Emma had avoided talking to her, though. She'd been either absent or busy during every pie delivery that week, making it pretty clear that having any kind of in-depth conversation with Charlie wasn't high on her priority list. Charlie had sent several texts, and the ones that Emma had responded to consisted of short phrases and noncommittal answers. Scratching at a spot on the table, Charlie knew she had to admit to her own complicity, given she hadn't really done much to force any sort of communication. She'd told herself Emma had a lot on her mind with her father's death. She reminded herself that she was not Emma's BFF, Danielle was. She used the crazy pace of running a restaurant as an excuse as well.

"Goddamn it, I'm important, too," she said quietly to the empty kitchen. Her eyes went immediately wide, and she sat with the words for a few minutes. Held them up. Studied them from different angles. And for the first time since before Darcy had dumped her, she actually believed them.

❖

Anytime, Emma. I mean it. Your brothers would love to get to know you.

Emma sat back in her chair and exhaled. She'd been communicating with Zaya off and on since last week, after she'd sent a message to apologize for not going to the funeral services. She knew she didn't owe Zaya an explanation, but she felt bad for just leaving without saying good-bye. It was the right thing to do at the time, but now, almost a week later, it felt weird, and while she'd expected to get an icy reply, she'd gotten the opposite. Zaya seemed to understand exactly how this all felt for her, and she wasn't sure how to react to that.

Tonight, Zaya had extended an invitation for Emma to come back for a visit any time she wanted. According to her, Calvin and Trey were very interested in getting to know the big sister they'd never had the chance to talk to. And Emma could admit that it was kind of a cool discovery to find out she had siblings.

"I have two little brothers," she found herself whispering aloud every now and then. "I have two twin brothers. Calvin and Trey. My little brothers."

It was late. Thursday. It had been a week since her trip to Nashville. She'd seen Charlie a couple of times since they got back, but there'd been no time for discussion. She'd been so busy at the restaurant, and her late nights and mornings had been spent on…

Stop it.

She halted her thoughts—no, excuses—because that's exactly what they were. Excuses. Reasons she was hiding behind so she didn't have to face the reality of what had happened in Tennessee. So she didn't have to face the reality of Charlotte Stetko and her return to her life and what that might mean. What she might hope it meant, might want it to mean.

With a snap, she closed her laptop and glanced at the clock: 1:27 a.m. She really needed to get some sleep. Too bad sleep hated her lately and had been avoiding her like a jilted girlfriend.

Speaking of jilted girlfriends, with Sabrina gone, she needed to hire a new bartender, pronto. And also go see her mother, have a very serious talk with her, but that was going to be a big one and she needed to be ready for it. There would be much gearing up needed. Right now, she just couldn't. She also had to start thinking about her fall menu for the restaurant...

The ringing of her phone startled her. Who the hell was calling at one thirty in the morning? A glance at the screen told her. Dani.

"Hey, everything okay?" she asked by way of greeting.

"I was going to ask you the same thing," Dani said, and she could tell by the background noise that she was in her car. "I just drove by your place and saw your lights on. You all right?"

She sighed and moved into her bedroom, stretched out on top of the navy blue comforter. That was the question, wasn't it? Was she all right? "I've got so much in my head, Dani. So much."

"I know, babe."

She'd risked Dani's wrath by filling her in on everything that had happened last week, every detail, and surprisingly, Dani hadn't blown up at her. In fact, she'd done the opposite. While Dani'd lamented being out of town, insisting she'd have taken her to Nashville without a problem, she'd been sympathetic about Emma's dad and *almost* supportive of the Charlie situation. Which made her feel like her world had slanted a bit, and things were slowly sliding out of place, because what the hell? Hadn't Dani been all about listing every issue Emma had ever had with Charlie in the past? She had been too exhausted to argue about it with her, so she put it on her pile of Things to Deal with Later, which had grown into a mountain at that point.

"Zaya wants me to come visit, meet the boys, spend some time."

"What do you think of that?"

"I'm considering it, which is so weird. I mean, I've known about them for more than a year. Why am I considering it now? Why not six months ago when I could've actually seen my father?" It was a question that had rolled around and around in her head for days now, driving her a little nutso. "The timing just sucked."

"All right, don't get mad at me, but I'm about to lay out some cliché on your ass." She chuckled and Dani continued, "They say everything happens for a reason. Maybe it was supposed to be like this."

Emma groaned. "But so much? All at once? My dad dies? I meet my stepmother and little brothers at his calling hours? I find out my mom is partly responsible for my having no contact with him? Charlie is suddenly amazing, and I sleep with her? It's a lot. It's so much. Why now and why all at once?"

"Have you talked to her yet?" Dani asked.

"Who?"

"You *know* who." Dani's tone said she knew Emma was stalling.

"No. I've been too busy."

"You've been too scared."

She couldn't lie to her best friend, but she also didn't have to admit to the truth. She was too tired to fight Dani on it. She was too tired a lot lately. Everything she'd listed to Dani felt like it weighed hundreds of pounds and had parked directly on her shoulders.

"You need to talk to her," Dani said, and her voice was gentler now. "You need to make some decisions, one way or another."

"I do? Why?" It was a snarky question, but it was late and she was frustrated and tired, and she'd been carrying so much around since her return from Tennessee, it was flattening her. Her coping skills were in the crapper.

"Because it's eating you alive, Em." Dani's voice was simple and matter-of-fact and part of Emma hated her a little bit for that. The rest of her hated Dani for being right.

"I know." She gave up, defeated. "All right. I'll go see her tomorrow."

"Good," Dani said. "I only nag because I love."

"Yeah, yeah."

"Try to get some sleep. You sound like you could fall over anytime."

They signed off and she lay there in the dark of her bedroom, all her clothes still on, and stared at the ceiling.

It was time to face the reality of her situation, which she had been clear on for a while now: the only one she really wanted to talk to was Charlie.

And she should. She *would*.

And also?

She was terrified.

CHAPTER TWENTY-FOUR

C harlie had become a weirdo. In one night. She was pretty sure.
It was the beginning of August, and rather than key lime, triple berry was the flavor of the month. Charlie had the dough chilling and was working on the filling, a mouthwatering combination of blackberries, raspberries, and blueberries that she wanted to scoop into her mouth with a spoon, to hell with the crust. The entire kitchen smelled warm and sweet and absolutely edible. More so than usual, given it was in a bakery.

As she worked, the noise from next door's construction creating a not terribly pleasant soundtrack, she recalled her plan, the one she'd worked through last night. The one where she'd pretty much written a speech. A speech that talked about how she was feeling, how she wanted to know what Emma was feeling, what the next steps might be, if there were any. An actual, honest-to-God speech. To give to Emma.

Weirdo didn't begin to describe her.

Fridays were always a little lighter, a little more fun at The Muffin Top. They were busier. Customers were in good moods. They took their time ordering. Lingered a bit. And now that the construction was underway next door, they were curious. Asked questions. Peeked through the windows on the sidewalk with curiosity. Sandy and Bethany had the front covered as Charlie worked in the back, Sandy flitting back and forth between the current part of the shop and the new one. And all the time Charlie worked, she went over her talking points.

My God, I have talking points? Am I running for office? I just want to be real with her. That's all. Why is this so hard?

Those thoughts had coursed through her mind on a loop. But she was a smart woman and while she could wail and drop her head back, roll it around in an animated display of frustration, she already knew the answer to why this was all so hard, the answer to why she'd waited more than a week to take the bull by the horns, sit Emma down, and make her talk. It was simple, really.

She was afraid.

Emma didn't trust her. And why should she? She had hurt Emma. Badly. Yes, they'd been young and that was the time in life when you screwed up adult things, but she'd left very, very deep scars on Emma. It only made sense that Emma would put walls up with her. Protect herself.

Charlie rolled out the dough, laid it into pie plates, as her mind churned and swirled.

And while she liked to think their night together was something more than just sex, she also knew of Emma's penchant for pairing with women in just that way: sex only. Look at poor Sabrina the bartender. She'd obviously wanted something more with Emma, and Emma had shut her down.

Would Emma shut her down, too?

It was a possibility she needed to be prepared for. A distinct one.

With a sigh, she filled her pies, covered them with the second layer. As she slid one into the oven, she felt her phone buzz in her back pocket. When she finished what she was doing, she took the phone out, gave it a quick glance. A text from the woman who had interviewed her on Skype. The one from the Boston firm.

We are happy to request a second, in-person interview with you.

Several dates were listed, all of them for the following week, and she had her pick.

Lily had been right.

Charlie's heart beat fast as she scooted to the back corner, out of sight of customers, and read the text again, checked the dates. This job could be hers. She could hardly believe it. It wasn't New York, true, but Boston was an amazing city, according to Lily. Charlie knew she'd like it there. The fast pace, the endless sound, the never-ending selection of things to do and see and taste.

She breathed out slowly.

"Everything okay?"

Charlie jumped as she turned to meet Sandy's eyes. A hand pressed to her chest, she let out a nervous laugh. "You scared me."

Sandy grinned. "Sorry. You looked so serious—I wanted to make sure nothing was wrong."

"Oh no." Charlie shook her head, probably more vehemently than she needed to. "Everything's fine." She hadn't mentioned to Sandy that she'd had an interview, and she decided to keep it that way for just a little while longer. As soon as she checked on flights, she'd need to take a couple days off from the bakery, and she was going to have to be honest with Sandy about why. A little seed of dread took up residence in the pit of her stomach.

"Good." Sandy interrupted her thoughts. "Emma's here to see you."

"Emma?" Charlie's heart rate suddenly jumped to double time as she followed Sandy through the kitchen. "Now?" She wasn't ready for this, was she? Her speech. Her talking points.

"Mm-hmm. She asked if she could talk to you." Sandy studied her for a moment, and her expression held something wise and knowing. Then she jerked her head toward the front of the shop and said softly, "Why don't you take a couple minutes? Go outside and talk. Bethany's okay for a bit."

"Okay." Charlie shook out her arms. She rolled her head around a couple of times, felt that satisfying pop. She bounced on the balls of her feet. When she turned her head, Sandy was grinning at her.

"Is it time for the big game?" Sandy asked quietly, trying—and failing—to hide her amusement.

Charlie shot her a mock glare. "Shut up." She pushed through the door.

"The pies look great," Sandy called, her laughter following Charlie out into the front area where Emma stood waiting in a corner away from the counter.

God, she was beautiful. How was it possible that she was always so beautiful? She must've stopped in on her way into the restaurant, as she wore her loose-fitting chef's pants, though not the coat. Just a white T-shirt that hugged her form nicely. Her hair was pulled back, as it always was when she cooked, but her chef's hat also hadn't made an appearance yet. She looked casual. Authoritative. Ridiculously sexy. Charlie's heart skipped a beat. It skipped several.

"Hey," Emma said as Charlie approached.

"Hi." She reached out, gave Emma's arm a gentle squeeze. She couldn't help it. "Everything okay?"

"Yeah." Emma nodded. "Yeah, I just wondered if we could talk for a minute. I know you're working…" She let the sentence trail off like she had no idea what the end of it was. She seemed…nervous was the wrong word. A little off, maybe? Uncertain?

"No worries. Sandy gave me a few minutes." She sighed internally, pretty sure she was about to get the brush-off. And even though she knew it was something she'd needed to prepare for as a possibility, it still sucked. "You want to go outside?" She gestured to the door with her chin.

"No, no, this is fine." Emma's unease was obvious as she looked around the bakery. They were in one of their lulls that happened on and off throughout the day. One customer was trying to decide between almond cookies and lemon ones. Two others sat at a far table sharing a Danish. The rest of the place was quiet—construction noise from next door aside—but Emma was fidgety. Either she didn't want to be there, or she didn't know what she wanted to say. Charlie wasn't sure which, so she pulled out a chair at the table for two near them and sat. Emma did the same and seemed suddenly relieved to not be standing.

"What's up?" She wasn't trying to sound snarky at all, but a little bit crept in, she was sure. *Because really, if you're going to blow somebody off, just do it.* Her muscles tightened on their own, her jaw clenched, and she knew she was bracing.

"I'm really sorry." Emma had her elbows on the table, her dark eyes focused on her.

And there it was. Even though Charlie had known it was coming, had been ready for it, it still sucked. Big time. Not wanting to let Emma see that, she waved a hand between them as if she was wiping a dry-erase board clean.

"Hey, no worries. It was just one night, right? Super crazy circumstances…" She watched Emma's expression change. Her brow furrowed. She pursed her lips.

"No, I'm not sorry about that."

"You're not?" Charlie blinked at her.

"No. Are you?"

"God, no. I just thought…" Now *she* didn't know what to think, and her talking points began rolling around in her head again. Emma was *not* sorry about their night together? She was at a loss. This was good news, something she realized right at that moment, right as she sat there looking into Emma's sparkling eyes, at the almost-smile on her face. "Then, what are you sorry for?"

"I'm sorry for not talking to you sooner. About important things. Things besides pie."

"Listen, pie is *very* important."

"Oh, that's right. I forget. My bad."

They sat there for a moment, both smiling, and Charlie felt a pang of what used to be, of how comfortable she'd always been with Emma, how relaxed and content she felt being with somebody who knew her as well as Emma did. Or at least used to know her.

"So, look." Emma wet her lips and sat up a little straighter, as if in preparation to say something super important. "I was thinking—"

Her words were cut off by the door of The Muffin Top being flung open, the small bell not given a chance to tinkle sweetly. Rather, it banged against the glass with a thwack. They both turned to see who had shoved their way into the bakery. A noisy group of what looked to be high school kids came in, shoving playfully at each other while cranking the decibel level up by several notches.

"I got a second interview," Charlie blurted before she realized she was going to, "with a really big marketing firm. In Boston."

"Oh." Emma blinked at her, obviously trying to regroup, to alter whatever path she'd been on when she'd walked in. "I see. Well. That's awesome. I mean, I didn't know you were interviewing, but…" She cleared her throat. "That's great. When do you go?"

Emma was having trouble meeting her eyes now, and somehow, that was almost worse than anything else. That Emma could barely look at her. She hadn't meant to just drop it on her, but part of her was glad she had because if she hadn't, she wasn't sure she'd have been able to tell her at all. And Emma, of all people, deserved to know. "I haven't set it up yet, but sometime next week."

"Oh, wow. Next week? That's…" Emma scratched her neck, looked around the bakery as if she wasn't sure where to settle her gaze. "That's soon."

"Yeah." Charlie swallowed. Hard. Words had left her. All of them. The air shifted drastically. She had no idea what to say. She wanted to erase the shock, the unease, the confusion on Emma's face, but she didn't know how.

"It's a good company, you said?"

"It is. My friend Lily works there. She's the one who got me in the door."

"Oh, good. Good. It's good to have friends like that."

"Yeah." God, this was painful. It was Charlie's turn to clear her throat. "So, what you started to say earlier—"

"Oh, no worries." Emma waved it off dismissively. "It wasn't important. Not a big deal." She stood from her chair, and while Charlie had the impression that it might have been a very big deal, she felt stuck. Paralyzed. Unable to make any kind of move that might salvage this disaster of a conversation. "Listen, good luck on the interview, okay? I hope you get what you want." And before Charlie could say another word, Emma turned on her heel and left The Muffin Top, left her standing alone and frustrated. When she looked back at the counter, Sandy was standing there, the look of confusion on her face telling Charlie that she'd likely heard the entire conversation. Sandy held her gaze, then turned and pushed through the doors to the back. She had some explaining to do.

No time like the present. She blew out a breath and followed Sandy.

❖

I am so stupid.
I am so stupid.
I am so stupid.

Emma couldn't get the words to stop playing in a loop through her head, but she also didn't want them to stop. She needed to hear them. To remember them. To grab on to them and hold tight until she learned her lesson. Again.

She grabbed a meat tenderizer and went to work on the chicken breasts for tonight's chicken French special. It really was a perfect job for how she felt, and she hammered away.

What in the actual fuck had she been thinking? Seriously? What? Had she somehow conveniently forgotten what it was like the last time a big-city opportunity had presented itself and swept Charlie away like an ocean wave? Like the two of them were standing together on the beach, and suddenly, Charlie was gone, waving at her from the bow of a really expensive yacht, sailing off to a better life. One that didn't include her. Had she forgotten what it felt like to have her heart split in two in the middle of her chest?

Well. She'd done what she'd had to do this time.

This time, she wasn't about to wait for Charlie to rip her heart out of her body, stomp it into a million pieces, and then hand it back to her. No. No way. Not again. This time, it was Emma who had taken the bull by the horns. Emma who had exited somewhat gracefully before she could be pummeled into the ground. She was not going to go through that again.

How could she have possibly thought they might have something again? She was an intelligent woman. Wasn't she? Charlie wasn't new and she obviously hadn't changed, had she? Nope. She was still the same old selfish Charlie, always ready to do what served Charlie best.

Okay, maybe that wasn't fair. Had she really expected Charlie wouldn't try to find another job in her field? That she wouldn't want to get back to the big city? Any big city? It's what drew her out of Shaker Falls in the first place, why wouldn't it again? So if she was being honest with herself, Charlie was simply doing what any person in her shoes would do. She had to admit that.

It still hurt, though. Goddamn it, it still hurt, and for that, Emma blamed herself. She'd let Charlie back in, and wow, it hadn't taken much, had it? It hadn't taken much to fall right back into old routines, old comforts, familiarity. It hadn't taken much at all. And she had loved it.

She'd *loved* it.

She had to admit that too.

Switching out the chicken breasts, she reloaded her cutting board with the next ones and pounded away. It really did help, the physical act of beating something into submission.

Charlie was going to fly to Boston, she was going to get a job offer, and she was probably not going to even come back. If she did come back, it would be quick. Boston was a little bit closer than New York, so at least that might make things easier on Charlie's parents. It would still crush Mrs. Stetko, Emma knew that, and she started making plans to pop in to say hi, make sure they were doing okay. Lord knew, Charlie wouldn't be visiting regularly.

Emma stopped hammering, stood there with the tenderizer setting on the chicken breast, as her heart pounded and tears threatened. She concentrated on her breathing. Focused on her lungs. Deep breath in through the nose. Hold it. Out through the mouth slowly. She did that three times and literally felt her heart rate slow.

This was her new normal. Which was such an odd thing to think because Charlie hadn't been home all that long. It wasn't a new normal at all. It was normal. That's all it was. Just normal. And Emma needed to get back to it.

CHAPTER TWENTY-FIVE

Charlie hadn't expected to be on a plane and headed to Boston on Sunday. That was crazy fast, considering she'd just gotten the request for the second interview barely three days ago. But the airline gods had been with her, and she found a flight that was reasonably affordable and got her into Boston with plenty of time for her to get her bearings, find her way around, and get to her interview on time.

Downtown Boston was gorgeous in August. Charlie wasn't surprised, and she also was. She'd never been to Boston before, but she'd seen photos and heard descriptions from Lily, and neither of those things had done the city justice.

Charlie could have strolled around Quincy Market for days if she'd had the time. The colors, the smells, the people, the *food*. So much food. The atmosphere was a festive one, but also relaxed. People were happy, and they were also chilling, hanging out with a drink here or a snack there. It had been a hot day, but the humidity seemed to decrease slowly as evening approached. She moseyed along in her sundress and flat sandals, taking in all the sights and sounds, and thinking about how much Emma would like it here, how fascinated she'd be with the seemingly endless array of food vendors. When she realized where her mind had gone, she shook it back to the present and focused on her surroundings—and her surroundings only—until she found the small café where she was meeting Lily.

"There she is!"

She heard Lily's voice before she ever saw her, but the next thing she knew, she was wrapped in the warm embrace of her friend she hadn't seen in much, much too long. Lily felt leaner, her muscles tighter, and she still smelled like oranges, the way she always had.

"Somebody's been going to the gym," Charlie said, squeezing Lily's upper arm as they parted.

"Yoga," Lily said with a proud grin. "Don't be fooled by the pretty clothes and relaxing music. It's hard work."

"I've heard this."

Lily led her a few feet to a metal outdoor café table, complete with two chairs and two glasses of white wine, condensation dripping down the sides. "I took the liberty of ordering you a drink. I hope that's okay."

"Oh, absolutely." Charlie took a seat. "But just the one. My interview is first thing and I want to be sharp."

"They already love you, so you're in good shape to start with. I wouldn't worry." Lily sat, too. "Though not showing up hungover would probably get you points."

"You think?" They laughed together and sipped their wine. Charlie looked around. "This place is so cool."

"It can be kind of touristy, but I love it." Lily was also from a small town. Hers was in upstate New York, and they'd bonded in college over that commonality. They took a moment to bask in their environment before Lily reached over to pat her thigh. "I'm so glad you're here."

"Me, too." It wasn't exactly a lie. She was glad to be there. But she had so many other emotions rolling through her head, through her heart, that she found it hard to be excited, to be as giddy as Lily seemed to be. Guilt sauntered in and sat on her shoulders.

The waiter came and took their salad orders. "So, your interview is at nine?" Lily asked when he'd left.

"Yep. And thank you for the hotel recommendation. I'm just a block from the office, so I'll be able to walk, barring any horrifying weather."

"You'll be fine. No rain tomorrow. Just humidity. But at nine, you should still be okay."

"You mean I won't be a mess of frizzy hair and sweaty clothes?"

"Not from the weather," Lily joked. They spent the next half hour going over strategy, probable interview questions. Lily filled Charlie in on who would likely be sitting in on the interview, what they were like, what she could expect. They were almost finished with their salads. Lily had moved on to a second glass of wine while Charlie stuck with

GEORGIA BEERS

water, and she took a sip. "You seem"—Lily squinted at her as if trying
to find exactly the right descriptor—"low key. You seem low key. Are
you just tired? Nervous? Something else?"

Charlie sat there quietly for what felt like a long while. She'd
known Lily for years now. They'd roomed together, they'd always been
open with each other, and there was love. Definite love. Charlie would
do anything for Lily, and she knew the reverse was also true. Finally,
she took a deep breath and answered her friend. "Yes, I'm tired. Yes,
I'm nervous. Yes, I'm something else."

Lily gave a nod. "Interesting. Okay, let's talk about the something
else. A girl? *The* girl?" Charlie was gobsmacked, and it must have
showed, because Lily chuckled. "Come on, Chuck. I know you. Talk
to me."

And Charlie did. She didn't so much talk as spew. Dump. Pour.
Open the locks. Smash the levees. Again. It occurred to her in the midst
of it that she'd *needed* this. She'd needed to talk to somebody about it
all because she really hadn't. Bits and pieces to people here and there,
but she hadn't laid it all out for one person who knew her well. So that's
what she did. She told Lily everything. From the beginning, even the
stuff she already knew. She ended with Emma's exit from the bakery
after she had told her about the interview.

"What do you think she came over to say?" Lily asked. Leaning
over the table toward Charlie, she'd been riveted.

With a sigh, Charlie shrugged. "I don't know. Well. Not for sure."
She let herself drift back to that moment, when she'd been sure Emma
had come over to let her down easy, tell her everything they'd done had
been fun, but it had to stop. Emma'd said she was sorry, and Charlie
had jumped to that conclusion, and then Emma had said that wasn't
what she was sorry about.

"Then what *was* she sorry about?" Lily asked.

Charlie fell back in her chair and groaned dramatically. "I don't
know, that we hadn't talked sooner? I had just found out about the
interview and I was so wired, and I blurted it out before she could
finish."

Lily's entire face fell. "Seriously? You interrupted her? In the
middle of that?"

"I was *freaking out*." Her shoulders slumped, and she frowned.
"Selfish Charlie strikes again."

• 224 •

"I don't know that I'd say that." Lily gestured for the waiter and ordered two more glasses of wine.

Charlie didn't protest, as she decided she could use some more alcohol to dull the realization that she'd been an idiot. Again.

"Okay, but there's one thing you haven't told me through all of this." Lily looked at her, eye contact intense.

"What's that?"

"How do you *feel* about everything? What do you think? And more importantly, what do you want?"

Charlie blinked. Blinked again. "I…" She blinked some more as a strange realization hit her. "You know, I've been so conscious of my past—I don't want to say behavior, but my past decisions that…" She inhaled as she looked off into the middle distance, thoughts chugging through her head.

"You decided you weren't allowed to think about what you wanted, didn't you?" Soft and gentle. That was Lily's voice in that moment, like she was afraid of hitting Charlie too hard with her words.

"I guess I just…" She looked up into Lily's concerned eyes as the waiter dropped off their wine. "Yeah. I did. I hurt so many people with the decisions I made that I'm terrified of doing that again." She picked up her glass and took a healthy swig.

"All right. Listen to me." Lily sat up straight, her posture shouting *I mean business here.* "How long will you beat yourself up? You're aware. You may have fucked up, but you know you did, and you feel bad about it, and you're sorry, and you've taken responsibility. That's a big deal. And PS, we'll revisit the whole fucking-up thing at another time because I don't believe that's what you did. But for now, remember this: everybody fucks up in life. Multiple times. I mean, it is part of life, after all. You're not that special." Lily winked as she sipped.

Charlie nodded, watched a young couple stroll by pushing a stroller with a sleeping infant.

"Charlie?"

"Hmm?"

Lily didn't so much look *at* her as look *into* her. It wasn't until she seemed sure she had every last ounce of Charlie's attention that she asked her question. "What do you want? What is it that you really want?"

CHAPTER TWENTY-SIX

There were quite a few reservations for a Monday, and for that, Emma was grateful. It would keep her busy, and that's what she needed right now. To be busy. To have her hands and, more importantly, her brain completely occupied by something other than the past month of her life. Seriously, how much stress was one person supposed to take?

She shook her head as she used a giant spoon to stir the tomato sauce on the stove. Tonight's special was lasagna, and she'd started her homemade sauce at noon, keeping it simmering, low and slow, so all the flavors would meld. Unlike the last time she made it, she remembered to make a small batch that didn't contain any meat, as having vegetarian options on her menu was becoming more and more important. Therefore, a second smaller pot also simmered on the stove, and she would make a second pan of lasagna that didn't contain ground beef or pork. It would sell.

Charlie loved her lasagna.

Emma groaned loudly at the intrusive thought. Her brain had been doing that to her since she left the bakery a couple days ago, knowing Charlie was headed to Boston for an interview and likely wouldn't be back longer than the time it took her to pick up her things. She'd spent her weekend trying to reconcile that, to accept it. It had been a whirlwind of a summer, and they'd run the gamut of emotion. Between their initial re-meeting, the barbecue, Emma's father's death and the subsequent trip to Nashville, and the night they'd spent together, they'd been all over the damn place.

The sauce tasted divine. When Alec arrived in a few minutes, she'd have him taste it, just to be sure, but she was pretty confident. She set a third pot on the stove filled with water so she could cook the pasta and construct the lasagnas to bake in another hour or two.

Thank God for her restaurant. Thank God for her ability to lose herself in her cooking. Emma wasn't sure how she'd survive otherwise. If she didn't have recipes to create or meat to tenderize or fresh vegetables to shop for? If she had spare hours in the day for simply thinking? Being lost in her own head? No. No way. She'd go nuts. They'd have to lock her up and throw away the key. When life was all too much—and it could be so, she knew from experience, case in point: the past month—all she had to do was submerge herself in food. Her job was what kept her sane, and she would be forever grateful for that.

An hour later, Alec was in and had given the sauce two thumbs-up, three large pans of lasagna had been constructed and were waiting to be baked, and Emma slipped out into the dining area to give herself a break and grab some much-needed caffeine from the bar. As she was squirting some Diet Coke into a glass filled to the brim with ice, her phone buzzed in her back pocket. Probably her mom.

With a sigh, she set down her drink and slipped the phone out, stopping dead when she saw the screen.

Charlie.

She could ignore it. She was a pro at dodging calls. Just ask Sabrina. She could let it go to voice mail, though Charlie might not leave a message. But then she'd text and the idea of endless texts showing up on her phone made Emma instantly feel weighed down.

She groaned.

"Might as well get it over with," she grumbled, then hit the green button. "Hey."

"Hi. It's Charlie."

She nodded, even though Charlie couldn't see her. "Yes, I know. I can read." Okay, that was unnecessarily snarky. She closed her eyes. "How was the interview?" She didn't really want to know but felt like she needed to be nice to make up for her snottiness. And then that annoyed her because what did she owe Charlie? Nothing, that's what.

"The interview went really, really well." Charlie paused, and there was an odd quality to her voice that Emma couldn't quite pinpoint. "They offered me the job."

Emma's stomach dropped. But why? Why did it drop? This was

exactly what she predicted would happen. Charlie would be offered a job in Boston and that's where she'd stay. It was no surprise. At all. Not even a little.

So why did she feel like she was going to throw up?

"Oh. Well. Wow. That's great." Air. She needed some air. Badly. Right now. Her body broke into a sweat and her stomach roiled sourly.

"I turned it down."

Quickly, Emma made her way around the bar and nearly jogged toward the door. Why was it so hot in the dining room? Air. She needed air. As she pushed through the doors of EG's, the words finally registered in her brain.

"Wait. What?" Emma stopped dead on the sidewalk, blinking rapidly, sucking in oxygen, and trying to understand what Charlie had said. Reasonably sure she'd headed off the vomit monster, she swallowed and inhaled again, blinking, as her eyes focused on the car parked across the street. The car that had Charlie leaning casually against it, her jean-clad legs crossed at the ankle, her arms folded, one hand pressed to her ear.

"I said I turned down the job." She looked directly at Emma as she said it, and even from that distance, Emma could make out the trace of a hesitant smile.

She simply stood there, her phone in her hand by her side. Staring at Charlie. Absorbing what her words meant. Charlie had also abandoned the call, and then they were both standing. Both staring across the not-very-busy street. Finally, Emma pulled herself together, bolstered her courage, and threw caution to the wind.

She crossed the street.

"Hi," Charlie said when Emma reached her.

"You're here."

"I am."

"What did you do?" she asked, her voice low, quiet. She still wasn't sure what was happening. She had an idea, but it terrified her, and she wanted to duck down behind the car and hide.

"I had an epiphany."

She squinted at Charlie. "What does that mean?"

Charlie toed the asphalt with the tip of her sandal and seemed to organize her thoughts before she gave voice to them. "I've been confused and lost for a really long time, Emma." She glanced up, held up a hand to prevent Emma from interrupting, but she'd had no intention of doing so. No, she wanted to hear this. Very much. "I know you may not necessarily agree with that. You may think it's a flimsy excuse to make my horrific choices in life seem out of my control. Whatever. That's okay. I accept that. Hell, I'd probably feel the same way if our roles were reversed." Focusing on her feet once again, Charlie continued, "I was young, and I was naïve, and young, naïve people do stupid things. That being said, they were *my* poor decisions to make, and I've had to live through the consequences. Knowing I've hurt people. Knowing I've altered the way some people look at me." With that line, she raised her face to meet Emma's gaze, and Emma saw nothing but strength and sincerity in Charlie's eyes. "I've grown. I've changed. I've learned so much about myself. And most of all, I've learned what's important to me. I've learned exactly what it is that I want." Charlie dropped her head back, eyes to the sky, and Emma couldn't help but trace the line of Charlie's throat with her eyes. "I lay in my hotel room last night and it was like a fog lifted. Like smoke cleared away and I could finally see everything just laid out before me. I saw my future, Emma."

Caught up. That's how Emma was feeling. That's what Charlie's words had done. She was caught up and she couldn't turn away now. She had to see it through, despite the white-hot fear that was coursing through her veins. Maybe she should've turned and run away as fast as she could. Maybe she should've laughed in Charlie's face, told her to fuck off once and for all. Maybe she should've clamped her hands over her ears and sung loudly so she couldn't hear any more of what Charlie had to say. But she did none of those things. Instead, she asked the question. God help her, she asked the question.

"What's your future, Charlotte?"

The smile that lit up Charlie's face then felt like magic. Like sunshine. Like hope. "You, Emma Grier. You are my future." She reached out a hand, laid her palm against Emma's cheek, and the love on her face was deep and clear and so genuine, it brought tears to Emma's eyes. "I've always known it. Since the very first time we kissed, I've known it. I don't know why I fought it, but I'm done with that. I'm so sorry for the pain I've caused you. I will regret that for the rest of my life."

The solid lump that parked itself in Emma's throat seemed to have no intention of moving, and she swallowed hard but couldn't seem to form words yet. Could this be? Was it really happening?

"I know that this is a lot," Charlie said, her expression shifting from slight dreamy to much more serious. "And I also know that you may not be on the same page as me. That I may have caused you to rip that page out and burn it, never to be read again. That this all may be too little, too late. I know that. Believe me, I know that. So there's no pressure here. I'm not asking for anything from you. I'm just telling you exactly what's in my heart. For once." The self-deprecating half grin, half grimace was the cutest thing Emma had seen in a long time. But then it morphed into a smile so bright and beautiful, it made her breath catch in her chest. "And what's in my heart is you. Only you."

Emma still hadn't spoken. But she stared. She looked at every aspect of Charlie's face. The tiny scar on her left eyebrow that she got from falling off her bike when they were ten. The soft, light down on her cheeks that Emma could only see because of the angle of the sun. Her gorgeous eyes and the love that so clearly shone from them. Yeah, that's what got her. That's what got Emma. The eyes. The love. It was so apparent, so obvious, that Emma would've sworn it radiated warmth. Warmth that encompassed her like a blanket. Like protective arms wrapped around her. It was something she hadn't felt in…well, years. Since Charlie left for college. And it hit her now how much she'd actually missed it, like a punch to the gut.

"I love you, Emma. I always have." Clarity. Everything about Charlie then broadcast it. Her eyes. Her overall expression. Her gentle, tender smile. She was speaking from her heart, and she was speaking the truth. The very least Emma could do was the same, right?

"My whole life, I've felt like an outsider," she began, her voice quiet. "In school. In college. Even in my own house sometimes. I was always the different one, the odd one out." She wet her lips and looked Charlie in the eye. "The only time I didn't feel that way was when I was with you. With you, I just feel like *me*." She took a deep breath and let it out slowly. "It took me a long time to get over you, Charlie. And when you breezed back into town, I realized that I actually hadn't. I have spent much of your time here reminding myself of all the reasons you and I are a bad idea, and I've been able to come to only one conclusion. We're not."

"We're not," Charlie agreed, shaking her head as her grin widened.

"You wanna give this thing a shot?"

"More than you can possibly know." And then Charlie's hands were holding her face and Charlie kissed her. Softly and sweetly and with such promise, and just like that, Emma's worries seemed to burn away like early morning fog.

"It won't be easy."

Charlie shrugged. "Maybe it will, maybe it won't. But it'll be worth it."

"You think so?"

"I'm sure of it."

"I like this version of you," Emma said.

"Yeah? Me, too."

She leaned in, kissed Charlie again. Deeply. Thoroughly. Could have kept at it endlessly until they heard "Hey, get a room!" from across the street. They parted and turned and there was Dani, sitting in her car, window rolled down, exaggeratedly ogling them until they both laughed.

Charlie turned back to her. "Work meeting?"

"Afraid so."

"No worries. I'll go home and unpack, and then I need to talk to Sandy. I've got a business to help run, you know."

"You really are staying." Emma's chest swelled.

"I really am." They stood quietly for a beat before Charlie said, "I love you, Emma."

Emma leaned in and kissed her. "Come by later. I'm making lasagna for the special."

Charlie's eyes went comically wide. "I *love* your lasagna."

"I know you do." She brushed a chunk of hair off Charlie's forehead, tucked it behind her ear. Then she turned, looked both ways, and started across the street. She heard Charlie open her car door and called to her. "Hey, Charlie?"

Charlie turned, brows raised.

"I love you, too."

About the Author

Georgia Beers is the award-winning author of nearly thirty lesbian romances. She resides in upstate New York, where she was born and raised. When not writing, she enjoys way too much TV, not nearly enough wine, spin classes (aka near-death experiences), and loving all over her dog (much to his dismay). She is currently hard at work on her next book. Visit her and find out more at www.georgiabeers.com.

Books Available From Bold Strokes Books

Face the Music by Ali Vali. Sweet music is the last thing that happens when Nashville music producer Mason Liner and daughter of country royalty Victoria Roddy are thrown together in an effort to save country star Sophie Roddy's career. (978-1-63555-532-5)

Flavor of the Month by Georgia Beers. What happens when baker Charlie and chef Emma realize their differing paths have led them right back to each other? (978-1-63555-616-2)

Mending Fences by Angie Williams. Rancher Bobbie Del Rey and veterinarian Grace Hammond are about to discover if heartbreaks of the past can ever truly be mended. (978-1-63555-708-4)

Silk and Leather: Lesbian Erotica with an Edge, edited by Victoria Villaseñor. This collection of stories by award-winning authors offers fantasies as soft as silk and tough as leather. The only question is: How far will you go to make your deepest desires come true? (978-1-63555-587-5)

The Last Place You Look by Aurora Rey. Dumped by her wife and looking for anything but love, Julia Pierce retreats to her hometown only to rediscover high school friend Taylor Winslow, who's secretly crushed on her for years. (978-1-63555-574-5)

The Mortician's Daughter by Nan Higgins. A singer on the verge of stardom discovers she must give up her dreams to live a life in service to ghosts. (978-1-63555-594-3)

The Real Thing by Laney Webber. When passion flares between actress Virginia Green and masseuse Allison McDonald, can they be sure it's the real thing? (978-1-63555-478-6)

What the Heart Remembers Most by M. Ullrich. For college sweethearts Jax Levine and Gretchen Mills, could an accident be the second chance neither knew they wanted? (978-1-63555-401-4)

White Horse Point by Andrews & Austin. Mystery writer Taylor James finds herself falling for the mysterious woman on White Horse Point who lives alone, protecting a secret she can't share about a murderer who walks among them. (978-1-63555-695-7)

Femme Tales by Anne Shade. Six women find themselves in their own real-life fairy tales when true love finds them in the most unexpected ways. (978-1-63555-657-5)

Jellicle Girl by Stevie Mikayne. One dark summer night, Beth and Jackie go out to the canoe dock. Two years later, Beth is still carrying the weight of what happened to Jackie. (978-1-63555-691-9)

My Date with a Wendigo by Genevieve McCluer. Elizabeth Rosseau finds her long-lost love and the secret community of fiends she's now a part of. (978-1-63555-679-7)

On the Run by Charlotte Greene. Even when they're cute blondes, it's stupid to pick up hitchhikers, especially when they've just broken out of prison, but doing so is about to change Gwen's life forever. (978-1-63555-682-7)

Perfect Timing by Dena Blake. The choice between love and family has never been so difficult, and Lynn's and Maggie's different visions of the future may end their romance before it's begun. (978-1-63555-466-3)

The Mail Order Bride by R. Kent. When a mail order bride is thrust on Austin, he must choose between the bride he never wanted or the dream he lives for. (978-1-63555-678-0)

Through Love's Eyes by C.A. Popovich. When fate reunites Brittany Yardin and Amy Jansons, can they move beyond the pain of their past to find love? (978-1-63555-629-2)

To the Moon and Back by Melissa Brayden. Film actress Carly Daniel thinks that stage work is boring and unexciting, but when she accepts a lead role in a new play, stage manager Lauren Prescott tests both her heart and her ability to share the limelight. (978-1-63555-618-6)

Tokyo Love by Diana Jean. When Kathleen Schmitt is given the opportunity to be on the cutting edge of AI technology, she never thought a failed robotic love companion would bring her closer to her neighbor, Yuriko Velucci, and finding love in unexpected places. (978-1-63555-681-0)

Brooklyn Summer by Maggie Cummings. When opposites attract, can a summer of passion and adventure lead to a lifetime of love? (978-1-63555-578-3)

City Kitty and Country Mouse by Alyssa Linn Palmer. Pulled in two different directions, can a city kitty and a country mouse fall in love and make it work? (978-1-63555-553-0)

Elimination by Jackie D. When a dangerous homegrown terrorist seeks refuge with the Russian mafia, the team will be put to the ultimate test. (978-1-63555-570-7)

In the Shadow of Darkness by Nicole Stiling. Angeline Vallencourt is a reluctant vampire who must decide what she wants more—obscurity, revenge, or the woman who makes her feel alive. (978-1-63555-624-7)

On Second Thought by C. Spencer. Madisen is falling hard for Rae. Even single life and co-parenting are beginning to click. At least, that is, until her ex-wife begins to have second thoughts. (978-1-63555-415-1)

Out of Practice by Carsen Taite. When attorney Abby Keane discovers the wedding blogger tormenting her client is the woman she had a passionate, anonymous vacation fling with, sparks and subpoenas fly. Legal Affairs: one law firm, three best friends, three chances to fall in love. (978-1-63555-359-8)

Providence by Leigh Hays. With every click of the shutter, photographer Rebekiah Kearns finds it harder and harder to keep Lindsey Blackwell in focus without getting too close. (978-1-63555-620-9)

Taking a Shot at Love by KC Richardson. When academic and athletic worlds collide, will English professor Celeste Bouchard and basketball coach Lisa Tobias ignore their attraction to achieve their professional goals? (978-1-63555-549-3)

Flight to the Horizon by Julie Tizard. Airline captain Kerri Sullivan and flight attendant Janine Case struggle to survive an emergency water landing and overcome dark secrets to give love a chance to fly. (978-1-63555-331-4)